COLD WRATH

*Recent Titles by Peter Turnbull
from Severn House*

The Hennessey and Yellich Series

ONCE A BIKER
NO STONE UNTURNED
TURNING POINT
INFORMED CONSENT
DELIVER US FROM EVIL
AFTERMATH
THE ALTERED CASE
GIFT WRAPPED
A DREADFUL PAST
COLD WRATH

The Harry Vicary Series

IMPROVING THE SILENCE
DEEP COVER
THE GARDEN PARTY
DENIAL OF MURDER
IN VINO VERITAS

The Maurice Mundy Series

A COLD CASE

COLD WRATH

Peter Turnbull

Severn House Large Print
London & New York

This first large print edition published 2019
in Great Britain and the USA by
SEVERN HOUSE PUBLISHERS LTD of
Eardley House, 4 Uxbridge Street, London W8 7SY.
First world regular print edition published 2018 by
Severn House Publishers Ltd.

British Library Cataloguing in Publication Data
A CIP catalogue record for this title is available from the British Library.

ISBN-13: 9780727892317

Except where actual historical events and characters are being described
for the storyline of this novel, all situations in this publication are
fictitious and any resemblance to living persons is purely coincidental.

Severn House Publishers support the Forest Stewardship Council™
[FSC™], the leading international forest certification organisation. All
our titles that are printed on FSC certified paper carry the FSC logo.

MIX
Paper from
responsible sources
FSC
www.fsc.org   FSC® C013056

Typeset by Palimpsest Book Production Ltd.,
Falkirk, Stirlingshire, Scotland.
Printed and bound in Great Britain by
T J International, Padstow, Cornwall.

It came to pass that in the land of Elizabeth, our Queen, in the city of York, which in the time of Augustus Caesar was called Eboracum, there dwelt a certain man who was named Anthony Garrett and who was within his own dwelling slain.

One

Wednesday 21 June, dawn – 11.30 hours

In which a man sees a human corpse for the last time, three women are seen to act in a most curious manner, and in which the gentle reader is introduced to Chief Inspector George Hennessey.

The day on which Miles Law came across a human corpse for the last time was also, by coincidence, the first day of the long-forecast heatwave which was created by a high-pressure weather system and which had tracked in a north-easterly direction from the Azores to enfold the British Isles. It was also, by further coincidence, the longest day of the year, being the 21st of June, the summer solstice. Miles Law had chosen for his bedroom a room with a south-east-facing window and had thus, that morning, as on all mornings, awoken with the sunrise, sleeping, as was his wont, with open curtains. Less than one half-hour later, having flung the light summer duvet off his naked body so as to try and obtain some release from the heat, he had attempted to return to sleep. Then, with no little annoyance, having found that nakedness brought him neither sleep nor tranquil rest, he observed the wisdom of the ancient adage '*do not fight the battle which you know you can't*

1

win', and had in consequence thusly risen and had showered and had shaved. Once dressed in white slacks and an old, baggy and much faded blue T-shirt, he had crept light-footedly down the narrow-angled staircase of the small cottage he rented and into the cramped narrow lounge and then he progressed to the equally cramped kitchen which was situated beyond the lounge. He had a light breakfast of cereal and three mugs of black sweetened coffee, taken in the lounge while listening with appreciation to the gently reassuring and effortlessly cultured sound of BBC Radio 4's morning programmes, *Today*, *Yesterday in Parliament*, and the first few minutes of *Desert Island Discs*. He remained in the lounge sipping coffee as the time crept slowly, all too slowly he felt, until just after nine a.m., upon which he switched off the radio and then left his cottage, which was set back from the road beside a stand of laurel bushes, and he collected his bike from the lean-to shelter which stood at the rear of the building. He wheeled the bicycle down the deeply rutted pathway of unsurfaced, baked-hard soil which led to the roadway, whereupon he mounted the bicycle and began to cycle steadily and quite contentedly towards the nearby village of Millington. At that moment the sun was rising behind him and so, as he rode, he was able to enjoy the view of the flat, rich landscape that was the Vale of York without having to half close his eyes and squint against the glare of the sun. He cycled in a relaxed and a calm manner along the pasty grey-coloured lane, which was, he had once learned, an ancient roadway,

2

probably dating to pre-Roman times, and he rode his bike between fields which were thick with ripening wheat, as indeed he had done many times before. He enjoyed the birdsong about him as he rode. His eye was suddenly caught by a red kite that was circling in a gliding manner seeking prey, and doing so against the blue and near cloudless sky. Miles Law watched with interest as the raptor suddenly folded its wings and dived, with evident purpose and determination, into the wheat field to his right, and then, moments later, rapidly rose to a height of about fifty feet, Law judged, and flew away.

Miles Law entered the village of Millington and as he did so he noticed a small amount of normal morning activity: the postman on his walk impudently reading with clear and evident curiosity the message on the back of the postcard that he was about to deliver; the lithe figure of the milkman in his blue smock attending to his bottle-clinking round; the middle-aged women walking side by side but not talking, carrying, at that time, empty shopping bags. Shortly after crossing the parish boundary into the village Miles Law dismounted from his bike and bent forward to remove the cycle clips from his trouser bottoms. He then began to push his bike up the long, narrow gravel-covered driveway which was the pedestrian and vehicular approach to an isolated Victorian-era house which, by the weathered name carved into the stone gateposts, which stood either side of the foot of the drive, was called 'The Grange'.

Miles Law pondered The Grange as he commenced what would be his slow walk up the drive, his feet crunching the gravel as he did so. The house did, that particular morning he thought, present quite a colourful spectacle, catching the rising sun and glowing most becomingly as it did so. The house that day in fact seemed to Miles Law to possess a particularly warm and most welcoming appearance.

The Grange stood, the dear reader might picture in their mind's eye, four square and solid upon a slight eminence, which Miles Law had learned some years earlier had been created by a glacier in the last ice age bulldozing the soil before it, as it progressed in a southerly direction, where-upon it had halted and over the vastness of geological time had eventually retreated as the global temperature had warmed and the ice had thawed. Or more succinctly, as Law has been told, 'it was as far south as the ice got', there being many hundreds of similar mounds stretch-ing across the United Kingdom and Ireland and which roughly corresponded to the 54th degree of latitude.

The driveway of The Grange was of recently laid dull yellow gravel and rose in a slight incline from the road to the house over a length, Miles Law estimated, of perhaps two hundred feet, before it widened out to form a large area in front of the house itself to offer car turning, or car-parking space. To the left of the driveway as one approached the house was a dense shrubbery which, at that time of year, was in full foliage of mainly green shades but was also speckled here and there with splashes of yellow and red and blue. To the right of the driveway as one approached the house was a large area of lawn which had evidently been mown so that strips of dark-green grass alternated neatly with strips of light-green grass of equal width. The building itself was of stone with large sash windows on the elevated ground floor, one at either side of the door, with similar sized windows above the ground floor and with a third window above the door. A generously sized skylight in the roof gave clear indication that the attic space had some function other than storage, although specifically what that function was Miles Law did not know, he having not once set foot in any part of the house, his place being in the garden, and there he was kept. Even his interview for his job had taken place outside the house, with he and his prospective employer agreeing on terms, and job description and remuneration, standing talking to each other at the foot of the front steps.

The Grange had been repainted within the last few weeks and Miles Law thought that the paint still looked fresh. The walls were, to Miles Law, a subtle and most pleasant pastel shade of blue, while the stonework surrounding the window frames had been picked out in gloss white which, at that moment, powerfully reflected the sunlight, while the blue caused the becoming glow. The door was painted gloss black and the large and heavy-looking handle and door knocker were both of highly polished brass. The roof was of red tiles and was, so far as Miles Law could tell, flawless, as if having been recently re-roofed, the owner of the house clearly subscribing to the belief that 'if you want to look after your house, then look after the roof because if you lose the roof, you lose the house'. At ground level airbricks betrayed the presence of a cellar which Miles Law knew to be something of a rarity, even a rare luxury in the Vale of York with its notoriously high water table. Law's modest cottage, situated as it was on the flood plain of a small river, could, by contrast, boast and offer only a shallow crawl space beneath the floorboards of the ground floor.

Miles Law, who had been a fit and a strong man when he was in his youth, now hesitated at the foot of the driveway of The Grange and 'pumped up' his body before pushing his bike up the driveway to the house. He began the ascent, making no attempt to soften his footfall, but actually twisting his feet so as to encourage the sound of his shoes crunching the gravel to carry over the ground towards the front aspect of the house. He knew his employer to be a man who did not seek friendship, a man who was not frightened of being disliked, and Law especially knew him to be a man who did not like being taken by surprise and so, as Law pushed his bike towards the house, he crunched and crunched and crunched.

Upon reaching the well-scrubbed stone steps at the front of the house he rested his bicycle against the side of the house and then climbed the steps up to the front door, and then he rapped out what was 'his' agreed knock on the large brass door knocker, being one knock then a slow count to ten then two more knocks, in rapid succession, which echoed loudly inside the house.

The head gardener, Miles Law had been told, also had his designated knock and the contract house cleaners had, he had found out, their specific knock. It was just the way the householder wanted it. The house owner paid the gardener's wages and he paid the cleaners' fee and so he got what he wanted. It was by the means of designated knocks that the householder knew who had arrived at his house and when they had arrived.

Miles Law, having announced his arrival, then turned and looked out across the front garden and back down the driveway towards the road. All seemed still. The postman and the milkman having progressed on their 'walk' and 'round' respectively had disappeared from sight, and the two middle-aged ladies had clearly reached the shops because they too had vanished from sight. Miles Law's eyes then rested upon the bungalow which stood directly opposite The Grange and which was also raised up a little from the level of the road, although it was of a slightly lower elevation than The Grange. He recalled when that particular plot of land had been occupied by a derelict barn which had subsequently been demolished. Shortly afterwards, about five years earlier, he thought, the bungalow had been built using the local grey stone. The garden of the bungalow with its two-car garage on the right-hand side as one faced the property had been laid out by a firm of landscape architects and the occupants, an elderly married couple, had then taken up residence. The couple had always seemed to Law to be well content. He had noticed the couple only in passing over the recent years and then he realized that he seemed to be noticing only the elderly lady occupant, quite thin looking, he always thought, even frail, but she was clearly a 'garden gate' of a human being, one that keeps creaking but never falls from its hinges and continues to do the job which nature intended it to do.

Miles Law descended the front steps of The Grange and walked, again deliberately crunching the gravel as he did so, to his left and then left again down the side of the house towards the rear of the property to where the outbuildings stood, hidden from the view of anyone on the road whether car driver or pedestrian. At the rear of The Grange were the greenhouses, the potting shed and also the shed where the gardening tools were kept. As he reached the rear corner of the building, Miles Law glanced to his left, ran his eyes along the back wall and instantly noticed, and with no little surprise, that one of the ground-floor windows was open – wide open, fully elevated so that the lower pane was almost parallel with the upper pane.

'Now that,' Miles Law spoke softly to himself, 'is very unusual. It is not like Garrett at all. Not like him at all.'

It was, in fact, most unusual indeed.

'And see here, once again he comes,' the woman spoke to herself, 'and always with that "shifty" something about him. So short and thin but he seems to be strong, he seems to be deliberately grinding the gravel beneath his shoes as he walks up the driveway, so much so that I fancy that if

I were outside my front door I could hear him at this distance.' The woman watched Miles Law arrive at The Grange and once again thought 'shifty' was the best way she could describe him. She had always thought that there was just something very 'criminal' about the man who would arrive periodically at The Grange on his bicycle. She had also noticed how the man seemed to come and go at odd times, as if arriving and leaving when it pleased him. *What*, she had often wondered, *sort of working arrangement is that?* The man was evidently a gardener, but one with no set hours. It was, she felt, a very strange working arrangement. Most strange indeed.

Linda Holyman sat in comfort in the deep armchair which stood against the wall of the sitting room of her bungalow. On the opposite side of the room, across a sea of dark green carpet, was the huge front window of her house. Very soon upon moving into her home she and her husband had come to learn that when she, or they, sat in the armchairs of the house which were opposite the window they could see very clearly out of it, but few people viewing from the outside could see them, being situated so deeply in the room as they were. It had become her practice, upon the sad but not unexpected loss of her husband, to sit in 'her' armchair each day during the daylight hours, often with a cup of tea on the low table beside the chair, listening to soothing Radio 3 or learned Radio 4, and to watch the world go by, such as what of the world was wont to go by in sleepy Millington. Usually Linda Holyman saw little of note or of interest but

9

occasionally, very occasionally, an incident would occur which would hold her attention, and which she would remember, as was the case a few days earlier, on the previous Saturday of that week.

It had been, she had noted, and now still well recalled, in the late forenoon of that day that a car had turned off the road which divided her bungalow from The Grange, and, unusually, she thought, had then halted at the very foot of the driveway rather than going all the way up to the front of the house. Intrigued, Linda Holyman had watched as three young women exited the car and then formed a particularly strange sight, so she felt. All three, she noticed, were dressed identically, in civilian clothing rather than in military wear, but so identical that it might, she fancied, be the uniform of a large commercial organization, in the way that air hostesses dress in the uniform of the airline for which they work. Not only did the three women wear identical clothing but what was also remarkable, she thought, was their identical handbags, each carried on the right shoulder, and also their hair-style and hair colour, being long and blonde, were also identical.

By then utterly spellbound, Linda Holyman watched as the three women walked slowly and calmly, very slowly and very calmly, she thought, up the driveway of The Grange, but they walked not as Linda Holyman had anticipated or expected, as a small group keeping station with each other, or in line abreast, but rather she saw that as they walked their paths interweaved, with one crossing in front of the other or others, or with one crossing behind the other or others, or when not in line abreast, with one at the rear moving forwards to occupy the place at the front of the group, or the woman at the front reducing her pace and re-joining the group at the rear. Linda Holyman watched as halfway up the drive the three women stopped to look at the expanse of the large lawn to their right-hand side and then resumed walking in their casual but constantly intertwining manner further up the drive. Once level with the shrubbery they turned to their left to look at it. The three women then began to walk towards the house. At the house two of the women stood at either side of the steps facing outwards, not, Linda Holyman thought, unlike two sentries. Linda Holyman watched as the third woman climbed the steps and knocked on the door using the brass knocker. She watched as the door opened and the woman who had knocked on the door entered the house immediately, too rapidly, she thought, to have been invited to enter. The door was then closed behind her, whereupon the other two women continued to stand motion-less, sentinel-like, as if not being permitted to move, nor to speak to each other. Within a few moments the woman who had entered the house was noticed by Linda Holyman to re-emerge, closing the door behind her, and then descended the steps and stood between the other two women. There was then a short but noticeable pause before the three women walked away from the house, moving as one, as if responding to some visual or audible cue or command which only they could see or hear. The three women walked back down the driveway, and once again their paths interweaved until they drew level with the car which was clearly waiting for them at the foot of the driveway. They got into the car, one in the front passenger seat and the other two sliding, in a lady-like manner in Linda Holyman's estimation, on to the rear seat. The car then carefully reversed on to the main road and was driven out of Millington in an easterly direction, opposite to the direction from which it had arrived. Linda Holyman had not seen the three women before, nor would she see them again.

And the owner of The Grange? Linda Holyman knew little of him. Very little indeed. Further, based on what she did know of the man, she wanted to know very little else. He was a strange fellow, she had always thought. She found him unwelcoming, cold, distant. She had met him once when a parcel had been delivered to his house which needed to be signed for, it being sent by Recorded Delivery, but the occupier of The Grange had not been at home to receive it. The postman, now retired and replaced, and known to Linda Holyman to be a cheery soul who always had time for a chat despite his long walk, had crossed the road from The Grange to her bungalow and had asked her if he could leave said parcel with her for the occupier of The Grange to collect upon his return home. Linda Holyman had been happy to agree to the request and had signed for the parcel. It was then, while reading the front of the package, that she had discovered that the owner of The Grange was called Anthony Garrett. The cheery, spindly postman, with his long, loping stride, had then returned to The Grange and left a note telling Mr Garrett from where he could collect his parcel. Some few hours later Garrett had returned home and, as Linda Holyman watched, he clearly found the note left for his attention by the postman and walked aggressively from his house over the road to her bungalow, whereupon he had rung the doorbell in an angry and an impatient manner. She had opened the door, parcel in hand, whereupon he had snatched it from her grasp mumbling only a cursory 'thank you very much', and had then turned away and walked back to The Grange angrily swinging his arm. Linda Holyman recalled a very clean man; bristlingly clean with piercingly cold blue eyes. She thought then that she did not want to know any more about her across the road neighbour, one Anthony Garrett esquire, nor did she ever wish to meet him again.

The open window at the rear of The Grange, the curiously open window, the suspiciously open window, the worryingly open window . . . Miles Law stood utterly still, hidden from view by any person who might, at that moment, have been looking at the building from the roadside of the house as he pondered the significance of the open window. It appeared to him to have been fully opened, slid all the way up, as it would have been so as to permit the house to ventilate on a hot summer day, but which had not been closed again once night had fallen. It was not, Miles Law thought, open in the manner of it being forced open by an intruder intent upon gaining unlawful entry. It was, Miles Law knew, opened too widely for that. When he, Miles Law, had burgled houses in his youth, he had always forced any window open just sufficiently to allow his egress like a lubricated viper. To leave a ground-floor window open, and so widely open, all night was totally unlike the Anthony Garrett whom Miles Law had come to know. It was totally out of character for the fastidious, every-thing-in-its-place Anthony Garrett, the Anthony Garrett who, despite his aggressive manner, still seemed to Miles Law to be frightened of his own shadow, who had admitted his fear of being burgled and who would shut his house down following the same routine each night, walking from room to room he had once told Law, dili-gently checking everything was as it should be, 'all off, all shut downstairs' being his mantra. Then checking that the gas was turned off in the kitchen, all the doors were bolted from the inside of the house and all windows closed and fastened shut. It was just not in Anthony Garrett's nature to leave a ground-floor window so widely open. It was such an invitation to crime and so unusual for Garrett, who had had his drive and the area surrounding the house freshly laid with gravel so that not even a cat could approach without making a sound.

Miles Law slowly walked towards the open window but he was most careful not to touch the frame for fear of leaving his fingerprints anywhere. He knew that his fingerprints should not be found, even if he was able to provide an acceptable excuse for having touched the window

14

frame. The window, he noted again, was indeed open to its fullest extent, as if in the manner of being opened to allow the house to 'breathe' on a hot day, as might in the present weather conditions be fairly expected, but which had not, as also fairly expected, been closed for the night. Miles Law turned and walked slowly and with a sense of mounting curiosity, and a mounting sense of fear for the safety of Anthony Garrett, back around the building to the front door. For the second time that morning he walked up the stone steps of The Grange to the front door and rapped the door knocker. This time he did not use his signature knock, but rather he banged the knocker three times in rapid succession and did so as loudly as he could. He elicited no response from within the house.

He turned the brass door handle and pushed the door, which opened smoothly and silently.

The open window.

The unlocked door.

Miles Law felt a growing sense of trepidation. This, was not like Anthony Garrett at all. It was just not in the nature of the man, the ever so, just so, private Anthony Garrett, the man who allowed so few people near him, and fewer still within his house, the man who seemed to Law to have few friends, and that is if he had any friends at all. Miles Law stepped gingerly into the foyer of the house, which he found to be light and airy and with no obvious sign of any disturbance having occurred there. He called out Garrett's name using the prefix 'Mr', as Garrett insisted on being addressed, and then adding 'sir' as he knew Garrett liked . . . 'Mr Garrett, sir . . .' Miles Law heard his voice echo within the entrance hallway and up the staircase to the upper floor. It was the first time that Law had been inside The Grange and he viewed with great interest the high ceiling of the hall, the angled staircase with the stone stairs protruding at ninety degrees from the wall without any visible means of support, clinging somehow to the wall so wide and confidently, as it climbed to the first floor. He saw the expensive, valuable even, paintings which hung on the walls above the staircase. He also noted the solid oak table standing in the middle of the floor of the entrance hall, the upright chairs of dark stained carved oak which lined the walls, all serving to give the impression of a wealthy homeowner.

'Mr Garrett, sir!' Once again Miles Law loudly called out Garrett's name. Once again Law heard his voice echo within the house, and once again there was not the slightest response to his shout. Law began to probe the house, walking softly, and as he did so, he noticed further indications The Grange had not been shut down properly for the night as he knew Garrett insisted on doing. Particularly he noticed that the ground-floor doors were left ajar rather than fully closed and bolted from the foyer side. He also noticed that the small wire cage behind the front door beneath the letterbox contained four or five envelopes, all of which appeared to be junk mail, but significantly their presence showed that the wire cage had not been emptied of mail for some days.

In the event Miles Law found Anthony Garrett in

a sitting position in an armchair in the drawing room. Or rather, he found the body of Anthony Garrett slumped backwards in an armchair, with his stomach beginning to bloat and his arms risen slightly with rigor. Flies in a black swarm hovered over the corpse. There was, Miles Law noted, a small circular hole in the middle of Garrett's forehead from which blood, now dry and blackened, had issued.

'Not again! Not another one!' Miles Law gasped in a voice which an observer might have thought to have a pleading quality about it. 'Not again . . .' he repeated, 'not again . . . not another one . . .' Miles Law steadied himself by grasping the back of a chair which he stood close to, and then he moved a little forward and then to his side and sank slowly into it. The chair in which he found himself sitting stood opposite the chair which contained the corpse of Anthony Garrett, separated by a distance of approximately, Law guessed, ten or twelve feet, with the man's head inclined backwards and his mouth gaping wide as if frozen in a moment of shock. Miles Law was not known to be an ethically steadfast human being, and even he himself would never claim that he was a man of unquestionable integrity, and yet, at that moment, when he was presented with a wonderful opportunity for theft on a large scale, the sort of opportunity he could only previously dream about, all he wanted to do was to sit quietly in an armchair and look at a dead man. Here within this large house which was clearly well stocked with easily portable items of value – and that was only what was in plain sight in

17

the drawing room – and with no one to stop him, and with no one likely to call at the house until the contract cleaners came in two days' time, there was, in short, nothing, nothing at all to prevent Miles Law from indulging in a high level of plunder. There was no obstacle at all, Law thought, to stop him collecting all he fancied from within the house and leaving it in a neat pile somewhere outside at the back, waiting there for him to return with a hired motor vehicle and then to remove said plunder under the cover of darkness. Nothing at all. It had, Law further thought, all come too late for him, this gift that he, as a young petty thief, could once only fantasize about. He sat silently and pondered the fly-blown corpse of Mr Anthony Garrett, sir, with the small hole in the forehead, and thought it had all come too late in his life.

Miles Law then stood and began to explore the house. He did so with a twofold purpose, the first being an inquisitive search of the building which he had never been permitted to enter with the knowledge that he would never again set foot within the walls and under the roof. The second reason was to survey the contents of the building with the eye of a lifelong thief, selecting in his mind the items of value which could so easily have been his had he been so inclined, and he did in fact find a drawer full of hard cash in used high-denomination notes, he also found a drawer full of valuable watches, men's as well as women's, he saw the silverware in the presentation cabinet with the easily broken glass front, he noticed the heavy furniture, clearly valuable, which, with help, he could run down to the Bermondsey Antiques Market in London in the back of a covered lorry and there sell for good money and with no questions asked. Said antiques market, it was rumoured, being the depository for the proceeds of burglary throughout the UK. Here, pondered Miles Law, was the means, the motive and the opportunity to enable him to acquire a very interesting amount of money. He would not be a wealthy man, but for him there would be no more pushing a lawnmower over the endless vastness of someone else's garden or the backbreaking weeding of someone else's flowerbeds. But it was all too late. All so late to be of use to him. As he wandered longingly from room to room he knew it. Even the wad of hard cash stayed where it was in a neat pile in the drawer and not one note was slipped into his trouser pocket, not one of the clearly valuable wristwatches was slipped on to his left wrist.

The little hole in the middle of Anthony Garrett's forehead said that it was all too late.

It was in passing that Miles Law noticed how neat the house had been kept. He noticed how Anthony Garrett had clearly been an obsessively neat man, despite the weekly contract cleaners calling. Garrett, Law saw, kept his house like he kept his garden, with precision, with a fastidious neatness about it, quite lifeless, Law thought, quite dead – as dead in fact as the householder.

It was, Miles Law pondered, the sort of detached observation that only a man also about to die would make. A bleak observation, he thought, and one with a certain detachment about it.

His leisurely tour of The Grange complete, save for the attic and the cellar, because for some reason he felt not the slightest desire to visit either, Law returned to the ground floor and specifically to the drawing room where Garrett's corpse sat in an armchair and where Law had noticed a telephone standing on a small, highly polished circular table by the door. He approached the telephone, picked up the receiver and, it being an old-style phone, dialled three nines and asked for the police. Law told the officer who answered his call who he was, his home address, where he was at that moment, and what he had found there.

George Hennessey instantly recognized the type, as indeed any long-serving police officer would. That pinched face of the petty criminal, those self-inflicted juvenile detention centre tattoos, the slight but wiry frame, those cold, piercing eyes of one of life's predators. George Hennessey thought there was something weasel-like about Miles Law. It was the only word he could think of to describe the man – weasel-like – and he further knew that he and Miles Law understood each other perfectly. He was the cop. Law, despite the irony of his name, was the criminal. They both knew each other's thinking. They both knew their attitude towards the other. There was a high fence between them, high and insurmountable, and both men liked it that way. Without being told, George Hennessey knew that Miles Law had a criminal record running through him like letters in a stick of Scarborough rock. Again, he saw those cold blue eyes of a human predator, the lithe frame adept at sliding through slightly forcibly opened windows. Hennessey estimated Miles Law to be a man in his mid-fifties, by then clearly a 'has-been', a burnt-out case and no longer an active criminal, and he further saw that Miles Law was one of the bad ones. He was not a sad one, nor a mad one, but a bad one, deserving of each of his fines and his prison sentences.

George Hennessey had arrived at The Grange in Millington, or to give the village its proper but barely used name, Millington-in-the-Vale, with Sergeant Yellich, with Yellich at the wheel of the unmarked police vehicle which they had taken from the car pool, and as they had approached the house Hennessey had noticed the two marked police vehicles, a third unmarked vehicle and the black windowless mortuary van already parked at the side of the road, near the foot of the driveway of The Grange. All neatly parked and pleasingly so, unlike a police car he had once seen when in Canada with three wheels on the road surface and the fourth left slovenly on the pavement. He noticed also, as Yellich slowed the car to a halt behind the hind-most police vehicle, as they approached the scene, that a blue and white tape reading *Police Do Not Cross* had been strung across the entrance of the driveway of The Grange from gatepost to gatepost at waist height. A single police constable in a white shirt and serge trousers stood on duty at the foot of the drive, midway between the gateposts. Hennessey and Yellich left their motor vehicle with one window wound down a few inches to permit the interior of the car to 'breathe'

21

in the growing heat of the day and they then walked towards the gateway of The Grange. Upon their approach the constable nodded, offered a warm, 'Good morning, gentlemen,' and lifted the tape to allow Hennessey and Yellich to walk beneath it.

'No one is going to be able to approach this house quietly,' Yellich observed as he and Hennessey began the walk up the gravel-covered drive, having replied to the constable's reverent greeting.

'As you say.' Hennessey looked ahead of him at the lone figure of Thompson Ventnor standing a little to the left of the house. Three constables in white shirts stood in a group in front of the door to the house. 'I always said and advised folk that gravel and a dog are the two best burglar deterrents that can be had. Either is good, but both . . . well, with both you have a very safe house indeed, especially if you have a security light permanently switched on within the building.' He glanced to his right and viewed the gently undulating landscape that was the Vale of York, approximately 1 degree west and 45 degrees north. 'But there is no need for me to tell you that,' Hennessey added with a smile. 'I mean one copper to another. No need at all.'

'Indeed, sir,' Yellich replied, also with a smile. 'Indeed, as you say, no need at all.'

Hennessey and Yellich walked on in silence save only for the sound of the gravel grinding beneath their feet, until they stood in front of Thompson Ventnor.

'Good morning, sir.' Ventnor addressed Hennessey,

22

being the senior of the two officers, but he also nodded respectfully to Somerled Yellich.

'DC Ventnor,' Hennessey replied. 'What have you got for us?'

'One deceased male, sir,' Ventnor informed him. 'The deceased appears to be in his late middle years. Dr Mann, the police surgeon, pronounced life extinct at . . .' Ventnor consulted his notebook, '. . . at ten thirty-three hours this forenoon, sir. Upon his declaration, I requested the attendance of a Home Office licensed pathologist and also asked control to notify the senior officers on duty and to request their attendance.'

'And here we are.' Hennessey further glanced about him.

'Yes, sir,' Thompson Ventnor stammered. 'Dr Mann extends his apologies. He said that he would have stayed as a professional courtesy until the senior officers and the pathologist arrived, but he had a suspicious death in Selby to attend.'

'It's all happening in the Vale today,' Hennessey growled. 'Very well, thank you, Thompson.' He noted the solidly late Victorian building that was The Grange, and the neatly mowed expanse of lawn which he thought was ready for another cutting. 'Do we know which pathologist is going to be attending?'

'I'm sorry, sir,' Ventnor mumbled, 'I didn't ask. It never occurred to me to do so.'

'No matter.' George Hennessey continued to look at the building that was The Grange; he especially noted how well maintained it appeared to be. 'It was just a matter of idle curiosity on my part; I dare say that we'll find out quite soon enough.

So . . . tell me . . . what have you done? Where are we . . . at what stage of this investigation?'

'Well, I've secured the location, sir,' Ventnor stammered. 'I've conducted a rapid search of the premises, calling from room to room as I went in the company of two constables. There appears to be no other person in the house, nor any other bodies. I have not yet been in the cellar or in the attic.'

'Understood.' Hennessey nodded and then commented with clear interest, 'This house has a cellar, you say?'

'Yes, sir.' Ventnor smiled. 'I know that cellars are quite rare in the Vale of York, but as you see, this particular building is upon a slight rise, or a hillock, or what the Victorians might have described as being a slight "eminence" . . . which has permitted cellarage to be included in the house's design.'

'Yes, so I see.' Hennessey nodded. 'An eminence . . .' he echoed. 'I like the use of the word . . . yes, it has an appeal. So, who found the body? Who found the deceased?'

'The gentleman standing over there, sir.' Ventnor pointed with a bent arm, so his finger was at waist height, to the solitary figure of Miles Law who was, at that moment, standing to Hennessey's left and in the shade of the shrubbery which stood at the top of the driveway and to the left of The Grange as viewed from the road.

'All right,' Hennessey growled. 'Have you taken a statement from him yet?'

'Not yet, sir,' Ventnor offered, 'just his details, but he does seem very willing to cooperate. I searched the house in the first instance. I gave that priority. It seemed to be the correct thing to do.'

'Fair enough.' Hennessey brushed an annoying fly from his face. 'Anything of note within the house?'

'Not that I could see, sir,' Ventnor replied. 'I was just concerned to determine that no other person, alive or deceased, was in the building, and it appears that there is not, although, as I said, the cellar and the attic both need to be searched. I was about to do that when the constable at the door announced the arrival of yourself and Sergeant Yellich. So the house still needs a detailed forensic examination.'

'Understood.' Hennessey nodded once more. 'What do we know about the deceased? What have you been able to find out?'

'Very little, I'm afraid, sir.' Ventnor consulted his notebook. 'The post in the mailbox, all of it, appears to be addressed to one Anthony Garrett. I have requested a criminal records check but the collator hasn't come back with any results yet. The collator has also agreed to check with the land registry as to the registered owner of the property.'

'Right.' Hennessey further looked at the house. 'Right,' he said again, 'you two, Somerled and Thompson . . . I want you two to please undertake a thorough search of the house, room by room, cupboard by cupboard, drawer by drawer, basement to rafter. Stay together, you know the drill. Meanwhile, I'll have a little chat with the gentleman who found the body. What is his name?'

'Law, sir,' Ventnor replied. 'Mr Law gives his age as fifty-three years and his occupation as being that of "general labourer".'

'General labourer,' Miles Law confirmed. 'I'm just that. Nothing special. I never amounted to much in life. I had a modest start and it looks like I am having a modest end. But that's better than falling from grace, I always think.'

'General labourer is good enough.' George Hennessey spoke softly so as to try to put Miles Law at ease. The pinched face, the gaol-house tattoos, and then he knew, as previously observed, that he was talking to a member of the criminal class. He knew that Law knew that he knew, and he also sensed that both he and Law were happy with that recognition having been made. There was a mutual understanding, even a mutual respect. Just so long as each stayed on his side of the fence, then they were both content.

'That job title can cover a multitude of sins.' George Hennessey continued to speak softly and he smiled warmly as he looked down benignly at Miles Law, whose head was level with George Hennessey's chest.

'Well, it's the honest truth, governor, that's what it is, and it's all I'm really good for. I reckon it's all I'm good for.' Miles Law shrugged. 'So that's me . . . lifting things, carrying that, fetching the other, so I reckon "general labourer" sums me up quite well . . . quite well enough, me and my little old life.'

'Very well, but do you think that you could be a little more specific, Mr Law, if you please,'

Hennessey pressed, though he still spoke in a calm and a gentle manner. 'I mean, can you tell me what you do for Mr Garrett? What is your specific area of responsibility here at The Grange?'

'Do you mean "did"? What my job was?' Miles Law looked to his left and sighed. 'I mean, I don't think I'll be doing much for Mr Garrett now, do you? Well, anyway, if you must know I was the "donkey gardener" here. That's me . . . that was me . . . the "donkey gardener". It's all I amounted to.'

'The "donkey gardener"?' Hennessey parroted. '"Donkey gardener"? What on earth is one of those? I confess I have never heard of such a beast.' He brushed another persistent fly from his face.

'That's probably because it's a name I gave myself.' Miles Law shrugged. 'My proper job title is the "under-gardener", sometimes I'm the "second gardener" and sometimes I am the "assistant gardener". I do the easy work . . . hard work in a sense but unskilled, the jobs that just need brute strength, just a bit of honest to God muscle. Like, I may not be clever but I can lift things. So today I was to mow the lawn. I like that job.' He pointed to the lawn. 'I did that a week ago. I came here this morning to do it again. That's one of the "donkey" jobs in this old garden.'

'Yes.' Hennessey viewed the garden. 'Very neat, if I may say so, the alternate light and dark strips. I really do like that effect. It's very easy on the eye.'

'Up one way and back down the other way,'

Law explained. 'It's very easy with the power mower. I also trim the edge of the lawn with a pair of long-handled shears, all round the edge, inch by little inch by little inch until the whole edge is neatly trimmed, just as Garrett wants . . . or wanted it. I like doing the lawn, I must confess – I can easily lose myself in doing the lawn. And you can see when the job is done. I also pull up the weeds from the flowerbeds and sharpen the tools and I wheel the cuttings to the compost heap in the wheelbarrow. I do all those things, so I do. But the pruning of the fruit trees, the grafting of saplings, the potting of new growth in the plant pots in the potting shed, all that sort of stuff is done by the head gardener. He should have just returned from his holiday about now. Him and his family.'

'I see,' Hennessey grunted. He was content to let Law talk, and the more Law talked the more Hennessey was prepared to accept that the man was no longer criminally active. No active criminal would be relaxed enough to speak to a police officer in the manner in which Miles Law talked about his job. 'I get the picture. I was going to ask of the whereabouts of the head gardener, but now you've told me.'

'Well, that's me, the old "donkey job" man out here in the garden of The Grange, working . . . or rather did work for Mr Garrett.'

'What did you intend to do today?' Hennessey felt the need to get Law on his side. He intuitively felt he was going to need the man's cooperation. 'I mean, it all still looks very neat. The lawn could possibly do with a trim, as you say, but it's far from being overgrown and untidy. So what brought you here today?'

'The heat,' Miles Law smiled briefly, 'the heat and the need to do something. I woke early, the sun woke me and it can get very hot in my little cottage. I knew I'd get fed up with my own company so I thought that I'd cycle over to The Grange and mow the lawn and water the garden.'

'And there's plenty of dry-looking soil at the moment, I see,' Hennessey grinned, 'plenty to point your hose at. It looks like it could do with a good drink; the whole lot of it looks a trifle thirsty.'

'Yes . . . well, any old and sad and stupid fool can water a garden and so that's why it's on my "to do" list. So I have a reason to leave my house and to do my job at The Grange. So I am felling two birds with one stone.'

'Yes . . .' Once again Hennessey brushed a persistent fly from his face. 'So you have no set working hours to adhere to?'

'No . . . nope . . . none,' Law replied, 'and I confess that that suits me nicely, suits me down to the ground, suits me very well indeed. It was as Garrett said when he first set me on, "*You can always tell when your gardener's working, or not, as the case may be.*" So long as I put in my hours, that's thirty hours a week in the summer months, do my "donkey" jobs, then I lift a reasonable pay packet on the Friday. But, of course, I only get paid in the summer when there's work to be done. So for me it's the old gardener's song, "Cigars in the summer and

29

roll-ups in the winter". Such is the lot for we poor sons of the soil.'

'So what happened this morning?' Hennessey asked. 'Just take me through the events of this morning, please.'

'So . . . this morning . . . well, this morning I arrived on my old bike, like normal, like I said.' Law pointed to his bicycle which stood by the steps of the house. 'I arrive and I hammer on the knocker, using the knock that Garrett gave me . . . one knock and then a long pause and then two knocks in quick succession.'

'That's your knock?' Hennessey queried. 'You have your own knock?'

'Yes, I have my own knock. That's how Garrett knows . . . or knew it was me who was at his door. He gave all his employees their own special knock. The head gardener's knock is three knocks in quick succession, a pause, then two more knocks in quick succession. It let him know who had arrived at the house without him having to get out of his chair and have a look see.'

'I see.' Hennessey nodded. 'I can see the value of that arrangement.'

'The house cleaners also have their own special knock. They have a key to let themselves in if he is not at home, but he likes them to knock anyway.'

'Interesting,' Hennessey mused, 'so Garrett was clearly a man who liked to be in control. He was a man who liked to know what is . . . or was . . . going on about him.' Then he asked, 'What do you know about Garrett? Much? Anything at all you can tell me will be useful.'

'Garrett.' Law shrugged and glanced to his left. 'Not much, to be honest with you, Guv, not much at all. He always struck me as a bit of a cagey sort of geezer, well cagey, did Mr Garrett. He didn't seem to want to let anyone in his house, so far as I could tell . . . except the folk who needed to be in there, like the cleaners. They're called The Maids and they arrive in their little yellow van once a week, so they're not known personally to Garrett . . . or were not known . . . and so far as I could tell it was not always the same women who called. It was different women from week to week, it seemed to me. They arrive and he lets them in and they do their thing – they vacuum and dust and polish and clean the bathroom then they drive away again. If he's not at home then they let themselves in anyway, like I said, but they have to knock first. He was very insistent on that point. Once they let themselves in without knocking and I heard him shouting at them from where I was down there by the gateposts. He had quite a temper, did Mr Garrett.'

'I see,' Hennessey nodded. 'So no personal visitors that you know of and he liked to keep people at a distance?'

'It seemed that way to me, sir . . . but I am not here all the time and The Maids, well, they're in and out in about an hour each time that they visit.'

'Just an hour, for a house of this size?' Hennessey gasped. 'And just how many cleaners each time?'

'Two, just two women. Well, I mean he was a single bloke, living alone. He probably only used just one bedroom, one bathroom, the kitchen and the lounge, or drawing room if you're posh,' Law offered. 'So, yes, I can see why they only needed to stay for an hour, probably keen to get away – he wasn't the world's most pleasant old boy. In fact, The Maids once asked me about his routine.'

'His routine,' Hennessey repeated. 'They asked you about that recently?'

'No . . . no.' Law shook his head vigorously. 'No, this was a year ago now, last summer. I was just finishing as they were leaving the house and it was their last job of that day so we just got chatting . . . nothing special . . . just about this and that, a sort of end of the working day natter between working-class folk. It happens all the time. Just a bit of a chinwag.'

'I see.' Hennessey nodded. 'But do go on, please.'

'Well, it was then that they told me that he shuts his house down at night because, on the few occasions that they have called in the morning, like it's their first job of that day, he lets them in while he is still wearing his pyjamas and his dressing gown and unlocks all the inside doors – locked so that if the house is burgled the felon cannot get past the room he has broken into, and they wanted to know if he has the some sort of security arrangement in the garden. They were just curious, you see – anyway, I told them it didn't seem that he did. There were no security features that I knew of outside the house, apart from the gravel drive . . . no alarms, no CCTV cameras. The outbuildings are kept shut by a latch but are not locked as such. He probably felt he didn't need CCTV – he thought he was safe. It's quite a remote house, difficult to approach without being seen. In the city . . . yes, he might need CCTV, but not out here. He wasn't particularly bothered about local villains poking around – he could live with that.'

'I see,' Hennessey repeated. 'So he is a single man who lives alone?'

'Yes . . . yes, I think he is that.' Miles Law again glanced to his left, then paused and turned to Hennessey. 'Look, governor, there's no use beating around the bush . . . you'll know him. You will definitely know him.'

'We will?' Hennessey raised his bushy eyebrows. 'You mean that he is known to the police? We would have checked anyway, but it's interesting that you say that. So tell me, how do you know that Mr Garrett has a criminal record?'

'Well . . . because it takes one to know one and you'll know him all right,' Law replied, 'just like you know me. Me and Garrett, we've both been inside. We both have criminal records.'

'You do?' Hennessey feigned surprise. 'So we'll know you, Mr Law?'

'Look, I'm trying to help you so don't pretend to be surprised,' Law replied sourly. 'I know you clocked me for an ex-con the very moment you set eyes on me, just like I could tell that you were a copper if I saw you walking down the street. You and me, we don't need no uniforms and labels stamped on our foreheads to recognize each other for what each other is . . . or for what we are. So I may as well tell you because you'll be checking up on me anyway, won't you?'

'Yes,' Hennessey nodded, 'yes, we will. As you say, we'll be checking on you anyway.'

'See, I know how the cops work. I know very well how the police work.' Miles Law spoke softly. 'If I ever learned one thing in life it's how the boys and girls in blue work. I picked it up along the way. But I have not done no crookin' for a long time. I mean nothing that you'll be wanting to hear about. I've gone straight, been straight for a while, but I've done some things in my past and while I could work for Garrett, I could keep on going straight. This is the only job I can get now and now he's gone . . . well, this job is not a position of responsibility – no position of trust is part of being a "donkey gardener". I got paid in hard cash so it kept me out of trouble, but now it looks like I'll have idle hands and we all know who makes work for idle hands. Don't we all know that?' Law paused. 'Well . . . I've got a plan hatching.'

'All right, so we'll have your name and address on file?' Hennessey asked. 'Your current address, I mean?'

'Yes, you will, but only because I gave it to the other detective – the younger geezer who arrived first, the one with the drink problem.' Law held a defiant eye contact with Hennessey. 'I gave my current address to him.'

'Why do you say that?' Hennessey growled. 'I mean about the drink problem?'

'Those bloodshot eyes, governor, the breath heavy with the smell of strong mints to cover up

34

the stale breath caused by last night's beer.' Law smiled. 'Come on. Don't tell me that you haven't noticed it, or are you pretending not to notice it? Is that it? What's that term, "an elephant in the room", something so big that it's more comfortable to ignore it ... pretend it's not there? Anyway, that's your business not mine, but you'll have my address on your file,' Law continued, 'or in your computer, and you'll have my real name – you'll have that also. I don't use an alias. I was just a very silly boy. I was never a major player, just a petty crook, that's the term to describe me, or to describe what I used to be. Just a petty crook.'

'Fair enough,' Hennessey murmured, though he still felt stung by Miles Law's reference to Thompson Ventnor's drinking habit. It was, though, an issue which he was uncomfortably aware of. 'So what,' he asked, 'makes you think that we will know Anthony Garrett, deceased?'

'Believe . . .' Law replied with a glint in his eye. 'There is just no thinking about it, squire. It's a belief, a dead certainty, a knowledge.' Law took a deep breath. 'Well, let's just say it was like love at first sight. It was like that. You know the way? The way it is when two people first set eyes on each other and there is an instant connection? Well it was like that with me and Garrett. Just like that. The moment we saw each other we knew that we'd both been inside. I figured him for an old lag, and he figured me for an old lag. Different league maybe, but old lags just the same. I knew that he saw me as a minor player because he sort of sneered at me with his eyes

35

. . . like I was beneath him, which I probably was, so I reckon that's fair. But that's the answer to your old question, governor, just like two ex-servicemen can recognize each other as being ex-military, so me and Garrett recognized each other as both being ex-cons.'

'Understood.' Hennessey wiped a bead of sweat from his brow. 'Yes, I know what you mean. So, do you know anything about his background? What sort of crime did he do? Did you pick up any information like that? Did he tell you anything?'

'Nothing, squire,' Law responded quickly. 'I know nothing about him, nothing about his history.' Miles Law glanced at the ground and rubbed the sole of his shoe in the gravel. 'He was a cagey sort of geezer, like I said. Very, very cagey, was Mr Garrett. Very cagey indeed. I never got to go inside his house until this morning, and he hardly ever spoke to me at all, not really . . . he just checked the garden had been done to his satisfaction and he gave me an envelope of hard cash once a week during the summer months when I was working for him. In the winter I got laid off, like I said. What I can tell you plain is that he was not from around these parts. He was not from the Vale. He was a Londoner, I would think. He had a London accent – East London, I'd say. I always thought that he was an East End boy. You see, he'd pronounce "with" as "wiv", for example, so I thought East London, but north of the river, a bit like your accent, governor. I'd put you as East London, but south of the river. I'd put you south of the river.'

'You'd put me correctly.' Hennessey smiled. 'You are quite right, quite right I am a Londoner, south of the river and east – I'm from Greenwich. I've been up here a good few years though, and so my accent is not as strong as it once was and I dare say that it has not been strengthened by spending years behind bars like you say Garrett seems to have done. That experience will strengthen any regional accent. He'd have to have kept it strong to gain acceptance.'

'I reckon the same,' Law replied. 'You see, governor, regional accents is a bit of a hobby of mine. I got interested in local accents when I was serving in the army. I was in the Royal Logistical Corps . . . the "Loggies". Three years I did. Not a long time. Anyway, we had boys and girls from all over the UK. Unlike the county or city-based regiments who'd recruit from just one main area, we came from all over we did.' Law paused. 'We had Scots geezers who'd call a woman "hen", English blokes who'd call a woman "duck", we had Lancashire girls who'd call an apple pie an "Eve pie", a Cornish bloke who'd call his mates "my handsome", London boys who'd call men "geezers" and call girls "Richards" – rhyming slang, you see . . .'

'Yes, I know,' Hennessey smiled once again, 'Richard the thirds – birds, so "Richards" for short.'

'That's it.' Law also smiled. 'Mind you, you'd know that. I mean, being from the Smoke. So, anyway, with all those accents and expressions all mixed up in one mob I got to develop an interest in accents, and when I heard Anthony

37

Garrett's accent I pinned him to the East End of London and I also clocked him as an ex-con. I'll be right on both counts, I bet you I will. It was after I left HM Forces that I came off the track, that I stepped on to the wrong path.'

'Sorry to hear that, but anyway . . .' Hennessey pulled the conversation back into focus by asking: 'So, this morning, tell me how you came to be in the house and find Mr Garrett.'

Miles Law then told Hennessey about the open window, so very unusual and wholly out of character for Garrett. He told Hennessey of there being no response to his urgent knocking on the door when he attempted to check on Anthony Garrett's welfare, of how the door opened, not being locked, again very unusual for Anthony Garrett, and of how he had entered the house while calling Garrett's name over and over again, of finding Garrett's body and of picking up the phone in the drawing room and dialling three nines. 'And,' he said, 'here you are.'

'Well, thank you, Mr Law,' Hennessey responded with an approving smile. 'We'll be calling on you at home later to take a full statement from you, but thank you for phoning. It was very public spirited of you.'

'Ha!' Miles Law scoffed. 'Public spirited! That's a turn up for the books. Nobody has ever called me public spirited before . . . especially not a copper. Me, public spirited! Me!'

George Hennessey walked slowly and calmly back towards the front door of The Grange and slipped his hand into his jacket pocket as he did so and extracted his mobile phone. He pressed a pre-selected number which was answered with a crisp, efficient male voice. '*Micklegate Bar Police Station, York, Constable Barnes speaking.*'

'DCI Hennessey here.' Hennessey identified himself.

'Yes, sir.' Barnes was eager, it seemed to Hennessey. He was clearly a good man to have on the switchboard.

'Put me through to the collator, please,' Hennessey requested just as he saw Detective Sergeant Yellich emerge from the house, accompanied by Thompson Ventnor.

The line clicked and a second voice spoke. '*Collator here, sir.*'

'Good man.' Hennessey took off his Panama hat and wiped his brow with his forearm. 'Can you please see what we have in terms of criminal records of one Anthony Garrett of The Grange, Millington-in-the-Vale, Vale of York, and also one Miles Law, address to follow. Both men are in their fifties.'

'*Yes, sir. Will do.*' The collator's voice was also eager, also efficient-sounding.

'Thank you.' Hennessey replaced his hat. 'Can you put me back to the switchboard, please?'

The connection then fell silent as Hennessey, waiting to be re-connected to the switchboard, pondered the ludicrous situation wherein he was speaking to people just ten miles away via a satellite orbiting the Earth. It was not though, he was able to reassure himself, perhaps so ludicrous as the young female he had once heard using her mobile phone as she entered a pub, in which he was sitting by the door, and asking where in the pub her friends were sitting, thus sending a signal into space and getting a reply, via space, so as to avoid her the trouble of looking in a maximum of three rooms.

'*Switchboard.*' The voice of PC Barnes remained crisp and alert.

'Yes . . . good man, Barnes, Hennessey here again. Can you put me through to the press officer, please?' Hennessey continued to walk towards the location where Yellich and Ventnor stood talking to each other.

'*Yes, sir.*' Once again the connection clicked and then fell silent.

'*Press officer.*' The voice was female, young-sounding, thought Hennessey, but equally keen and eager.

DCI Hennessey halted when he was within an arm's length of Yellich and Ventnor. 'Can you issue a press release, please? "*Police are investigating the suspicious death of a male, believed to be one Anthony Garrett of The Grange, Millington, Vale of York. Anyone with any information should contact Micklegate Bar Police Station, York, etc . . .*" You know the sort of thing.'

'*Yes, sir,*' the press officer replied confidently, '*leave it with me, I know exactly what is needed.*'

Hennessey pocketed his phone and glanced at Yellich and raised his eyebrows as he did so.

'There appears nothing out of order in the house, sir,' Yellich replied in answer to Hennessey's raised eyebrows, being by then well aware of his senior officer's way of requesting information.

'There appears to be no sign of disturbance or of theft . . . no sign of any forced entry that we could detect. The house appears well stocked with items of value which would appeal to any housebreaker. I mean items like jewellery, watches, antique furniture, bundles of banknotes . . . but nothing appears to have been removed. Nothing at all. There are no obvious gaps where something once stood for example. We did find a number of building society passbooks in the names of persons other than Anthony Garrett. We also found chequebooks, also in names other than Garrett.'

'So . . . a monied man,' Hennessey observed dryly, 'and keeping account details for other people, or what I think is much more likely is that he is a man using assumed names. That is difficult to do these days but not at all is it impossible. It's still too easy to obtain another person's birth certificate. Alarmingly easy if you ask me.'

'Indeed, sir,' Yellich replied. 'We are also satisfied that there is no other person in the house, and also no animals are present, not one living thing apart from the flies hovering over the deceased. And, as you requested, we checked basement to rafter, cellar to attic, and so we feel the building can be secured once the deceased has been removed.'

'Good . . . good . . . thank you.' Hennessey then saw what Miles Law had meant about Ventnor's bloodshot eyes and his mint-laden breath. It possibly was an issue he had to address, he thought, but while Ventnor's functioning as a police officer remained at an acceptable level,

41

Hennessey decided that he would not broach the subject for the time being. It was, though, he felt, something to keep an eye on. 'So, all very shipshape and Bristol fashion would you say? Apart, that is, from the body in the drawing room. Can I ask, did you notice any female jewellery?' Hennessey paused and then grinned at his own inadvertent double meaning. 'What I mean is did you notice any jewellery which would be worn by a woman?'

'No, we didn't, sir.' Yellich also grinned. 'I know what you meant. All the indications in the house are of one man who lived alone, in some luxury it has to be said, but a man with no significant other in his life.'

'All right,' Hennessey nodded, 'I have the picture. Thank you.'

'We did a very thorough search of the house,' Ventnor added, 'opened every drawer and every cupboard . . . top to bottom, just a detailed forensic examination to be done now . . . and photographs taken, of course.'

'Yes. Did you request SOCO?' Hennessey half closed his eyes against the glare of the sun.

'Yes, sir. They're on their way.' Ventnor glanced at his watch. 'In fact, they're overdue really.'

'All right, so long as they're on their way,' Hennessey replied calmly. 'So all is in hand. The press officer is putting out a bulletin so we can expect TV crews and the newshounds also to arrive at any time now. There's only one officer at the foot of the drive at the moment, so we'd better reinforce that. Can you see to that, please, Ventnor? At least three other constables I think.

It's going to be quite a media scrum. You'd also better post a couple of uniforms at the rear of the building. No one except those on police business are to set foot in the grounds.'

'Yes, sir.' Ventnor turned and walked briskly towards where a uniformed sergeant and a group of constables were standing.

'And I,' Hennessey turned to Yellich, 'I will take a tour of the house so as to familiarize myself with the building whilst we wait for SOCO and the pathologist to arrive.' Then he added, 'If the pathologist is Dr D'Acre we'll have a long time to wait, I think.'

'We will, sir?' Yellich asked. 'You think so?'

'Yes, I think so.' Hennessey permitted himself the briefest of smiles. 'Now, please do not misunderstand me, Somerled, I have a lot of time for Dr D'Acre, an awful lot of time. She is one damn good pathologist and we are more than fortunate to have her services but good heavens, I swear, Somerled, I have come to learn that that woman has no sense of direction at all, none whatsoever. She'll get from one place to another by following the bus route without considering that the bus might make all sorts of detours to collect and to deposit passengers, rather than taking the direct route. So if she wants to go from A to B, she'll drive from A to C to D to E and then to B because that's the way the bus goes. I hitched a ride in her car once to attend a crime scene and I found myself having to be very patient with the lady. Very patient indeed.'

'Yes . . . I know what you mean, sir.' Yellich

43

smiled. 'I too have met drivers like that, male as well as female.'

'I'm sure you have, Somerled.' Hennessey paused. 'Now, let us get back to the matter in hand. I have a job for you.'

'Yes, sir,' Yellich replied eagerly.

'Now, Mr Law, the self-deprecating, self-styled "under-gardener", painted a clear picture of Mr Garrett not only living alone, but not encouraging any contact from the outside world. The only people he allowed in his house, it seems, was a crew of contract cleaners, who will have to be visited.'

'Yes, sir.'

'Now it seems to me that the only house with a clear view of The Grange is the new-build bungalow over there, directly opposite, on the other side of the road. Do you see it?' Hennessey nodded towards the bungalow.

'Yes, sir,' Yellich replied. 'I also noticed it for the same reason . . . it affords a good view of the front of this house.'

'Yes. So can you please be so good as to cross the road and interview the occupants. See what, if anything, they can tell us. I mean, a man shut himself away from the world, discouraged callers, yet someone can walk into his house and shoot him at point-blank range . . . drill him between the eyes from a few feet away and then just leave again – not interested in stealing anything despite there being much to steal. See if they can tell us anything, Somerled. Meanwhile I will, as I said, familiarize myself with the interior of The Grange.'

George Hennessey, Panama hat in hand, turned and walked slowly and silently through the house, room by room, making his own general, rather than detailed, survey of The Grange. He saw clearly what Miles Law and what Yellich and Ventnor had meant when they described a man who was fastidiously neat, with, he noted, not an item appearing to be out of place, and he pondered that Anthony Garrett would most probably not have been an easy man to live with. Living with Garrett, Hennessey reflected, would have been like walking on broken glass: one would, he felt, be frightened of breathing too loudly or even of blinking too often in this house. The man, Hennessey believed, would drive any person who lived with him into a state of 'frozen awareness', like abused children who are too frightened to move. He also saw what Miles Law and his officers had meant when they had severally reported that there was, in The Grange, much of interest to any burglar, but similarly he noted that nothing appeared to have been stolen. It was all there, no obvious gaps where some valuable item clearly once stood. Hennessey walked into a front bedroom, not, he noted, one which seemed to be used, by virtue of the unmade bed and the open wardrobe door which revealed that it contained nothing, being in fact just as empty as it would have been had it been on display in a furniture shop. Hennessey glanced out of the window of the unused room in which he stood, and saw Somerled Yellich striding manfully up the driveway of the bungalow which stood on the opposite side of the road, about to knock on the door of the house, as he had asked Yellich to do. He also saw, with a great sense of pleasure and pride, a red and white Riley RMA circa 1947, half on the kerb, behind a line of police vehicles. He watched as Dr D'Acre stepped lithely out of the car and began to walk up the drive of The Grange, having negotiated the blue and white police tape which had been held up for her by one of the constables who had been stationed there, reinforcing the original lone constable as Hennessey had requested. Hennessey enjoyed the image Dr D'Acre presented, tall, slender, elegant, close-cropped hair, dressed in white coveralls and carrying, as she always did on such occasions, a highly polished black Gladstone bag.

Hennessey glanced up at the blue and near cloudless sky and said, 'He'd know his attacker. His attacker knew him. His attacker came here to kill him, and that done, left the house. Job done. That's what happened here. This was no burglary gone awry. This was calculated and premeditated.'

'Well, life is extinct, as Dr Mann has stated.' Dr D'Acre considered the corpse of Anthony Garrett. 'Most extinct indeed.'

George Hennessey, upon noting the arrival of Dr D'Acre, had turned from the window of the unused bedroom and had casually descended the angled staircase to the foyer, timing his arrival on the ground floor just as Dr D'Acre stepped into the building. Dr D'Acre and George Hennessey permitted themselves the briefest of smiles and of eye contact, after which Hennessey

said, 'Just through here, ma'am,' and had indicated the open door of the drawing room. 'The
police surgeon, Dr Mann, pronounced life extinct
about one hour ago. Dr Mann regretted he could
not remain until you arrived, ma'am, but he
reported that he had to attend a suspicious death
in Selby.'

It was then, after walking from the foyer into
the drawing room, that Dr D'Acre stood over the
corpse of Anthony Garrett and had said, 'Life is
extinct, as Dr Mann had stated, most extinct
indeed . . . and the flies I see have been usefully
busy, leaving us their little gifts. They will help
us . . . help me to determine the time of death
with a reasonable degree of accuracy, which I
know is something you are always very keen to
find out. There must be an open window in the
house somewhere. I mean for them to have gath-
ered like this, they must have had ready access
to the corpse,' Dr D'Acre commented as she
considered the black swarm which buzzed and
hovered over the corpse of Anthony Garrett. 'Did
you know,' she asked, 'that the common house
fly, the so-called "bluebottle", can detect deceased
flesh from a distance of two miles within ten
minutes of death occurring?'

'I believe I did once hear something like that,
yes, ma'am,' Hennessey replied. 'Fascinating.'

'And the larvae they lay . . . those maggots,
you see, they develop at a consistent rate once
they are laid. At a glance the larvae have not
developed into the pupa stage from which the
maggots emerge . . . so . . . he has been deceased
for less than six days. Approximately.'

47

'Indeed,' Hennessey replied, noting again Dr D'Acre's slender but well-toned figure. The muscle tone he knew was developed because of her passion for horse riding, her hair was close-cropped and dark, and she wore just the slightest trace of lipstick of the palest shade.

'Well dressed.' Dr D'Acre turned her attention to the corpse. 'Casually dressed,' she commented, 'but those clothes, that footwear, they don't look cheap to me. He kept himself clean shaven, the stubble on the chin which you can see is post-mortem. Facial hair will continue to grow for a day or two after death has occurred as I am sure you will know, but that will further assist me to determine the approximate time of death which, as I said, I know that you will be asking for, and which I cannot give. Not officially anyway. The cause yes . . . if I can . . . but the when of it . . . no . . . although I will try my best to accommodate you, even if it is off the record.'

'I appreciate that, ma'am.' Hennessey kept a distance from the corpse, permitting Dr D'Acre room to manoeuvre as she made her initial examination of the corpse. 'I really would appreciate that,' he repeated.

'Do we know his identity?' Dr D'Acre turned to Hennessey. 'It's early days yet I know, but do you know who he is?'

'He is believed to be one Anthony Garrett, ma'am,' Hennessey replied, 'of which we believe something is known, but I know not what as yet.'

'Known to the police, you mean?' Dr D'Acre stood up.

48

'So we believe, ma'am,' Hennessey replied. 'Yes, known to the police.'

'A very neatly kept house . . .' Dr D'Acre surveyed the room. 'Nothing seems to be out of place in this room. Nothing at all. It is fastidiously neat.'

'Yes, ma'am.' Hennessey waved his hat and created a draft which disturbed the swarm of flies which promptly re-settled over the corpse. 'We also made that observation. We believe he lived alone.'

'That I can well understand.' Dr D'Acre glanced once again around the room. 'Magnificent house that it may be, I would think that only another totally obsessively neat person could live with this man and they would both have to agree exactly about what went where. Can you imagine that collusion of minds? Horrible. I mean, that would really be a meeting of two minds, and not a meeting I would want to be part of. I certainly could not live with a man such as this.' Dr D'Acre once again looked down on the fly-covered corpse of Anthony Garrett.

'I too made the same observation,' Hennessey stated. 'That is to say that I made it to myself and only myself, not yet to my team. He seems to have somehow managed to sanitize all the humanity out of this house. The rooms upstairs are all in the same manner, with such a precise ordering about them.'

'No humanity in the house.' Dr D'Acre repeated the observation. 'You know, Chief Inspector, that is quite a succinct way of putting it. It really is a lifeless house. I do not find such obsessive

49

neatness to be particularly endearing.' She paused. 'Well, back to work. Can you help me to turn him and to remove his lower clothing, please? I have to take a rectal temperature and also a reading of the room temperature and, once that is done, then all I need to do here has been achieved. So once all the photographs you need to take have been taken, then the corpse can be removed to York District Hospital. We are, in fact, enjoying a very rare quiet period at the moment and so I will be able to conduct the post-mortem this afternoon. Will you be observing for the police, Mr Hennessey?'

'Yes . . . yes, I think I'd like to be there for this one. I'd like very much to observe this one for the police,' George Hennessey replied in a soft but determined voice. 'I confess that I think that this murder has an intrigue about it. I feel that there is a story here. A man living alone in a huge house, packed with valuables, a single gunshot wound to the head and yet there is no sign of forced entry, so he must have known his killer . . . or killers, and he let him, or her, or them, into the house. Yet, despite that the execution seems to have been carried out in a calm manner. Totally without emotion, almost like a professional execution by the criminal underworld. It seems to have been cold, and ruthless and efficient.'

'Yes . . . I do see what you mean, but that is more your department than mine, although I do fully see what you mean.' Dr D'Acre leaned forward and withdrew the rectal thermometer from her bag. 'To wholly misuse the word, but I do fully see what you mean about this murder being "professional". He seems to have invited his murderer into his house and then calmly sat down in this chair whereupon he, or she, or they, shot him. Just once . . . right in the middle of his forehead, a small-calibre bullet by the look of it . . . a real assassin's weapon. You know it is an observation that I have heard, that the

closer the murderer gets to his victim, the more ruthless they are. A high-powered rifle with a telescopic sight, or a small-calibre gun fired from a few inches away . . . of those two the ruthlessness is with the latter. So let's get him turned and clothes off. Shall we say two p.m. for the post-mortem?'

'Suits admirably.' George Hennessey advanced on the corpse of Anthony Garrett, scattering the swarm of flies as he did so. 'Two p.m. it is. I'll be there.'

It was Wednesday, 11.30 hours.

Two

In which Detective Sergeant Somerled Yellich hears of the three women who recently called on Mr Garrett at The Grange, hears also of Mr Garrett's use of a pathway at the rear of his house, and is later at home to the always too kind and most gracious reader.

'They arrived, or visited perhaps I should say . . . they visited on Saturday last. One really could not miss them: they made quite a striking impression. It really was just the sort of thing that one would not forget in a hurry and indeed, could not forget. Identical . . . identical . . . identical, all three of them, clothing and hair colour and style, weight and figure. Identical. Totally identical. There was just nothing to set one of them apart from the other two. Not one small detail. Perhaps if you were close enough to shake their hand, or hands, then you'd notice some small detail of difference but at this distance they were identical in appearance. You see their clothing was like a civilian uniform, if you understand what I mean, the way air hostesses dress in the same uniform, or receptionists in large hotels?'

'Yes . . . yes, I know what you mean, ma'am.

52

I know exactly what you mean.' As he had been requested, Somerled Yellich had walked from The Grange, across the road and knocked reverentially on the door of the bungalow which stood directly opposite Anthony Garrett's house. As he approached the bungalow, the drive, which was similarly lain with gravel, caused his feet to 'crunch' it as he walked. As he drew closer to the building he noticed the pale-grey brickwork of the bungalow which contrasted strongly with the red tiles of the roof. He further noticed the two-car garage beside the building. Although he knew little about house construction, the bungalow did seem to him to be particularly solidly constructed, and it also seemed to him to have been particularly carefully built. The bungalow was clearly new, but it was not a 'thrown together' quick-build. It was certainly no 'Friday afternoon job', as so many modern houses seemed to him to be. Yellich stood at the door which he found to be set in the side of the building rather than the front aspect and waited until his knock was answered. As he waited for the door to be opened he looked about him with a police officer's eye, searching for detail. He noted a very carefully tended garden but one which was, at that point, in need, he thought, of a little attention as though the contract gardener was due his regular visit, or as though the home-owner had been too busy with other projects to cut the lawn and trim the privet.

The door of the bungalow was opened soon upon his knocking, silently so, but widely, by a frail, elderly-looking lady in a lavender-coloured

53

dress who Yellich estimated to be in her seventies. She had carefully kept silver hair which was cut neatly and short. Her feet were encased in black patent-leather shoes with a modest heel.

'You'll be the police, I would think?' The woman spoke in a strong, clear tone of voice which Yellich found to be both warm and welcoming. She looked up at him with a generous smile and alert brown eyes.

Yellich returned the smile. 'Yes, madam, I am the police.' He took out his ID card and began to show it to the elderly woman.

'Oh . . . it's all right.' She held up her hand. 'I don't need to look at your identity card. You look like a police officer and I have been keenly observing the police activity at The Grange all morning. Something of note has happened at that house methinks . . . and I saw you walk from amongst the police officers there and I watched as you walked up my drive. I don't open my door so widely and so readily to strangers. I have a security chain and I usually keep it across the door.'

'I am pleased to hear that,' Yellich replied with a nod and a smile. 'I am Detective Sergeant Yellich of Micklegate Bar Police Station in York.'

'Linda Holyman,' the woman responded. 'Mrs Linda Holyman, and you'll be wanting to know if I saw anything of note occurring at The Grange recently and in fact I think that I may very well have done. Do come in and I'll tell you about the three little maids from school.'

'Three little maids from school?' Yellich repeated and grinned as he did so. 'What on earth do you mean, madam?'

Then, once seated in Linda Holyman's lounge, she then said, 'Identical . . . identical . . . identical.'

Mrs Holyman then proceeded to relate what she had witnessed the previous Saturday morning, being that of the three women who seemed to her to be identical in dress, hair colour and style, build, figure, age . . . in fact, so identical that she could not distinguish one from the other two, especially when they started to weave.

'Really . . . weave?' Yellich reached into his jacket pocket and extracted his notepad and ballpoint pen. 'What do you mean?' he asked for a second time.

'I mean that they weaved in and out of each other. I mean that their paths weaved in and out of each other.' Linda Holyman then went on to relate how she had watched as the three women had walked in paths which interweaved with each other as they progressed from the car to the house, and how she saw just one of the women enter the building while the other two remained outside, standing either side of the front steps which led up to the door, 'like sentinels,' she added, and how then just a few moments later the woman who had entered the house re-emerged, and how the three women then took another similarly interweaving path back to where the car in which they had arrived waited for them. 'I really could not tell one from the other,' she explained. 'I very rapidly could not tell which one sat in the front and which two got in the rear seat, and I could certainly not tell you which one of the three women was the one who entered the house.'

'I see . . .' Yellich wrote on his notepad. 'So can you describe them, please? Clothing first, that's always a good place to start. You said they seemed to be in uniform?'

'No . . . no . . .' Linda Holyman held up a long admonishing finger. 'No, I didn't say that.' She inclined her head. 'No, I said that their clothing looked like it might have been a civilian organization's uniform, in that you might say that they were uniformly dressed, but probably not a uniform as such. Each wore a grey skirt . . . with hems about knee length, a red blouse, open-necked, a black handbag which they each had slung over their right shoulders, and black shoes with a small, sensible heel. Their height? Well, what can I say? Average . . . say over five feet six but less than five ten . . . so I can't really help you there very much. Their hair seemed long and blonde, so really very ordinary.'

'Did your husband also see them?' Yellich asked. 'You did, I think, mention that you were a married lady?'

'I doubt it.' Linda Holyman smiled gently. 'Malcolm, my husband, passed away peacefully in his sleep about ten years ago, and so I do really doubt that he saw anything.'

'I am so sorry.' Yellich felt awkward.

'No reason to be sorry, young man, no reason at all.' Linda Holyman continued to smile warmly. 'You were not to know. But then that is the way of it, so it seems to me. Men live a short life and we women just go on and on which is why there are always more women than men in the UK, and probably the world over. That statistic doesn't mean rich pickings for men, it means that all the excess women are frail and elderly and who are very patiently waiting for the end so that they can join their husbands. Anyway, I can see an awful lot from this chair, which was Malcolm's chair when he was still with us, and as you can see, I have a very good view of The Grange, the gardeners who call seemingly when they feel like it, and the house-cleaning service, in their yellow van. I use "Mrs Mop" in a white van, but Mr Garrett uses "The Maids" in their yellow van.'

'So,' Yellich asked, 'to confirm . . . you saw the three women last Saturday morning, so four days ago? It is important that you're sure of the day that they came.'

'Yes.' Linda Holyman held eye contact with Yellich. 'It was last Saturday in the forenoon. I am seventy-eight years of age but my eyesight is still good and my memory is still good. The old instrument . . .'

'Instrument?' Yellich queried.

'Instrument,' Linda Holyman repeated. 'I used to be an actress, and thespians, let me tell you, do not have bodies, they . . . we . . . have "instruments". At drama school you are taught how to move in a three-dimensional way for example and to stand a little at an angle to the audience in a theatre so as to help develop said three-dimensional look. It's a practice called "projecting your instrument".'

'How interesting.' Yellich inclined his head. 'That really is very interesting.'

'Yes. So the instrument is failing,' Linda Holyman continued. 'I have rheumatics and lately have

57

developed an arthritic knee. I feel unsteady on my feet from time to time and sometimes I feel unbalanced. It's age, you see, and it happens to all of us if we live long enough and I always say it's a damn sight more preferable than dying young. But anyway, the top bit of me . . . the head, still works a treat and the eyesight is still first class.'

'Good for you,' Yellich replied. 'Good for you. I hope I'll be able to say the same thing if I reach your age.'

'Yes, nobody's future is guaranteed but I do consider myself very lucky . . . very fortunate. So I can confirm that it was Saturday last, in the morning, that I saw the three identically dressed women call on Mr Garrett.' Linda Holyman paused. 'So what else can I tell you about those women? Well . . . they arrived in a silver car, I can tell you that, but it wasn't a taxi, of that I am sure. It didn't have that white plastic box thing on the roof which all taxis have and which glows all the time to signify that it is available for hire. It was just an ordinary car.'

Yellich wrote on his notepad.

'They arrived in the late forenoon, at eleven a.m.,' Linda Holyman continued. '*The Week in Westminster* had just started on the radio and that is broadcast each Saturday from eleven a.m. to eleven-thirty a.m.'

'That is a very useful observation,' Yellich commented, 'very useful indeed. This is all very good.'

'And they departed before the programme had finished,' Mrs Holyman added.

'Again, so very useful. A date and a very exact time. This is excellent. Excellent.'

Yellich sat adjacent to Linda Holyman in her sitting room, so that he had to turn his head to the left to look out of her window at The Grange opposite. Mrs Holyman sat in a chair facing the window. Yellich found the room to be neatly kept, with a pale blue carpet and pale blue painted walls decorated with prints of paintings by Vermeer and Van Gogh. There was a modest-sized bookcase in an alcove beside the right-hand side of the hearth. The room smelled gently of furniture polish. A fly buzzed angrily against the windowpane. Yellich glanced at it with annoyance.

'I'll let it out later,' Mrs Holyman offered in an apologetic tone. 'My husband, Malcolm, was a builder. He built this house and he was very concerned about the environment. Malcolm always ensured his houses were on a generous plot of land and not crowded together on top of each other. So it was the case that if another small-scale builder might squeeze three or even four houses on a plot of land, Malcolm would build only two, sometimes even just one on the same-sized plot. "People need houses," he would say, "but they also need grass and trees and space for their children to run about in." It reduced his profit margin but not by a great deal and people valued "Holyman Homes". They still do. A "Holyman Home" retains its value. If you buy one you'll be able to sell it again.

'And . . .' again Linda Holyman held up a long finger, 'and he would never swat a fly. That was the sort of man he was, and I have very fond

59

memories of him. He would always be reminding people about nature's food chain. He would say that if you remove a layer from the food chain, everything above it will die of starvation, and insects are at the bottom of the food chain. So don't ever swat a fly, open a window and let it fly out, he would say, a bird will find it and eat it.'

'I have never thought of it like that,' Yellich replied. 'I confess that that has never occurred to me. From now on I'll think twice before swatting a fly.'

'That was just Malcolm,' Linda Holyman continued. 'You know, each time he completed a house, he'd find a length of wood and bury it just below the surface at the bottom of the garden, so it would rot and insects would find it and by that means he'd start a food chain. He was just a very caring man, very caring indeed . . . a lovely man . . . a very lovely man.'

'It certainly does seem so,' Yellich replied. 'But can we get back to the matter in hand, please . . . the three women who called on Mr Garrett last Saturday?'

'Yes, of course. What else can I tell you . . .?' Linda Holyman glanced down and to her right. 'Oh, yes . . . all three wore a pair of white gloves. I'm sorry, I should have told you that when I was describing them,' Linda Holyman apologized. 'That small but important detail slipped my mind.'

'No matter,' Yellich replied, gently so. He wanted to keep the interview at a slow, conversational pace. 'Would you say that the three women were in a hurry . . . or that they seemed anxious?'

'No, just the opposite in point of fact, just the opposite.' Mrs Holyman looked up at the ceiling of her sitting room. 'It was as if they had all the time in the world. It was like that. They strolled, or you could say that they sauntered, up the drive to the house and then they returned to the car in the same relaxed, oh-so-casual manner.'

'All right,' Yellich wrote on his notepad. 'So . . . the car . . . what can you tell me about the car? Did you notice the colour of the vehicle . . . did you say that already?' He scanned the notes he had taken. 'I don't think I wrote anything about the colour of the vehicle.'

'Silver. That I do remember because silver has a certain significance for me in terms of its being a car colour,' Linda Holyman replied confidently. 'Definitely silver.'

'Oh,' Yellich inclined his head, 'what significance is that, can I ask?'

'Well, yes. You will probably have noticed the two-car garage beside my house?' Linda Holyman asked.

'Yes, yes, I did,' Yellich replied, 'same type of bricks as the house, same sort of roof tile. It blends very well, very sensitively with the house.'

'Yes, it would do, it was built at the same time as the house, not added later,' Linda Holyman explained. 'But I mention the garage because it contains two cars, an Austin Healey 3000 . . .'

'Oh . . .' Yellich drooled. 'That is a serious car . . . three litres and no weight to carry . . . it's a real flying machine. I am in fact familiar with

61

those cars, although I have never got nearer to one of them than photographs in motoring magazines. But I do know those beasts. I know them well.'

'Yes, it is a man's car all right. It was my late husband's pride and joy. He loved that car. He cherished it. It is of a light metallic blue with white sides. It is a lovely car and is worth a lot of money. It is fully insured but it doesn't go anywhere, not any more. In fact, it hasn't moved for a few years now. It will be sold by auction when I die and the money generated by the sale will go to my estate, and God only knows where that will go. I have no children and I still have to make a will. I am really dragging my feet there, for some reason I keep putting that off. But the other car in the garage is a 1959 Mercedes Benz saloon. It is a bulky round-shaped sort of car with the gear lever on the steering column. Later models of Mercedes Benz were of a more angular design with the gear lever on the floor beside the driver's seat.'

'Yes, I know the type,' Yellich commented. 'I am also familiar with those cars.'

'Good,' Linda Holyman nodded. 'Well that was "our" car whereas the "Big Healey" was Malcolm's. He'd take me for a spin in the Austin Healey but we'd go to Cornwall in the Mercedes each year for our annual holiday. We both loved Cornwall.'

'I understand,' Yellich replied. 'The Mercedes was the family car.'

'Yes, that's a good way of putting it,' Linda Holyman smiled. 'But to continue . . . when we acquired the Mercedes, it was black and my husband had it re-sprayed silver. He did that for a number of practical reasons. A silver car is cooler in the summer and warmer in the winter than cars of other colours. That is one reason. Silver also hides bumps and scratches more effectively than other colours and a silver car doesn't look as unclean as it would were it any other colour being the other reasons and which explains why one sees so many silver-coloured cars on the road.'

'That is interesting,' Yellich commented. 'Confess I never knew that.'

'It is apparently the case,' Linda Holyman smoothed down her dress with her bony hands, 'but every upside has a downside, as my husband was fond of saying, and the downside of a silver car is that sometimes they are difficult to see. They are not as easily noticed by other road users and pedestrians as are cars of other colours. They are, if you like, unintentionally camouflaged, so my husband always drove the Mercedes with the headlights on during the day, on dipped beam of course.'

'Of course,' Yellich echoed, 'of course.'

'It always irritated him when other road users would flash their lights at him. "*Stop flashing your lights*," he'd shout as though the other motorists could hear him; "*I know I've got my damned headlights on. I'm not brain dead*" . . . but anyway it is for that reason that I clearly remember the car which brought the three women to The Grange last Saturday morning and which stopped at the foot of the drive was silver in colour. Silver cars have a personal significance for me. It was a silver four-door saloon.'

'Did you notice the make?' Yellich asked hopefully. 'Or the registration number, or any other distinguishing features?'

'No, and no and no,' Linda Holyman replied with a distinct finality. 'I'm sorry but had I known how important it was going to be, I would have taken more notice. I would even have taken a photograph. I do keep a camera to hand, you see, but at the time it did not seem to be anything more than Mr Garrett being called on by three young women.'

'Young women?' Yellich repeated. 'You thought them to be young?'

'Well, it's all relative. These days pretty well every woman is young to me, Mr Yellich.' Linda Holyman held eye contact with Yellich. 'They were certainly all three beyond the first flush of youth, but they were still short, well short, of being in their middle years. They were more *Cosmopolitan* readers than they were readers of *Woman's Own*, if you see what I mean.'

'Yes, I do,' Yellich replied. 'I know exactly what you mean. So . . . three identically dressed youngish ladies returned calmly and casually to the silver car, they got into it, and then I assume it drove away?'

'Yes, you assume correctly. That way. It drove away in that direction.' Linda Holyman pointed to her right. 'It arrived from that direction,' she indicated to her left, 'from the direction of York and it drove away in the direction of the coast.

So the car arrived from the west and drove away towards the east.'

Yellich wrote on his notepad.

'Are you going to tell me what has happened to Mr Garrett?' Linda Holyman pressed. 'It is obvious that something hugely significant has occurred. That is plain. It is more than plain.'

'We can't hide the police activity.' Yellich paused. 'We can't do that and we wouldn't do that. So, yes, I can confirm that a major incident has happened. I can tell you that Mr Garrett is no longer with us.'

'I knew it was something like that. I knew it had to be something of that sort.' Linda Holyman spoke softly. 'I mean, all those police vehicles and that black van without any windows. It was just that sort of van which took Malcolm's body away after I found him when I had returned home after a week visiting my late sister in Scotland. He was lying on the floor, about where the coffee table is. I called for an ambulance, it arrived, and so did the police surgeon, and it was he who arranged for a mortuary van . . . black and windowless, just like the one parked in the road, which took Malcolm's body away. Oh . . . look . . . it's just going up the drive now.'

Yellich turned to his left and saw that the mortuary van was indeed making a slow and steady progress up the driveway towards The Grange. 'Well yes, as I said,' Yellich continued, 'Mr Garrett is no longer with us and yes, the police presence means that we have reason to be suspicious about the cause of death, but any more than that I am afraid I cannot tell you.'

'Well, I dare say it will be the talk of the George and Dragon this evening, of that I am sure, and the talk of the Post Office, and also the talk of our small supermarket this afternoon. Things are noticed in this village like they are in all villages. The last bit of excitement we had in this little village of ours was when Tom Hopper's Gloucester Old Spot made a run for it.'

'What's that?' Yellich grinned. 'His what?'

'His Gloucester Old Spot . . . his pig, an "Orchard Pig". Gloucester Old Spots are the official name of the breed, but they are also known as the "Orchard Pig". They have a fondness for apples and because of that they produce the sweetest pork. Well, Tom's pig and his mates, they escaped from their enclosure, four of them, but poor Tom Hopper, I felt sorry for him. He had a devil of a job rounding them up, him and any other villager who'd help him. The pigs were not dangerous because they were recently fed. A hungry pig is probably the most dangerous animal that can be had because they'll eat anything, even humans. A pig is just an eating machine.'

'I know,' Yellich commented. 'I do know about hungry pigs. Frightening really. Terrifying.'

'Yes, indeed. But Tom Hopper had fattened them up so they were not at all hungry. It seemed to be the case that four took a sudden dislike to their pen. Well, he got three of them back pretty quickly, but the fourth; well that one was having none of it. Up and down the main street he went with men chasing after it . . . the pig squealing

66

and the men shouting and waving sticks. That was a few years ago now but folk here still talk about Tom Hopper's pig. They got him back in the pen eventually but he was a game old animal, that one. So now, Anthony Garrett's been murdered. It all happens in Millington-in-the-Vale.'

'I didn't say that,' Yellich smiled. 'Please don't put words into my mouth. I did not say that he had been murdered.'

'No . . . no . . . you didn't . . . that's a fair point to make, but you implied it, you very strongly implied it, Mr Yellich.' Linda Holyman spoke sternly. '"*Reason to be suspicious*", is what you said.'

'Well . . . to continue . . .' Yellich growled. 'Did you know Mr Garrett at all?'

'Hardly,' Linda Holyman sniffed, 'hardly at all. He was not a pleasant man, so I found from what little contact I did have with him.' She then proceeded to recount the incident when Garrett had collected the parcel which the postman had left for him at her house. 'Nothing but a cursory "*thank you*", and then a rapid walking away. He was just a man who lived alone and was a man who seemed to me to like it that way. He was not a social type. I never thought that I would, but I have really quite taken to living alone so I can well understand him.'

'Yes.' Yellich then returned to the question of the three women, and asked, 'Can I assume that you had not seen them before?'

'Yes, you can assume that,' Mrs Holyman replied. 'To confirm I had not seen them before, and they did not return, not that I saw, not that I ever noticed from my little spy perch here and I see most things during the day and the evening. Particularly, these long summer evenings as we are enjoying now. So I did not see them return, either singly or as a pair or as a trio. I am also sure that they did not visit before Saturday last, nor did they return since Saturday last. I saw nothing at all to be concerned about. The lights in Anthony Garrett's big old house went on and off as they normally did. I assume now that they were security lights on timer switches, and they were timed to go on and off at varying times so as to give the impression of the house shutting down for the night. The downstairs lights went off about half an hour before the upstairs lights, for example, but I observe that from my bed, not from here,' she explained. 'But it all served to make things look very normal and then about ten a.m. this morning one of the gardeners arrived on his blue bike which he pushed up the drive as is his usual manner. Or rather is his constant manner I should probably say. I have never seen him ride up the incline, you see.'

'You seem to be very sure about the time,' Yellich observed warmly. 'Very sure.'

'Well . . . again the radio told me what time it was. I like routines, you see, getting into routines leads to efficiency, or so I find.' Linda Holyman smiled. 'Really, I kid you not, routines do help a lot, and one of my routines is to make myself a cup of tea each morning and arrange a plate of two digestive biscuits, carry them into the sitting room, and sit back and relax as I listen to *Woman's Hour*, and this morning I can tell you that *Woman's Hour* was starting at ten a.m. which was when I saw the gardener arrive, or perhaps I should say, that the gardener arrived just as *Woman's Hour* was starting, but you know what I mean. The gardener got off his bike and began to push the thing up the drive just as the lady on the radio said, "... *and in today's programme* ..."'

'That's good enough ... that is well good enough.' Yellich wrote *Gardener 10.00 a.m.* on his notepad.

Linda Holyman went on to relate how she watched the gardener announce his arrival by knocking on the door and then him walking round to the back of the house, as was normal, and then how, unusually, he rapidly reappeared at the front of The Grange without his tools and then him knocking on the door a second time, then him clearly trying the door handle and indeed opening the door and entering the property.

'Yes,' Yellich advised. 'He told us that he found the door unlocked shortly, very shortly after he had arrived.'

'And, you know, I should tell you something else,' Linda Holyman continued. 'I should tell you that a full forty-five minutes or so, probably more, elapsed between the moment the gardener entered the house, and the first police arriving. In fact, I am certain that the first police officer didn't arrive until *Woman's Hour* was concluding. So there was almost an hour's delay in reporting whatever he found.'

'That is interesting,' Yellich replied softly, 'very interesting indeed.'

'Yes, he clearly had to search for Mr Garrett's body, or . . .' Linda Holyman paused, '. . . or else he found it very quickly and he then went on a tour of the house before calling the police.'

'That,' Yellich slipped his notepad and pen back into his jacket pocket and stood, 'is something we'll be asking him about. He's clearly got some explaining to do there.'

'The body.' Dr D'Acre quietly cleared her throat and adjusted the microphone so that it was level with her mouth. 'The body,' she repeated, 'is that of a well-nourished white European male. He is particularly well nourished, in fact.' She paused and considered the corpse which lay face up on the extreme left-hand table in a row of five stainless-steel tables which were in the pathology laboratory of the York District Hospital, as viewed from the wall, opposite the bench and drawers which ran the length of one side of the room. Above each table was a microphone which was attached to an anglepoise arm which was, in turn, attached to the ceiling above the table. The laboratory was strongly illuminated by a series of powerful filament bulbs, the epilepsy inducing shimmer of which was contained by the transparent Perspex sheeting which encased the bulbs. 'Immediately obvious,' Louise D'Acre calmly continued for the benefit of the microphone and tape recorder, 'is the single gunshot wound to the forehead, quite central to the forehead in fact. Powder burns are noted around the wound, which indicates that the muzzle of the firearm was approximately twelve inches from the deceased when it was discharged. This,' Dr D'Acre added, 'was not, I feel, an accidental shooting, nor was it suicide. There is insufficient powder burn for suicide. The single bullet was well aimed, and there seems to have been a cold deliberateness about the act. I can safely conclude that this gentleman was murdered.'

'Thank you, ma'am.' George Hennessey stood reverently against the wall of the laboratory opposite the bottom end of the table upon which the body of the deceased lay with a starched white towel draped over the coyly termed 'private parts', and with a cardboard label tied round the big toe of the left foot. Hennessey pondered that in the hundred or so years since the initial development of forensic pathology had been practised, no one had devised an alternative method of labelling a corpse by case number and name (if known) other than by the use of a cardboard label tied to the big toe of the deceased. 'That clarifies things for us,' he added, 'and it helps greatly. Thank you.'

'Yes . . .' Louise D'Acre nodded and half turned towards DCI Hennessey. 'I know how the police do so very much like to be clear about things. So, murder it is. Murder most foul.'

'Again, thank you, ma'am.' George Hennessey was, like Dr D'Acre and Eric Filey, the pathology assistant, dressed from head to foot in green paper wear-once-and-dispose-of coveralls which included matching head covering and matching slippers for his feet. There were no badges of rank in the pathology laboratory, there was no need. Each person knew his or her role, his or

71

her purpose, and knew the designation of the others. Hennessey quickly glanced at Eric Filey who, he noted with little or no surprise, was fully engrossed in the post-mortem procedure. George Hennessey had, over the years that he had known Eric Filey, grown fond of the young man, always finding him to be jovial and good humoured unlike so many other pathology laboratory assistants he had met and who seemed to him to be drawn to their calling because of a morbid fascination with death, and many indeed, Hennessey further thought, had a death-like quality about them. But not Eric Filey, who Hennessey could easily see being a trainspotter or a real-ale enthusiast in his free time. He seemed, to Hennessey, to be that sort of man, a man who would seek gentle and harmless pursuits when not at work.

'I note a tattoo on the right forearm of the deceased.' Dr D'Acre's sudden observation caused Hennessey's thoughts to rapidly re-focus on the post-mortem. 'It appears that it reads "Sylvia" and underneath is observed a second tattoo which appears to read "Pilot".'

'"Pilot"?' Hennessey repeated with a clear note of curiosity. 'That's quite unusual, "Pilot"?'

'It is, isn't it?' Dr D'Acre stepped back and rested her hands on the lip of the stainless-steel table. 'The tattoo is professionally done, that I can tell you. It's not a crude, self-inflicted tattoo. I confess that from an investigative point of view, "Sylvia" won't be much help to the police to confirm his ID, but I confess that I have never come across "Pilot" as a tattoo. It's very unusual indeed. In fact, it is probably unique. Do you have any clarification of the identity of the deceased, Chief Inspector?'

'None,' Hennessey replied. 'He is believed to be one Anthony Garrett, as previously stated, but that still has to be confirmed. But I think that the tattoo you have just noted, "Pilot", will go a long way to confirming his ID. I also have never come across any similar tattoo. It must be unique.'

'Which is, of course, what I meant when I said that it was going to be useful for the police from an investigative point of view.' Dr D'Acre once again leaned over the corpse. She then raised her head slightly and addressed the microphone, 'The deceased is probably one Anthony Garrett,' she spoke clearly and slowly, 'whose identity is still yet to be confirmed. The tattoos reading "Sylvia" and "Pilot" are noted on the right forearm, both appear to be of the same age and both are professionally applied, but we'll stay with case number 124/7 for now, thank you, Sylvia.' Dr D'Acre turned to Hennessey. 'Our audio typist is, by sheer coincidence, also a "Sylvia",' she explained, 'just to help me make my point about the name probably not being of much help to you, but "Pilot" . . . that intrigues me. There is a history there, I feel, a real significance. But that is your department, of course, not mine, although I'd be most interested in knowing the story there, if you find it.'

'I'll certainly tell you if we do find it.' Hennessey shivered slightly as he suddenly felt the chill of the laboratory. '124/7,' he commented. 'One hundred and twenty-four post-mortems and it's still only July. That's an unusually high number, is it not?'

'Yes . . . it is, as you say, an unusually high number for this time of year. It's quiet at the moment, but it has been an unusually busy six months for us. We have been working like Trojans since January. We'll easily reach the two hundred mark before the end of December at this rate. That is a very high number of post-mortems in one year for our little city.' She stepped back from the table. 'So . . . Eric, photographs please, of the two tattoos. A single close up shot of each and then a more distant shot capturing both.'

'Yes, ma'am.' Eric Filey promptly picked up a 35-millimetre camera and advanced on the corpse of Anthony Garrett, took the requested photographs and then silently retreated to where he had been attentively standing next to the bench and to the right of Dr D'Acre, and opposite to where George Hennessey stood.

'I see that you have taken the fingerprints of the deceased,' Dr D'Acre commented, noting the black ink staining on the tips of the fingers and thumbs of the deceased.

'Yes, as a matter of routine, ma'am.' Hennessey once again shivered slightly. He had become used to the air within the laboratory being heavy with the smell of formaldehyde, but the chill continued to reach him. 'Though there are certain indications that the deceased will be known to the police. We have not yet had any feedback from the Police National Computer, early days yet though. Very early.'

'Of course.' Dr D'Acre drummed her long,

74

latex-encased fingers on the rim of the dissecting table. 'I mention that because I am going to have to destroy his face and head, pretty as it is, so identification will have to be by scientific means, DNA, fingerprints, dental records, and not with the mark-one eyeball of a next of kin. We'll take a photograph, of course, but that won't be sufficient to determine identity for evidential purposes. I have to extract the bullet, you see, and that means cutting off the top of his skull and sliding his facial skin over his facial features. Once that has been done we can't put the face back where it was, as it was.'

'Fully understand, ma'am,' Hennessey replied, 'but I am quite sure the scientific methods you mention will suffice. As I said, there are strong indications that he is known to the police.'

'Good . . . good . . . then we'll crack on. Eric . . .' She turned to Eric Filey. 'A photograph or two of the face, please, before I destroy it.' She stepped back and allowed Eric Filey to photograph the face from both sides and also at oblique angles, then closed on the corpse once Eric Filey had withdrawn. 'So, rigor is established and the stomach is beginning to distend. I will examine the stomach contents to help establish the time of death by determining the extent of digestion of his last meal, though I think the fly larvae I collected this morning will do that more accurately, but we'll be thorough, and we'll never know what we might find of interest in his stomach. I'll say now, though, as I have said before, and doubtless I'll say again,' Dr D'Acre insisted, 'as I have oft times said, the best and most accurate way to determine the time of death is that the deceased died sometime between when he was last seen alive by a reliable witness or a CCTV camera, and the time the body was found. Anything else is pure conjecture, learned speculation, but speculation all the same. And we don't presume to determine the time of death anyway, as you know, just the cause. Determining the time of death is for television dramas, but I am prepared to suggest it as an adjunct, and an unofficial adjunct at that, to my findings.'

'That is appreciated, ma'am.' Hennessey shifted his weight from his right foot to his left. 'Unofficial or not, it's greatly appreciated.'

'But it's only a suggestion. I emphasize that most strongly, it is not a scientifically proven finding. It can't be.' Dr D'Acre glanced sternly at Hennessey. 'It will only be transmitted verbally to you.'

'Understood, ma'am,' Hennessey reverentially inclined his head, 'understood and noted.'

'I'll look at the stomach contents later. I'll do that last of all in fact, but I can tell you now that it won't be too bad an experience for us, certainly not as bad as the "bloated floater". Did I tell you that story? His body was found floating in the River Foss a few summers ago, and a hot summer at that.'

'No, ma'am, I don't think you did,' Hennessey replied diplomatically, being all too aware of the presence of Eric Filey. 'I don't think that I have heard that incident.' He had in fact heard of the 'bloated floater' many times before and indeed he had once visited the grave of said 'floater', and had done so in the company of Dr D'Acre.

'He was found floating in the River Foss, as I said, he was about to burst and I think that the police were very fortunate to get him here before he burst in the van. Had that happened, it would have been a very unpleasant experience for the constables who were crewing the van. But Eric and I put the extractor fans on full blast . . . all of them. Eric left the laboratory before me. I took a deep breath and then I stabbed the stomach with a scalpel and ran for the door as there was an almighty hiss. And, what would you say, Eric?' Dr D'Acre turned to Eric Filey. 'It was about half an hour before we could come back in there . . . that sort of time?'

'About that, ma'am.' Eric Filey nodded in reply. 'A very good half an hour, probably longer, in fact.'

'Yes, it probably was longer than half an hour, come to think of it. Anyway, in the event I couldn't find a cause of death and the police were never able to give him a name so the Coroner's Office gave him the name John Brown, and he was eventually buried in a pauper's grave in Fulford Cemetery. I was there, at the funeral, just me and the priest, as well as the four men from the funeral directors, who lowered the coffin into the ground. Well, strictly speaking, it was a "shell", so called, the most basic form of coffin. I go and visit the grave from time to time. I find that I need to do that. It's unmarked, as all paupers' graves are, and he shares the plot with two other unidentified deceased. But he was once a living, breathing human being. You can't escape from that fact. He had parents, maybe siblings, maybe even children, and no one relative of his knew where he was when he died, or even that he had died. It was a dreadful end, a terrible way to fetch up. No identity, floating in the river for several days, and wedged under the bridge at Walmgate before someone noticed his body, and that was only when it was set to explode.'

'Yes, ma'am,' Hennessey responded with continuing diplomacy. 'Indeed, it was an awful way for any person to end their days.'

'Well . . .' Dr D'Acre sighed, 'let's get back to the here and now . . . but as you say, just an awful way to end one's life. Well, at least this gentleman won't suffer that fate. At least he'll avoid all that. He seems to be known, and if he's known he'll be missed and then he'll be reported to the police as a missing person.' Dr D'Acre continued, 'He appears to have been in a good state of health when he died, as already stated. His house was well appointed. He is clean and well nourished. He will definitely have a social network even if he did live alone. He would have received a set of cards at Christmas, of that I am sure.'

'I would assume so, ma'am,' Hennessey responded from his position against the wall of the pathology laboratory. 'As you so rightly say, someone some-where must know him, and someone somewhere will be missing him sooner or later.'

'So, let us look in his mouth.' Dr D'Acre took a stainless-steel rod of about one foot in length from the instrument tray, 'always a real Aladdin's cave of information in your olde mark-one gob. You know, I confess I do so love that word "gob"

78

for mouth. It's only apparently used in Yorkshire now but it was once widespread throughout the length and breadth of the British Isles and a "gobbet" is a word from early medieval times meaning "mouthful". "Gob" was eventually replaced by the word "mouth" which apparently comes from the Old High German "mund" as well as an Old French source, but anyway, I still prefer the word "gob", it's so solidly Anglo Saxon.' Dr D'Acre forced the stainless-steel rod between the teeth of the deceased and then levered the jaw open. It gave with a loud 'crack' which echoed around the laboratory. 'I can just see the Merrie Men of Sherwood Forest, having felled and roasted one of the King's deer, passing a leg around as they sat round the camp fire and each man in turn taking a "gobbet" of roast venison.'

'Yes, ma'am,' Hennessey grunted softly, 'a "gobbet" of roast venison, now that does sound mouth-watering . . . it sounds very appealing indeed.'

'So . . .' Dr D'Acre peered inside the opened mouth. 'Well, I can tell you that this gentleman certainly knew the value of dental hygiene, he has very little plaque. There are a few missing teeth, but the majority of his teeth are still there. I note British dentistry. So, if the tattoo or the DNA don't help in the search for his identity, then dental records will. In the UK dentists have to retain their records for eleven years, a minimum of eleven years, and dental records are as unique as fingerprints or DNA.'

'Yes, ma'am,' Hennessey replied, despite

knowing very well of the uniqueness of dental records and of their importance in assisting with the identification of deceased persons.

'Very well.' Dr D'Acre took a deep breath, and exhaled. 'He was not at all a bad-looking man but I'm afraid that sadly I am going to have to ruin his face and remove his jaw to obtain an impression of his teeth to match against dental records. I doubt he'll mind though . . . in fact, I am sure he won't mind in the least.'

'Yes, he's past caring, ma'am,' Hennessey quipped. 'He's long past caring.'

'Indeed . . . and he won't feel anything either.' Dr D'Acre picked up a handheld battery-operated circular saw which had a blade of approximately three inches in radius. She switched the machine on and it whirred loudly, causing Hennessey to avert his gaze and then wince as Dr D'Acre applied the rapidly spinning blade to the side of the skull of the deceased. 'Well, if you need the bullet from within his brain, Chief Inspector,' Dr D'Acre smiled apologetically, 'I have to do this. It is as the French say, "*you cannot make the omelette without first you must crack the egg,*" and so the top of his skull must come off. It's a question of needs must.' Dr D'Acre sawed around the circumference of the skull, just above the ears. She then laid the saw on the instrument trolley and then, with the help of Eric Filey, she turned the body upon its anterior aspect to enable her to access the rear of the head so as to enable her to complete sawing round the circumference of the skull. When the body was once again lying face up on the table and the

80

starched white towel replaced, Dr D'Acre then, using both hands, lifted the top of the skull away causing a slight sucking sound as she did so, and thus revealing the brain of the deceased. She then took a long surgical knife and cut the brain in cross-section at the point that it protruded the skull; that done, she carefully lifted the top of the brain and placed it gently on a dissecting tray. Taking a long pair of surgical tweezers, she probed the bullet hole until she made contact with the bullet and, grasping it, she slowly extracted it. 'It is a .22 methinks and it appears to be a hollow point. Very nasty, but that is a job for a ballistics expert to comment on.' Dr D'Acre considered the bullet and then placed it in a stainless-steel bowl. 'I'll label it and send it off to the forensic science laboratory at Wetherby,' she added, without looking in Hennessey's direction. 'They can tell you all about it, or they can tell you all that they can about it, anyway . . . not quite the same thing, but you know what I mean.'

'Indeed, ma'am,' Hennessey replied. 'I fully understand the difference.'

'So, the stomach.' Dr D'Acre reached for the scalpel. 'Take a deep breath, gentlemen. Are the fans on, Eric?'

'Yes, ma'am.' Eric Filey glanced at the fans. Then he breathed in deeply.

'OK, here we go.' Dr D'Acre also took a deep breath and, turning her head to one side, she pierced the stomach. The gases therein escaped with a distinct hiss as Dr D'Acre stepped back from the table waving her hand from side to side. 'Well,' she announced after a few moments of silence, 'not as bad as it could have been and nothing like the previously mentioned "bloated floater".' Dr D'Acre then advanced on the corpse and then fully exposed the contents of the stomach by making an incision from just beneath the ribcage to the upper intestines. 'The stomach contents are little,' she remarked for the benefit of the tape recording. 'His last meal has been fully digested, indicating the time of death as being about forty-eight hours or so before his body was discovered. I'll trawl for poisons in his blood as a matter of course, as procedure dictates, but the single gunshot wound to the skull will be the cause of death, of that I am certain. The gun was fired at a distance of about twelve inches from his forehead, or about thirty centimetres in Euro-speak, or so I would estimate, and that means we can safely rule out suicide as I say, because there would be gunshot residue on his hands, and because the gun would have been found in the vicinity of his body when it was discovered. He was a long-time resident in the UK and he was in good overall health when he died.'

'So, definitely murder?' Hennessey sought to clarify the issue.

'If you like.' Dr D'Acre peeled off her latex surgical gloves. 'You could say that he was assassinated. I dare say you could say that. I can only determine the cause, if I can, but off the record, it seems to me to be a cold and deliberately planned murder. So yes . . . the police could say murder . . . but in the manner of an assassination, clearly so. Someone wanted this man,

Garrett, dead and that person or persons unknown got exactly what he or she . . . or they . . . wanted.'

George Hennessey took his leave of Dr D'Acre and Eric Filey, went to the male changing rooms and took off the disposable green coveralls and dropped them into the yellow 'sin bin'. He re-dressed in his own clothing and walked out of York District Hospital. As he did so his eye was drawn to the red and white Riley RMA which he had noticed earlier that day when it was driven to The Grange, Millington, and which had been parked half on half off the kerb behind the police vehicles. Owned by Dr Louise D'Acre, it was by then parked in her designated parking bay, held, he knew, in place by the engaging of the reverse gear not the parking brake as was the owner's custom, so as to preserve the efficiency of the parking brake when it was needed to help control the car in traffic. It was a practice that her late father had taught her, so she had once told Hennessey, her father being the car's original owner. George Hennessey had become very familiar with the car, having enjoyed occupying the front passenger seat on not a few occasions and having discovered the cramped interior, by comparison to modern vehicles, and that despite the car's generous outside dimensions. One had, he had found, to step up into the vehicle and then climb down to exit it. But that, he reasoned, was just how cars were made in the UK in the imme- diate post-Second World War years, appearing to be quite large on the outside by comparison to modern cars but with space at a premium within the passenger compartment. The car was lovingly maintained by a service and repair garage in Skelton, to the north of York, the proprietor having elicited a promise from Dr D'Acre that he would be offered first refusal should she ever come to sell the vehicle. Dr D'Acre had once told Hennessey that she had been willing to make the promise in the knowledge that the car would never be sold. She had inherited the car from her father and had promised it to her third-born child, her only son, when he was of age, and it would thusly be retained in the D'Acre line until the line ceased, or the car eventually deteriorated to nothing. Whichever came first.

That day being warm, very warm and sunny, George Hennessey chose to walk the walls to Micklegate Bar and the police station, being, as any resident of the city knew, the speediest way to transit the medieval centre of the city. Joining the walls at Lendal Bridge, he threaded his way in and out of groups of brightly clad tourists of all ages, in groups large and small, and the occasional local man or woman clearly doing what he was doing and being easily distinguished because they looked straight ahead as they walked, and not from side to side, and by being more soberly dressed and not laden down with cameras. He left the walls at Micklegate Bar and, as he did so, he glanced with horrific fascination up at the spikes across the front of the Bar where, in medieval times, the heads of traitors to the Crown had been impaled and left to rot for three years before being removed. Hennessey crossed the road when the traffic lights showed the green man in the pedestrians' favour and entered Micklegate Bar Police Station. He signed in at the enquiry desk and walked through the 'staff only' doorway. He nimbly took the stairs, two at a time, to the upper floor of the building and walked confidently down the CID corridor and, entering his office, swept the Panama hat from his head and skimmed it through the air towards the hat stand which stood in the far corner of the room.

His hat, the gracious reader will not be surprised to learn, missed the hat stand by a comfortable two feet and hit the wall above and to one side of the Chief Inspector's filing cabinet. He bent forward to pick it up from the floor mumbling that disposing of one's hat in such a manner is a lot harder to do in actuality than it appears to be in films. Hennessey placed his hat on a vacant hook on the hat stand and then sat behind his desk, feeling more than a little thankful that none of his team had witnessed his forlorn and utterly theatrical attempt to hang his hat. He sat forward to ponder the papers which lay upon his desk top, when, at that moment, Somerled Yellich appeared on the threshold of his office.

'I thought I heard you come in, boss.' Yellich tapped the door frame of Hennessey's office. 'Here is something which you should see.' He held up a computer printout.

'Ah, Somerled.' Hennessey leaned back and smiled warmly at Somerled Yellich. 'Something I should see, you say?'

'Yes, sir, it's the results of the trace we asked criminal records to run of the deceased at The

Grange. He is known, as was indicated to us by the gardener, Miles Law.' Yellich strode forward and entered Hennessey's office and handed him the sheet of paper.

'Well, so let's have a look.' Hennessey reached out and took the sheet of paper from Yellich and began to read it. 'Do sit down, Somerled.' He indicated the half-circle of chairs which stood in front of his desk. 'So . . .' he continued. 'What do we have?'

Yellich slid on to one of the chairs as invited by Hennessey. 'He is quite well known, in fact. As you see, he has quite a few aliases.'

'Anthony "Tony" Garrett . . .' Hennessey read the names aloud, 'a.k.a. Anthony "Tony" Guest, a.k.a. Anthony "Tony" Graham . . . a.k.a. Anthony "Tony" Glenn . . . so all with the same initials, A.G.,' he observed, 'and all fairly common names, all allowing him to answer to Anthony or Tony, and that is the aliases we know of . . . there'll be others.'

'Doubtless, sir,' Yellich placed his hand on his knee, 'doubtless others, as you say. It's always very useful for a criminal to have a number of aliases.'

'Oh, yes, it certainly is and it confirms his criminality being long term, a "career criminal", so called.' Hennessey continued to read the computer printout. 'I mean, who but a career criminal would want a string of aliases like this. All different, but also all have a distinct similarity.'

'Who indeed?' Yellich glanced to his right and out of George Hennessey's office window at a solitary man, amongst the crowds of tourists, who was wearing a yellow shirt with a camera slung over his shoulder, walking the walls towards Lendal Bridge and looking keenly and curiously to his left and right as he did so. 'And quite a criminal, as you will see, sir,' Yellich added as he turned once again towards Hennessey. 'All white-collar stuff in the main.'

'So what is he . . . a Mr Fix-it?' Hennessey asked as he continued to scan the sheet of paper.

'It does indeed seem that way, boss. It reads like he is the sort of bloke who will put a team together, plan a job, but let other people do the dirty work,' Yellich advised. 'Lots of conspiracy to steal, defraud and so on, but having said that, as you see . . . he was convicted of murder a few years ago.'

'Yes, so I saw, that did leap out at me.' Hennessey held the computer printout in both hands. 'But . . . look at this . . . did you read this . . . he collected his nominal life sentence for murder, as he would, but, I mean, stone the crows, he was released on licence after just three years.'

'Yes,' Yellich sat back in the chair, 'yes, I did notice that. I did. It's not the sort of thing one could easily miss. He served just three years for murder. There's a story there.'

'Indeed,' Hennessey sighed. 'That really makes life seem quite cheap. In fact, it makes it seem very cheap indeed. Someone was denied justice there methinks, most unjustly denied it.'

'Yes, sir,' Yellich then leaned forward in his chair, 'that was my feeling when I saw that . . . a deprivation of justice. As you say, sir, I also feel that there is a story to be told there. A tale to unfold.'

'But his age is confirmed as being sixty-two, that's useful to know, as is his identity, the tattoos being the identifying features . . . being "Sylvia" which helps a little, and also "Pilot", which helps muchly. It is the single word "Pilot" tattooed on his right forearm which pretty well confirms his ID. Not many "Pilots" about. We'll have his DNA and his fingerprints on file so we'll be able to double-check but "Pilot" seems to me to clinch his identity by itself. So I would have thought.'

'Indeed, boss.' Yellich shifted his position in the chair. '"Pilot" is unique.'

'Yes. I see he started his sentence in Wormwood Scrubs in London.' Hennessey glanced up at Yellich. 'I do so love that name for a prison. That and "Strangeways" Prison in Manchester, you couldn't invent those names for prisons.'

'Indeed, sir,' Yellich held eye contact with Hennessey, 'and Leavenworth Prison in the USA. I always think that name sounds like it ought to be an English country house.'

'It does rather, doesn't it?' Hennessey grinned. 'Confess that has not occurred to me . . . but since you mention it. Anyway, let's press on. So he was transferred to Full Sutton up here in Yorkshire to complete his sentence, but then he was released on licence, after three years . . . can we dig into that? We have to contact the Metropolitan Police, see what they can tell us.'

'Oh . . . they're coming here, sir,' Yellich smiled. 'They're on their way up here as we speak.'

'They are?' Hennessey raised his left eyebrow. 'We're going to be visited by the Metropolitan Police?'

'Yes, sir, it was one of the things that I was going to tell you. I contacted them. I anticipated you there, once I read that Garrett was a London con. I can tell you that they seemed delighted that we have found Garrett, a.k.a. whatever, because he had dropped off their radar, and they have been anxious to trace him for some time, so it appears.'

'His discharge address can't be false,' Hennessey protested. 'That has to be verified before he can be released.'

'He is always on licence, of course, that will never alter unless he is recalled following any conviction, but his aftercare supervision lasted only twelve months.'

'So then he was in the wind?' Hennessey groaned and put his hand to his forehead. 'I hear the old, old story . . . that same old song . . .'

'It certainly seems that way, sir,' Yellich replied. 'Anyway, the Met are sending someone up from London with the, excuse me, rather odd request that he be permitted to photograph Garrett's unique tattoo.'

'Photograph!' Hennessey gasped. 'That's a bit macabre, isn't it? Don't they trust DNA evidence or fingerprints?'

'I am afraid that I do not know the answer to that question, sir.' Yellich spoke with a defensive tone of voice. 'That a tattoo is already photographed as part of his prison record. It must be perhaps that they just want a comparison.'

'Well, I can't see the harm in that request, macabre as it might seem, and we do need their cooperation.' Hennessey glanced up at the ceiling of his office. 'But I ask you, of all the weird requests . . . anyway, we don't want to sour our relationship with the Metropolitan Police, and we need to know what they can tell us about Anthony Garrett, deceased.' Hennessey paused. 'You said you had other things to tell me? In fact, if I may say so, you look like the cat that got the cream. There is a certain smugness about you, Somerled. You have some good information, I think. That gleaming look in your eyes tells me so.'

'Indeed I do, sir.' Yellich then related to a dumbstruck Hennessey the information about the three identically dressed women who had called on the deceased late in the forenoon of the previous Saturday, and also of the fact that Miles Law appeared to have waited for some time, an hour at least, Yellich emphasized, before calling the police to report his finding of Anthony Garrett's body.

'Did he indeed?' Hennessey frowned. 'That is interesting. An hour, you say? That is very interesting indeed.'

'Yes . . . confess I thought so too, sir,' Yellich nodded, 'all seen by an elderly lady who lives opposite The Grange, in the bungalow you asked that I call on, and whose mind is as sharp as a tack and whose eyesight is top-notch. She was a very credible witness, I thought. She was very calm and collected and she was very good on detail. It's all in my report.'

'So . . . progress. We are making progress.' Hennessey clasped his meaty hands together.

'So, tell me, when can we expect the Metropolitan Police to honour us with their illustrious presence?'

'Any time now, sir,' Yellich glanced at his watch, 'any time now. They seemed to be most anxious to come up here. They said it would only take two hours to get to York once they're on the A1. So, as I said, any time now. I phoned them as soon as I had the CR records check printout and noticed the London connection. You were witnessing the post-mortem at the time.'

'Yes . . . I assumed that . . . and which I can tell you concluded with a finding of death by a single bullet fired at the forehead of the deceased. So, with the absence of a gun beside Garrett's body, unless there is any trace of poison in Garrett's bloodstream, which Dr D'Acre thought to be highly unlikely, we have a murder to solve. Dr D'Acre was very succinct, she hit the nail bang on the head, I thought, by saying that Garrett was not so much murdered, as he was assassinated.'

'A very neat way of putting it,' Yellich commented. 'An assassination.'

'But I have to say that I think she's correct.' Hennessey sighed. 'A single shot, close up, but not as close as a suicide would be, nothing in the house was disturbed, nothing appears to have been stolen, and nothing seems to have been done in panic. Those three women you mention, who called on Saturday last, the time that they called seems to coincide with Dr D'Acre's estimated, unofficially, that is, probable time of death. Dr D'Acre won't be drawn on the time of death, as usual, she insists that that is for television dramas, but she will help us and she will give a nod and a wink off the record. But you know I feel that this is shaping up to be a gangland job. We'll be lucky to get a conviction here methinks, but we'll run with the ball as far as we can now that we've got it.' Hennessey paused. 'I'll entertain the boys from the Met . . . when they arrive. Two hours they said . . . well, I think that is a little optimistic, so we'll say three hours. I think I'll send Carmen and Reginald to talk to Miles Law. I am curious to know why he waited so long to call 999, and yet nothing appears to have been disturbed in the house. As I said, I'd like you to go and chat with The Maids, remember, they are the contract-cleaning crew with the little yellow van.'

'Yes, sir,' Yellich stood. 'I know who you mean.'

'Then if you'll call on the other gardener . . . Millom by name, see what he can tell us,' Hennessey added.

'Millom?' Yellich repeated. 'Millom . . . like the town in Cumbria?'

'Yes . . . same spelling,' Hennessey confirmed. 'He's the head gardener. We were given his name when you were talking to the elderly lady, she of sharp eyesight and who is good on detail. I have added his name and address to the file,' Hennessey advised. 'Mr Millom is not a priority but he has to be interviewed for the sake of completeness . . . so when you can, please.'

'Very good, sir.' Yellich turned and left Hennessey's office.

* * *

92

'Well, you know, we did wonder what had happened at The Grange, of course we did. Who wouldn't?' Muriel Staples revealed herself to be a plump, middle-aged woman who sat behind a small, almost child-sized desk, and which caused Yellich to ponder that the desk made her look larger than she was. A much larger desk would, he reasoned, do much to improve her image, but it was not, he was fully aware, his place to comment. Behind Mrs Staples was a large coloured photograph mounted on the wall which showed a fleet of six highly polished yellow vans of Japanese manufacture with two broadly grinning women holding mops upright in front of each vehicle. The women's grins were, thought Yellich, too broad to be sincere. There was, he further thought, a sense of 'smile or you don't work' about the photograph. Mrs Staples' office, as befitting the owner of a house-cleaning company, had an everything-in-its-place neatness about it and it smelled strongly of furniture polish and air freshener. 'One of our vans drove past the house this morning after visiting another customer and the two ladies in the van noticed the police activity and the blue and white tape strung across the entrance to the drive with a constable standing there who they said was looking very serious indeed. Very solemn indeed, so they said,' Mrs Staples explained. 'So what has happened to Mr Garrett . . . can you say? It has to be something very serious for the police to visit and to remain in such numbers.'

'He is no longer with us, I can tell you that.' Yellich glanced out of the window at the industrial estate in which The Maids' office and garage was situated. 'He is, sadly, deceased.' He turned back again to look at Muriel Staples, who he thought seemed to be crestfallen at the news. Almost, he thought, as if Anthony Garrett had been a relative or a close friend.

'Oh, my . . .' Muriel Staples gasped and placed her left palm against her chest revealing as she did so many rings upon her fingers and many bracelets around her wrist. 'We thought it must be something like that. My girls said there was an awful lot of vehicles and uniform and plain-clothed men who were among the uniforms. She said there were about six cars parked at the foot of the drive and also a black van with no windows, apart from the driver's cab, of course.'

'Yes . . . that was the mortuary van,' Yellich advised. 'It and other vans like it are used to convey bodies from where they are found, back to the mortuary.'

'But the police . . . and in such numbers . . . there must be something suspicious about his death?' Muriel Staples sat back in her chair, heavily so. She seemed to Yellich to be a woman who was used to asking questions and used to receiving answers.

'There is,' Yellich nodded, 'there is indeed, but I am afraid that I can't say anything. I can't tell you anything.'

'Of course.' Muriel Staples smiled, although Yellich thought she seemed to be disappointed by his answer. 'I quite understand,' she continued. 'But this is something of a blow. I'm sorry . . .

you must excuse me . . . I must compose myself. Oh dear . . . deceased. Well, I never . . .'

'So, tell me,' Yellich asked, 'on which day of the week did you call on Mr Garrett? I presume you called weekly?'

'Yes, we did. We usually, really most often, called on Friday; each Friday afternoon. He was, in fact, one of our last calls of the week. We have six vans, so we have six last calls and Mr Garrett was one of them. We're there from 3.00 p.m. until about 4.00 p.m. That is unless we have a cancellation in which case we ask if we can call earlier such as on the Thursday or the Friday, but earlier than normal. If that happens, the girls can finish earlier in the week which they always appreciate doing and Mr Garrett is very obliging in that respect. So long as his house is done each week he is quite happy. Or was . . . I must get used to saying that now. Oh my . . .'

'I see.' Yellich took out his notepad. 'But an hour, only an hour for a house the size of The Grange, that doesn't seem very long to be there for just two cleaners. Is that all the time it takes?'

'Ah . . .' Mrs Staples lifted a heavily ringed finger causing bracelets to fall from her wrist down to her elbow, 'that is because we don't clean the whole house, you understand, just the parts of the house where he lives . . . or lived. That being his bedroom, the bathroom, the drawing room, the dining-kitchen, the hallway and the stairs, and we also iron his shirts, seven of them. He has more, of course, but we iron just seven, any seven, from his weekly wash, so he has a clean and ironed shirt to wear each day. All part of the service.'

'I see.' Yellich tapped his notepad with his ball-point pen. 'So you saw him . . . that is to say your employees called on him last Friday?'

'Yes, we did. His regular cleaners called there at about two-thirty p.m. We were running early that day due to a cancellation of a planned cleaning that morning.'

'All right,' Yellich replied. 'And all seemed well, I assume?'

'Well, I assume so,' Muriel Staples replied. 'The girls got back here at four or four thirty, as I recall. They gave me his cheque for services rendered and they scooted away, being happy to get home early for the weekend. Usually they'd finish at five thirty p.m. All must have seemed normal. I am sure that they would have said something had that not been the case. I am sure of it. I know my girls. I have a very settled workforce. Yes, I am sure that they would have mentioned if anything was unusual about Mr Garrett or his house that day. So I think that you can rest assured that all was well with Mr Garrett on Friday last.'

'What do you know about him?' Yellich spoke in a calm, unhurried manner, as he wrote *3.30, Friday – all well* on his notepad.

'Very little, I'm afraid, really not very much at all. It is true that house cleaners tend to find out a lot about their clients, as one would expect, but Mr Garrett seemed to the girls to be a quiet sort of gentleman with a bit of a cold manner, though he always insisted that the girls help

96

themselves to tea or coffee if they wished to do so. He was most appreciated by the girls because he would keep out of their way when they were there. He used to go out for a walk or he went up to the top of the house where he had a little den. It wasn't what you'd call a study, so I am told. He wasn't a very bookish person, apparently. It was just a little sitting room with a couple of armchairs and a radio. He'd sit there to stay out of their way.' Muriel Sparks paused. 'The girls quite liked him, I can tell you that. I mean, they liked working for him for that reason. He was a bit of a cold fish, as I said, but he'd give them space . . . he'd keep out of their way. Some of our clients, you see, well they insist on occupying the living room when the girls are there, even having guests when we call, chatting to their guests whilst we clean round them. That sort of attitude makes the girls feel invisible. But Mr Garrett was not like that, so they liked cleaning for him. Let's see, what else can I tell you? He had a calm, self-assured telephone manner, quietly spoken with a southern accent . . . London, I would think. Once he phoned me to tell me that the girls had left some of their cleaning gear behind, and he said . . . *"they've gone off without their cleaning gear"*, and when I mimicked the account to my husband later that day I said, *"they've gorn orf wiv aght der cleanin' gear"*.' Muriel Sparks smiled apologetically. 'Sorry, that was not a good imitation of his accent, but you might see what I mean about him being a southerner. He was definitely not local, not local to these parts anyway.'

'Yes,' Yellich nodded, 'I understand. That's interesting.'

'He pays by . . . or he paid by, cheque each week. So he was not a man with anything to hide. There were no locked rooms in his house, the girls could wander freely but only cleaned certain parts of the house.'

'You visited?' Yellich asked. 'You sound like you know the building.'

'Yes,' Muriel Staples admitted. 'I did invite myself over there one day when the girls were cleaning. I was passing anyway and so it was an unplanned on the job inspection. I jollied them along. I told them that they were doing a good job. I gave them that sort of encouragement but really I was hoping that Mr Garrett would be out so I could have a quick tour of The Grange. I don't mind admitting to you that I was burning with curiosity to explore that huge, lovely old house. Anyway, I lucked in and he had gone out when the girls arrived on that day so I had a good look round the house. He had a lot of valuables but no room was locked, although we came to know that he would lock rooms at night as a security measure, but he'd unlock them each morning. I didn't go up into the attic as I wasn't dressed to do that. I was in my "office smart" clothes and I did not go down into the cellar for the same reason but I did notice that neither the attic nor the cellar were locked. I felt it was safe to let the girls go there . . . I should add that, I think. Sometimes we have to be wary of single male clients, but not Mr Garrett . . . he was a gentleman in that respect.'

'I see. So how long,' Yellich asked, 'have you been cleaning for Mr Garrett?'

'Oh . . . probably about five years, I would say. I well recall that because I became a first-time grandmother at about the time that Mr Garrett contacted us and my grandson is now about five years old.' Mrs Staples beamed. 'He is now in his first year at school and he wants boys' toys, like train sets and toy soldiers and a football. My friend has a grandson of the same age who wants to wear dresses and skirts and play with dolls. They are worried, very worried about him and think he might have been born with gender dysphoria. He's having psychiatric evaluations and medical checks – but not my grandson Tom, he's going to be one hundred per cent testosterone I am relieved to say. But sorry . . . I am getting off the track; you want to know about Mr Garrett, not about my family.'

'When Mr Garrett left The Maids cleaning his house, you said that he either went out for a walk, or he stayed out of their way by sitting in his little "den" upstairs,' Yellich probed. 'When he went out of the house, do you know where he went? We were surprised to find that he didn't seem to possess a motor vehicle, yet his house is quite remote.'

'Yes, actually now that you mention it, there is a strange thing . . . well curious, perhaps . . . and I might be able to help you there.' Mrs Staples glanced to her left. 'You have visited the house, I assume?'

'Yes,' Yellich replied, 'just this morning.'

'Well, you'll recall that it has a large area to

the front of the house, a vast lawn and a long driveway . . . you'll remember that the house is well set back from the road?'

'Yes,' Yellich nodded. 'A huge expanse of lawn, as you say, to the front of the house.'

'Well, the back of the house, if you have not been there, is quite the opposite. There is very little ground behind the house,' Mrs Staples informed him. 'The field at the back of the house is separated from the building by only a matter of . . . perhaps twenty feet at most.'

'About that . . .' Yellich agreed. 'I did take a wander round the back of the house.'

'Yes,' Mrs Staples continued. 'Well, one day my girls saw him leave the house after giving them the cheque before they'd completed that week's clean, telling them to pull the door behind them because the gardener was working that day so the house would be safe until he returned . . . and one of the girls happened to be cleaning the kitchen, which is at the back of the house, and she saw him walking at the rear of the house and then force his way through the privet hedge which separates the field from his property, and then he turned to his left and walked towards the village. It was like a private pathway he used.'

'Interesting,' Yellich wrote on his notepad, 'we'll take a look at that. It sounds very interesting.'

'Oh, that's just his escape route,' Harry Millom shrugged his shoulders, 'his bolthole. It leads to a pathway through a cornfield and wasteland to the village. There is no gate as such, just a little bit of a gap in the privet where a man can

100

slide through if he turns sideways. You'd have to know the grounds to know it was there unless you saw Garrett using it. He'd know that it was there, so would Miles Law, but a stranger would only see a line of green privet. But, as you know, I'm one of the gardeners. I have got to know Garrett's territory very well. I reckon that I know every inch of his little bit of England.' Millom was a slender, lithely built man, so Yellich observed, and he thought that such a physique was a common feature of gardeners. He had certainly yet to meet an overweight gardener, and assumed that it was their occupation which kept them enviably slender, always in good physical shape without looking like heavyweight wrestlers. Millom had a large cherry red birthmark that covered the left side of his face but he did not seem to Yellich to be self-conscious about it. Clearly, thought Yellich, he had accepted the blemish as something he could do nothing about and courageously had just got on with his life. 'All the garden work at The Grange is in the front of the house; at the back there is only the privet hedge and a couple of fruit trees. The outbuildings, the tool shed and the potting shed, are at the rear but ninety per cent of the garden work is at the front of the house. I once found the gap Garrett uses to try to escape unnoticed into the village, but often he's seen without him realizing he has been seen. Little goes unnoticed in the country.' Millom spoke with a calm, steadfast matter-of-fact manner. 'If you go through the gap in the privet and turn left, you'll pick up the path easily, very easily. It's used by others, other than Garrett I mean. It's a partially established footpath which runs alongside Garrett's hedge, so Garrett can ease his way through the hedge and join the footpath. So what has happened to him? Can you tell me? I was in the village earlier today and there was much talk about the police activity at The Grange.' Millom paused. 'It's all right . . . I know, the old boy's dead, isn't he? And in suspicious circumstances?'

'How do you know that?' Yellich asked suddenly.

'I don't,' Millom replied equally quickly. 'I just assume it to be the case. I mean, why else all that police activity? Why else all that police interest?' Millom raised his eyebrows. 'There can be no other explanation, other than that he is deceased and deceased in suspicious circumstances.'

'Well, I dare say it doesn't take a rocket scientist to work that out.' Yellich inclined his head in a gesture of concession. 'Yes, Mr Garrett is deceased, that I can tell you, but any details I cannot divulge, I'm afraid.'

'Fair enough,' Millom nodded. 'That's fair enough. So how can I help the Vale of York constabulary . . . whom I'm always happy to help, by the way. Always happy to help the boys and girls in blue.'

'By telling us what you know about Anthony Garrett.' Yellich glanced round Harry Millom's council house in Millington. He saw it to be neatly kept, seemingly well ordered, with a copy of the *Daily Mail* lying, folded neatly, on the settee on which he, Yellich, was seated. Mrs Millom had shown Yellich into the living room and had then hurriedly withdrawn to let the men talk 'man talk'. The garden, as far as Yellich could see through the back window, was, as one would expect for a gardener, kept meticulously in order. Millom was dressed in a yellow T-shirt and white summer flannels with open-toed sandals upon his feet. 'I am growing to be more than a little interested in Garrett's "little escape route", as you call it,' Yellich prompted. 'So why don't you tell me about that, if you'd be so good.'

'I followed it one day,' Millom advised. 'I did so out of the selfsame curiosity that you seem to be feeling. I knew that Garrett was at the front of The Grange talking to Miles Law about something or other and I had completed all the work which I needed to do that day . . . this was a couple of summers ago now . . . and I had put the tools away in the tool shed at the rear of the house and had closed up for the day. So I was then just a few paces away from the narrow gap in the privet hedge so I grabbed the opportunity. It was on impulse, really, and I slid sideways through it and I found myself on the pathway. It wasn't . . . and it still isn't, a clear pathway, you understand. It is not worn down to the soil with continuous use, it's not like that, but if you can read a landscape close up you can pick the route by scanning the ground ahead of you.'

'Yes, I'm with you.' Yellich nodded. 'I know exactly what you mean.'

'So . . . I followed the path over some scrubland and it led to a cornfield and then into more scrubland and wasteland, and eventually it came out into this very housing estate, here

103

at the edge of the village. If you follow the path you'll find it comes out at the garages.'

'The garages?' Yellich asked. 'What are they? Garages for the use of the residents on the estate?'

'Yes.' Millom nodded. 'They are rental garages, about ten in all, and are arranged in a sort of cul-de-sac round a concreted-over area in one of the roads in the estate. If a tenant on the estate owns a car, then if they so wish, they can rent a garage, if a garage is available to rent, that is. So far as I can tell, all the garages seem to be rented and so the greater number of car owners on the estate have to leave their cars in the street. But the children who live on the estate seem to respect the cars and do not vandalize them. I like living on this estate for that reason, it's quiet; people know each other and are well behaved. It isn't like an inner-city sink estate. I couldn't live on one of the estates . . . all that crime, all that violence . . . horrible.'

'Yes.' Yellich glanced up at a framed print of Constable's *The Haywain* which hung over the fireplace in Millom's living room. 'I had just that impression of this village when I arrived. It does indeed seem to be a very civilized place to live.'

'Yes . . . so, the footpath comes out at the garages,' Millom continued, 'but why Garrett should want to walk along the footpath to get to the village is a bit of a mystery, unless he enjoyed the walk, and if that was the case, I can understand him. Give me the choice of a walk through fields and woodland, or along a road, then I know which I'd choose. But . . . Garrett, well he wasn't really one for taking exercise so far as I could tell, and of the two routes the walk on the road to the village would have been a lot easier on the leg muscles for him. You know, come to think of it, he was never seen in the village . . . he never went out for a beer or to the post office, or to our little supermarket, otherwise we would have run into each other, I'm sure of that.'

'So what are you suggesting, Mr Millom?' Yellich asked.

'Harry . . . you can call me "Harry".' Millom sat back in his armchair. 'Let's keep it casual and relaxed, shall we? No need to be formal.'

'If you like.' Yellich detected the gentle aroma of wood polish in the room. 'So what are you suggesting, Harry? What are you driving at?'

'Well . . . I am not really suggesting anything. It is not really my place to do that.' Harry Millom looked up at the ceiling and then across at Yellich from where he was sitting in an armchair in front of the window. 'But . . .' he held up an index finger, 'what I suspect, and this is only my impression, is that Mr Garrett is . . . or was . . . a bit of a fly-by-night.'

'Meaning?' Yellich became intrigued and sat forward.

'Meaning that I reckon he has . . . he had . . . a car in one of those lock-up garages,' Millom explained. 'Meaning he slips in and out of Millington with few people noticing. So I would suspect.'

'Few people,' Yellich echoed.

'Well, as I said, you can't guarantee you won't be seen, can you . . . especially not in this village?' Millom smiled knowingly. 'Someone always sees something. What's that expression, "the fields have eyes and the woods have ears"?'

'Dare say that that is a fair point,' Yellich acknowledged. 'So, a car, and which garage . . . do you know? And do you know how he can get a garage if they're for council tenants only to rent?'

'I don't know which garage,' Millom replied. 'I'm never there when he comes and goes. That is if he comes and goes by car because, remember, I am just guessing here. I don't have a car and so I don't use the garages . . . and how can he get a garage when he's not a council tenant?' Millom shrugged his shoulders. 'Well, he does that by subletting from a tenant who doesn't use their garage any more. You know . . . a little private arrangement that the council doesn't know about. That wouldn't be so difficult to make happen. That would be Harry Millom's little old guess. It would be useful for Garrett and it would mean a little extra cash for a hard-up council tenant. You scratch my old back and I'll scratch yours, that sort of number. In fact, I bet it happens all the time.'

'Seems logical,' Yellich mused. 'Yes . . . yes . . . I can very easily see that sort of agreement being reached. As you say, it suits both people, if they keep it hush-hush just between the two of them.'

'Well, I don't want to be too suspicious. I try to be fair-minded, and you know gardening does make you a fair-minded soul.' Once again Millom shrugged. 'But I reckon that is what is happening because, like I said, the easiest way to get to the village from The Grange by foot is to walk along the road in full view of the public. The path is a bit of a long way round, a bit . . . well, it's a significantly greater distance in fact and it would be muddy in the winter.'

'Don't be too upset about appearing suspicious,' Yellich replied warmly, 'there's nothing wrong with being suspicious. In fact, you would have made a good police officer. You seem to have a good eye for detail and a certain scope for suspicion.'

'I was one once.' Millom smiled. 'I used to be a boy in blue, which is why I am always pleased to help when I can.'

'Really?' Yellich sat back on the settee.

'Yes, really, but not for long, I reckon it just wasn't for me, it is, or was, as simple as that. You know I tried to put my finger on the reason . . . I gave it much thought at the time. I didn't like being in uniform for one, even if the girls went for a young man in a uniform, which they did, and that was pleasant, as I am sure you know . . . but there were definitely other reasons. I didn't like the hours for one, the shifts seemed to upset my body's system.'

'Yes,' Yellich nodded, 'the shifts do take some getting used to. Not everybody can cope with the shifts, turning day into night, going to bed and getting up again and it's still the same day.'

'So I left the police force.' Millom slung one leg over the arm of the chair in which he was sitting. 'There were no hard feelings, no ill-will on either side. In fact, my inspector said much

107

the same as you just did . . . it's not for everyone. He said that a person is either a copper or they're not. It's as straightforward as that . . . and I clearly wasn't cut out to be a copper. I was of no use to the police and I was of no use to myself being a police officer. So there was no use sticking at it so as to try to make it work. I did eighteen months and so I can say I gave it a good try.'

'Fair enough,' Yellich nodded in agreement. 'And sensible as well, if you and the police were not for each other it was a good move to go your separate ways.'

'Yes . . . so as I said, I left the police with no hard feelings. I wrote my resignation and left the building feeling very happy with myself and very happy for myself. It was handshakes all round and all that, and then I started to shop around until I found a job I liked and then it was one long holiday, that's how I found gardening to be. I took a job with the local authority department and once I got my City and Guilds Certificate in Gardening and Horticulture, well, then I was set for life. I never earned any real money, but it was safe work with an inflation-proof pension at the end of it all, modest, but a pension all the same. Then I got a job with Garrett during the summer months just to ease me into permanent retirement . . . that was the plan. So it looks like I am now in permanent retirement if Garrett's no longer with us, a bit earlier than planned, looks like that anyway. Mind you, working for Garrett was easy, nothing too heavy and all with power tools. So it was all easy gardening really, as gardening goes. I do . . . or I did . . . the skilled work, Miles Law did the "donkey jobs".'

'Yes . . .' Yellich stroked his chin, 'so he said. In fact, he called himself the "donkey gardener", mowing the lawn and cutting the hedges.'

'And the weeding,' Millom added. 'It is hard, back-breaking work and never a pleasant job in itself. And he had no skill. There was no skill involved in anything Miles Law did, to tell you the truth. I planted new growth in the potting shed, and re-planted them when they were ready to go into the ground, prune the fruit trees, grafted new stems on to existing stems . . . I did all that . . . all the live long day to myself in the open air during the summer months. It was heaven. So, no, I wasn't cut out to be a copper but I was a born gardener . . . I still am really . . . growing things,' he glanced out of the window towards his rear garden, '. . . and you see so much . . . a weasel running across the ground like an old autumn leaf being blown on the wind . . . and a swarm of bees once looking for a place to live. They settled in a hut on a bowling green in a park in York. The door of the hut was open you see because the bowling greens were in use and the bees just flew in and set up home. We got a local beekeeper to come and remove them to where he had a vacant hive they could use. You see nature like that all around you as a gardener. I do so pity those poor souls who work in offices. That must be a form of prison sentence, if you ask me.'

'Yes, I wouldn't much like a job like that either,' Yellich agreed. 'I like getting out and about. So,

109

tell me what you can about the assistant gardener, Miles Law, if you will? What do you know about him?'

'Law . . .?' Millom cupped his broad and smoothly shaved chin in his slender but strong-looking hand. 'I can't really tell you much, I'm afraid. Not much at all. Garrett introduced us, we shook hands and we stood, the three of us, outside the front door of The Grange and we agreed on our areas of responsibility and I hardly ever saw him after that. It was always a case of me arriving at Garrett's house to put a few hours in and noticing that the lawn had been mowed, or the flowerbeds had been weeded, and so realizing that Law had been there that day or two days earlier. It was like that most of the time. We might meet in passing now and again, but most times we were like ships which pass in the night.'

'I see,' Yellich mumbled to himself.

'But I can tell you that Law is not a gardener,' Millom added. 'Not in himself.'

'No?' Yellich raised his eyebrows. 'Why do you say that?'

'He's got cold icy eyes, steely eyes,' Millom explained. 'He hasn't got soul. You might not have soul when you start out, I don't think I had soul when I started, but I developed soul by working as a gardener. Working with living things you see, it makes you care and it makes you want to give, but Law, he took much and gave little, or so it always seemed to me . . . a bit like a thief, but I don't mean that in a criminal sense, I never saw him steal anything. There wasn't much he could steal anyway. He never went inside the house where there might have been goodies, neither of us did, but he is more of a thief than a gardener, if you ask me, in himself that is. Why do you ask? Do you figure him for topping Garrett? "The gardener dun it" . . .? Frankly, I can't see him for that . . . he's not a violent man. Not that I could tell.'

'No.' Yellich shook his head slightly. He thought rather of the three identically dressed women who were seen calling on The Grange on the previous Saturday forenoon, but he said only, 'No . . . no, we don't suspect anyone for the murder of Mr Garrett, not yet, but it's still early days yet. Very early days.'

Somerled Yellich drove away from Harry Millom's house feeling much confused about the man. He didn't know what to make of Millom. Enigmatically, on the one hand, Millom seemed to be a hail-fellow-well-met type, yet he clearly had a downtrodden wife. Millom claimed that he had 'soul', yet all the 'soulful' people Yellich had met never claimed to be in possession of the quality, rather it was an observation made about them. But, Yellich reasoned, he didn't need to understand Millom, Millom was a source of information and the information he had provided about the pathway which led along the rear of The Grange to the village of Millington, and the fact that Garrett was seen using the path, but was never seen in the village itself was, Yellich thought, valid. He too, like Millom, found himself wondering if Garrett had kept a motor

111

vehicle in a garage which had been illegally sublet to him by a council tenant. It was, Yellich believed, something to follow up. It was something to add to the 'to do' list.

Yellich arrived at York and drove through the steadily increasing volume of rush-hour traffic to Micklegate Bar Police Station and parked his car in the car park at the rear of the building, being for the use of officers and members of the public attending on police business, leaving the window of the car on the driver's side wound down so as to permit the car's interior to 'breathe' in the heat. He pondered that he wouldn't be able to enjoy the luxury of leaving his car window fully wound down in a public car park, but in the car park at the rear of a police station such an indulgence was possible. It would indeed be a foolhardy fellow who would steal cars themselves, or from cars, parked in such a location, so Yellich pondered. Yellich walked across the black tarmac surface of the car park in a calm but authoritative manner, enjoying the late afternoon sun as he did so, and entered the Victorian era building by the 'staff only' entrance. He signed in at the enquiry desk and then took the stairs, two at a time, to the CID corridor. He walked along the corridor to George Hennessey's office and tapped reverentially on the door frame.

'Ah . . . Somerled, I am pleased that you have returned. Do come in.' Hennessey, sitting behind his desk, smiled at Yellich's arrival. A solidly built man in a sports jacket also turned and beamed at Yellich. 'This is Detective Constable

Kelto from the Metropolitan Police.' Kelto stood smartly and he and Yellich shook hands.

'Pleased to meet you, sir.'

Yellich found Kelto's handshake to be warm and vigorous, and of just the correct pressure, in Yellich's mind, not overly tight, nor was it offensively loose. 'Welcome to the frozen north.' Yellich was astounded at Kelto's age, which he thought to be near retirement, but yet the man clearly was of lowly rank. Kelto's career had doubtless been worthwhile, if unspectacular, and he was clearly happy to address Yellich, who was junior in years to him, as 'sir'. He was not, thought Yellich, a man born for high places, and was evidently content to accept that fact about himself.

'I'm just calling in for the Garrett file, boss.' Yellich turned to address Hennessey. 'I have a couple of things to add and then I'll get off home, if that's all right?'

'Yes . . . certainly.' Hennessey took the file in question from his desk top and handed it to Yellich. 'Yes, by all means do so; it's been a long day for all of us.'

Yellich took the file to his office and wrote up the account of his interview with Mrs Staples of 'The Maids' and also of his visit to Harry Millom, detailing the information that both had given. He returned the file to Hennessey's office saying, 'Interesting but not urgent, boss.' He nodded warmly towards Kelto and left the office.

'Thank you, Somerled,' George Hennessey called after the departing Yellich. 'I'll read it asap.'

Somerled Yellich drove thankfully home to

Huntington on the northern outskirts of York. He drove down a narrow road in a new-build estate and halted outside a house with a front door which was painted loudly in canary yellow. As he halted the car, the door of the house was opened and a well-built boy of primary school age ran from the house towards Yellich with his arms outstretched and crashed into Yellich with such force that he, Yellich, gasped for breath. Yellich took the boy's hand, and they, father and son, walked up the short drive to the house and entered it.

'He's been a very good boy all day.' Sara Yellich flung her slender arms around her husband's neck and kissed him.

'Good boy,' Somerled Yellich smiled approvingly at the beaming Jeremy. 'Let me have a quick cup of tea and then we'll go for a walk, shall we?'

Jeremy nodded, still beaming. 'Yes, please, Daddy,' he replied enthusiastically.

'That is what I do so like to hear . . . a good boy and a good boy all day as well.'

A short time later Somerled and Jeremy Yellich walked into the fields near their home, identifying what birds they saw and both mimicking the 'ee-aw' of the horn of the mainline railway train arriving and departing from the north, or going from York towards the north, to Newcastle and Edinburgh and beyond, which echoed across the landscape, they being close to the East Coast Mainline. They sat and watched a group of boys playing cricket.

'Hard ball,' Jeremy commented as the 'thwack'

of the cricket ball being struck by the bat filled the air.

'Yes,' Somerled Yellich replied, 'they're made of cork wood.'

'Like the town in Ireland?' Jeremy Yellich asked. 'Cork? I saw it in the atlas.'

'It is spelled the same.' Yellich felt a glow of pride in his son. It had, he calculated, been fully ten days since he and Jeremy had sat down at the dining-room table and looked at the place names in Ireland, having already looked at place names in England and Scotland and Wales. 'But yes . . . good boy . . . you remember things well. I am pleased with you, Jeremy, very pleased.'

Jeremy Yellich curled into his father.

It was not politic, Yellich reasoned, to tell Jeremy that the atlas which they had looked at was quite old and that Cork was now spelled Cobh and was pronounced 'Cove'. It was the fact that Jeremy had remembered the name which Yellich believed was the important thing. 'But the cricket ball is made of cork wood, which is a type of tree grown in Spain,' he told him. 'So not really anything to do with the town in Ireland, they just happen to have the same spelling.'

When Somerled and Sara Yellich were told their son, their first, and subsequently only, child, had been born with Down's syndrome, they had felt the great rush of disappointment that all parents of such children experience, but they had then found that a whole new and hitherto unknown world began to open up to them as they met and made very good friends with other parents of similar children. They had also come

115

to appreciate the skill of the medical profession as they learned that even as late as the 1940s such children rarely lived beyond the age of ten or twelve years, yet now could live into their fifties or sixties and could achieve the functioning level of a normal twelve-year-old. With love and encouragement and support, Jeremy, they had been assured, could live a semi-independent life, in a supervised hostel, and could even take employment such as replenishing shelves in a supermarket.

Still later that day Somerled and Sara Yellich sat in silence, side by side, in the living room of their house listening to Ralph Vaughan Williams' 'Wasp's Suite'. When the music faded Somerled glanced at his wife with a raised eyebrow, as if to say, 'shall we?' . . . and his wife nodded her head slightly, just once, as if to say 'yes, we shall'. As they climbed the stairs of their house, he following she, the bells of the church in Huntington struck eleven.

It was Wednesday, 23.00 hours.

Three

Wednesday 21 June, 16.04 hours – 22.15 hours

In which the reason why Miles Law delayed calling the police upon discovering the body of Anthony Garrett is revealed, and Reginald Webster and Carmen Pharoah and George Hennessey are severally at home to the urbane and always too forgiving reader.

The principled and most virtuous reader will doubtless recall that when Somerled Yellich returned to Micklegate Bar Police Station to record the outcome of his visits to Mrs Staples of 'The Maids' cleaning services and to the modest but very cleanly kept home of Harry Millom, the head gardener at The Grange, he encountered Chief Inspector Hennessey in his office in conversation with Detective Constable Kelto of the Metropolitan Police, lately arrived from London. It is to that conversation, dear reader, that we must now return.

'Thank you, Somerled,' Hennessey called after the hurriedly departing Somerled Yellich. 'I'll read it asap.' He paused and, pointing to the open door of his office, he said to Kelto, 'That is one damn good detective sergeant. Damn good. I'm indeed very lucky to have him on my team. But

117

there's nothing else for him to do at the moment. It's been a long day for him. He's worked hard and well and he's got a son with special needs and so he has to get home to his family.'

'Indeed, sir,' Kelto nodded approvingly. 'Mine are up and away, flown the coop, making their own way in life.'

'So is mine,' Hennessey replied, 'all one of him. But he's done well. I don't worry about him and his future.'

'Two daughters in my case, Juliet and Sara without an "h", both married. I'm a grandad three times over and with the promise of more planned. I never had a son but I've got three grandsons now, so I dare say it's true that good things come to those who wait.' Kelto glowed with pride. Hennessey was pleased for him. He, like Yellich, had been surprised at Kelto's age for one of such a junior rank. Kelto seemed to Hennessey to be useful but unspectacular and so he had pigeon-holed Kelto as being one of the police force's 'foot soldiers'. Thinking, as Yellich had thought, that high office was just not for him. Kelto did not appear to Hennessey to be particularly self-conscious about his lack of promotion, being seemingly warm-hearted and happy to defer to rank by addressing all those senior to him as 'sir', despite their age. 'I still have two officers out there interviewing people but there is nothing else for Somerled to do today.'

'That's an interesting name he has,' Kelto remarked. 'I don't think . . . in fact I am sure I have never come across it before today.'

'It's Gaelic, apparently.' Hennessey leaned back

in his chair, causing it to creak loudly. 'It is spelled s.o.m.e.r.l.e.d., as if it should be pronounced "Somerled", but is in fact pronounced "Sorley", as you have heard. But to business . . . how can we help the Metropolitan Police?'

'Well, sir,' Kelto leaned forward, 'my governor sent me up here to view the body of Anthony Garrett. He also said that I could provide you with any and all information I can give, and be of what help to the Vale of York Police that I can be.'

'Fair enough,' Hennessey clasped his hands behind his head, 'all help is appreciated. But please tell me, why on earth do you need to see the body? It did seem a strange request when we first heard it. It still does seem strange in fact.'

'I don't want to see it but my governor, Mr Allardyce, Detective Chief Inspector Allardyce, the same position as you, sir, he said he just wouldn't rest until he's seen Garrett's body, or a photograph of it. Garrett has slipped the net so many times over the years that Mr Allardyce won't believe he's dead until he's viewed the body or has it viewed for him, by proxy as it were.'

'And so he sent you all the way to York to look at a dead body?' Hennessey gasped. 'The DNA will prove it's Garrett. Can't he wait for the test results? He seems a trifle impatient to me. It doesn't strike me as being an efficient use of police time. We could have taken photographs of his tattoos and faxed them to Mr Allardyce.'

'You could, sir, but that's just Mr Allardyce. Anthony Garrett has been a thorn in the side of the Met for years,' Kelto explained, 'and it's

119

become almost personal with Mr Allardyce, so it seems, but it's not my place to comment. I am told to be particularly on the lookout for a unique tattoo . . . you just mentioned it, sir.'

'Pilot,' Hennessey suggested, 'that is the tattoo in question, I assume?'

'That's it, sir . . . Pilot.' Kelto grinned. 'That's the tattoo. It seems you have the right man.'

'Well, I am sure we can arrange for you to view the corpse.' Hennessey drew a deep breath and leaned forwards in his chair but still kept his hands clasped on his head. 'I'll make a phone call to let the hospital know you'll be visiting their mortuary. You do have your ID to hand?'

Kelto proudly patted his sports jacket. 'Yes, sir, I showed it to your officer at the enquiry desk, as I was obliged to do. Do you want to see it, sir?'

'No . . . no,' Hennessey held up his fleshy right hand, palm outwards, 'but the mortuary staff will need to see it. They won't let you into their quiet, chilly little world without verifying your identity. But "Pilot", I confess that puzzled us as a tattoo. Useful as it may be as pretty well unique and good for identification purposes, but what is the story there? Do you know?'

'There is nothing especially mysterious about it, Mr Hennessey.' Kelto wore a light-weight chequered sports jacket, brown trousers, a white shirt with a police tie depicting a candle burning at both ends. 'He served in HM Forces, briefly, specifically in the Royal Navy.'

'Interesting,' Hennessey commented.

'Well . . . he had quite a reputation for wriggling

out of trouble, so we were once told by a fellow matelot who served with Garrett and whom we also had an interest in. It can be a small world sometimes,' Kelto explained. 'It was the case that if you fell foul of those draconian naval rules and regulations, then Garrett was a handy sort of geezer to have on your side. Well handy in fact, because Garrett could always find a loophole to squeeze through. In other words he could navigate his way out of trouble, him and his shipmates. Or he'd tell his shipmates what to say to help them wriggle out of trouble if he wasn't in the soup with them. He just had one of those minds, just as aircraft and merchant ships have "navigators" and the Royal Navy has "pilots" to tell them where their ships are . . . different name for the same animal you might say, so then, by that means, Garrett acquired the nickname of "pilot". He was what the army would call a "barrack-room lawyer", I would think.'

'I see. I know the type.' Hennessey unclasped his hands and folded his arms in front of his chest. 'Nothing mysterious there, no intrigue at all . . . it's a bit of a let-down really. But at least it's explained.'

'No intrigue at all,' Kelto shrugged, 'but apparently he quite liked his nickname, he really took quite a shine to it, so we were told, and so he had himself tattooed with it. It is very convenient for us that he did so because it's a unique identifying feature.'

'As you say,' Hennessey replied. 'It's very useful for the police.'

'I did three years in the army,' Kelto continued,

'more or less straight out of school, and my father warned me about tattoos when I went in. He said, *"Don't get tattooed, you're a marked man if you get tattooed."* I took his advice and I am quite glad that I did so, but it's fortunate for us that no one gave Garrett that advice.'

'As we have already agreed,' Hennessey growled, annoyed at the repetition of an observation already made. He was beginning to sense a certain emotional immaturity in Kelto, he was beginning to understand why the man had never risen in the police force, he was beginning to see why his 'governor' should have chosen him rather than another officer to send north to look at a corpse. 'So,' Hennessey continued, 'what do you know about Garrett? Why has he been a thorn in the side of the Metropolitan Police for so long?'

'Living up to his nickname,' Kelto advised. 'Always seemed to have been one step ahead of us, and always had been able to walk on some technicality or other if he had been arrested. He is believed to have been behind some big jobs in London and the Home Counties . . . I mean organized crime. He's put together some jobs, so we have been told, one of which resulted in the murder of a police officer.'

'Oh . . .' Hennessey groaned. 'I begin to understand Detective Chief Inspector Allardyce's need for the confirmation of Garrett's identity.'

'We were not, and still wouldn't be, able to nail him for murder for that crime, he was far too distanced,' Kelto explained, 'probably not even as an accessory before or after the fact, but he's been a wanted man for many years. But Anthony

"Pilot" Garrett has always found a way of slipping through the net. He's as slippery as a cup full of jellied eels.'

'So then despite that he was convicted for murder, as we have learned, he served only three years,' Hennessey commented. 'Three years for murder. Just three years! What's the story there?'

'Yes . . . offensively short,' Kelto replied. 'It seems that there is a story to be told about those three years he served, despite being sentenced to life. But why he got out so early? Well, I'm afraid I don't know. I suppose I just don't have the right level of security clearance.'

'All right . . . so tell me about the murder he served time for,' Hennessey asked. 'What happened?'

'It was a domestic murder,' Kelto explained. 'He murdered his wife. It was apparently very plain and very messy. A few men do, and few trouble and strifes murder their better halves. But few domestic murderers are career criminals, because career criminals know how difficult it is to get away with a domestic murder. I don't know much about the murder itself but it seems Garrett's old trouble and strife walked out on him and went to live in a refuge with their children. Garrett went round to the refuge and ran her through with a carving knife. He did that in broad daylight and in front of a large number of witnesses. Refuges are supposed to conceal their address but one or two don't, or are careless, or Garrett found out about the address somehow and that would not be difficult for him. I mean, a career criminal . . . he'd have contacts, or maybe it was someone with a loose tongue. But whatever the

123

means, Garrett went round to the refuge and offed his old lady. He collected life, as he would, but as you point out, he was out in three short years. The strange thing is though that he never returned to London, and that must have been hard for him. London has a strong pull on Londoners.'

'I know.' Hennessey smiled softly. 'Believe me, I know. I'm from Greenwich and I know all about the "pull" you speak of, well I know all about it. I also understand it's even stronger for criminals. For them it's not just about the streets and their roots, it's also about the comradeship of organized crime.'

'That is indeed probably the case, Mr Hennessey, sir.' Kelto nodded in agreement. 'I confess I have not thought of it like that. I just know the bond between London and Londoners. It is very strong. We're just not happy anywhere else.'

There then occurred a lull in the conversation, during which the two officers held eye contact with each other. After approximately ten seconds, Kelto broke the silence.

'I do know just a little about one incident which Garrett was believed to have some involvement. But this is just police canteen talk, you understand?' Kelto leaned back in his chair.

'Understood.' Hennessey conversely leaned forward and rested his forearms on his desktop and clasped his hands together.

'It appeared to be the case that Garrett was behind a job which went very badly wrong in that yet another police officer was murdered. He was in the wrong place at the wrong time. He apparently identified himself as a police officer,

124

but the felons stabbed him anyway, possibly in a state of panic. The police got a conviction against said felons, but despite great efforts could not get anywhere near Garrett. But the police officer had a son, a young man at the time, who became obsessed with finding Garrett and settling things. He was reported to the police on the QT by a police informer who told his police contact that the young man was asking people how and where he could buy a shooter.' Kelto paused. 'The police handled it unofficially, the son of one of theirs and all that . . . So they had words with the boy and advised him, strongly so, to leave town and cool off. "Your mother has just lost her husband – she doesn't need to lose a son as well." You know, that sort of advice.'

'Yes,' Hennessey grunted.

'One tragedy is sufficient for one family,' Kelto continued. 'No family needs two, not at the same time.'

'We would do the same,' Hennessey commented. 'Do go on.'

'And . . . and by sheer coincidence I believe he left London and settled up here in this very neck of the woods.'

'Really!' Hennessey gasped. 'Now . . . he has just become a person of interest.'

'So I can understand.' Kelto smiled briefly. 'He was also known to have gone off the rails after his father was murdered,' Kelto further informed. 'So you'll have some track on him.'

'Will we indeed?' Hennessey replied quietly. 'He is becoming very interesting now. What is his name, do you know?'

'I'll say I do.' Kelto smiled broadly. 'He is Francis Badger. It is a name I will always remember because I married one Frances Badger, it being my wife's maiden name, she of course being Frances with an 'e' and he, the son of Constable Badger, being Francis with an 'i'."

'I see . . . fair enough . . . and he has a record, you say?' Hennessey confirmed. 'For violent crime?'

'Oh yes. So I believe,' Kelto replied. 'He has a history of violence. But all this was quite some years ago, obviously before Garrett was arrested.'

'That is very helpful.' Hennessey smiled his thanks. 'Very helpful indeed.'

'Well, I don't think I have anything else to add, sir, with respect. Can you please direct me to the hospital you mentioned? I am sorry I could not provide any information, sir. I just don't have the seniority.'

'Nonetheless it has been useful.' Hennessey inclined his head. 'So don't feel unhappy. The mystery of the tattoo has been solved. There's no intrigue there, as we said. The question has been answered, and we know a little of Garrett's background, so it has been useful. I'll draw you a map. You won't find the hospital without one.'

'Will I need a taxi or to catch a bus?' Kelto stood. 'I have never been to York. I have never been this far north, in fact. It's a bit of an adventure for me, is this old trip. It's something to tell my grandsons about.'

'No . . . no you won't.' Hennessey reached for a sheet of paper and began to draw a simple map. 'York is nominally a city but in fact in terms of its population size it's smaller than some London boroughs that I can think of, a lot smaller, in fact.'

'Will I have the opportunity to walk on those ancient walls?' Kelto asked with what Hennessey thought to be childlike enthusiasm. 'I see them from here, through your office window . . . they must be the walls I have read about and I see people walking on them. Will I be able to do that?'

'Yes . . .' Hennessey replied with impatience as he drew the map which would take Detective Constable Kelto to York District Hospital. 'In fact, the best way to cross the city is to walk the walls . . . and they are not ancient, they were reconstructed in late Victorian times. Well, that is to say the stones are ancient but the re-building of them is comparatively recent. But thank you, Mr Kelto. It has been very useful.'

Carmen Pharoah carefully but discreetly read the room. She found it somewhat cramped but there was a certain undeniable neatness to it. She had the strong impression that a determined attempt had been made to keep everything in its proper place. The room, she thought, was manly with an overriding functional feel, rather than it being womanly with a certain gentle and softening homeliness about it. Most importantly the room told her that it was all age- and social-standing appropriate. There was no display of wealth that she could detect, for instance, that could not be afforded by a man who self-effacingly described himself as a 'donkey gardener'. She asked, 'How long have you been working for Mr Garrett?'

'Well . . .' Miles Law shuffled in his chair and turned to Carmen Pharoah, '. . . like I said, I only do odd jobs at The Grange and I don't put in a full week's work. Or, I did only odd jobs there. I'm just the "donkey man". If the grass doesn't need cutting or the hedge doesn't need trimming, well, then I don't go in, and of course I don't go in at all during the winter. I feast in the summer and I fast in the winter. Feasting, fasting and feasting again, that is the way of it for we poor gardeners. But how long I have been cycling over to The Grange for a bit of cash-in-hand work for Mr Garrett and his garden? Well . . . dunno . . . possibly seven or eight years, something like that. Yes, I'd say about that sort of time.'

'Have you ever been inside the house?' Reginald Webster asked.

'No!' The reply Miles Law gave was short, sharp, defensive. 'Never,' he insisted. 'I have never been inside the house.'

'Not before this morning, you mean?' Carmen Pharoah clarified. 'You went into the house this morning, didn't you? You went in and you found the body of Mr Garrett?'

Miles Law shot Carmen Pharoah a cold, hard stare.

Carmen Pharoah in turn was suddenly grateful for the controlling presence of Reginald Webster.

'Yes, all right, I meant that,' Law conceded. 'But not before this morning. Not once.' Law relaxed. 'I don't make no secret there. I saw the open window at the back of the house. I thought it was not at all like Garrett to leave the ground-floor window open all night. I mean, talk about

128

an invitation to crime, and Garrett, well, he was always so very hot on home security. Very hot on it. It just wasn't like Garrett to leave a ground-floor window open like that . . . not the Anthony Garrett I knew. So yes, I went into the house, banged on the front door a few times first and then, only then when I got no answer, did I enter the house. Only then. I didn't sneak in like a thief . . . and that is . . . was also unlike Garrett . . . window open *and* front door unlocked . . . that was definitely not the Anthony Garrett I got to know over the years.'

'It's hot right now. This is a particularly hot summer.' Carmen Pharoah continued to read the room. It all still looked to her as being appropriate for Miles Law. 'Mr Garrett could have left the window open to allow the house to ventilate. That could have explained the open window.'

'Not a ground-floor window,' Miles Law snarled his reply, 'an upstairs window yes, possibly, but not ever a ground-floor window. Not Garrett. And leave the front door unlocked? Garrett? Never,' Miles Law persisted. 'Garrett would not leave a ground-floor window open all night and it was not warm enough for him to want it open when I arrived. So, when I saw it open, I knew it had been open all night. So I did what anyone would have done – I checked on his welfare, didn't I? Anyone would have done that. Then I found what I found, and I saw what I saw. I went to find his phone because I don't carry one of those mobile things. I am an old-fashioned land-line merchant, that's me. So anyway, I dialled three nines, called the police, didn't I? Would anyone have done different?' Miles Law looked at Webster, then at Carmen Pharoah, and then at Webster again. 'So what are you going to say is wrong with that? You think I should have just left him there and got on with my little donkey job? I mean, at least you found out today. If I hadn't gone in the house like I did he wouldn't have been found until Friday afternoon when the contract cleaners call in their little yellow van. We have been told that the maids have a key and would have let themselves in if Garret had not answered their knock on his door. So I done you a favour. A big favour.'

'True.' Reginald Webster also read the room as Carmen Pharoah had done, and he also noticed an attempt at neatness, and he also found it to be age- and social-class appropriate. There was, he felt, nothing of suspicion in the room. No 'bad news' at all.

'So you see, you're on the case earlier than you might have been otherwise. So you owe me,' Miles Law insisted. 'So I did you a good turn, didn't I? So why the suspicion? So why the third degree like I am some sort of criminal?'

'Well, you are some sort of criminal,' Reginald Webster replied, 'by your own admission, but admittedly no recent convictions against your name. So why the third degree . . .? Well, we'll tell you. We want to know why it took you so long to report finding Anthony Garrett's body?'

A cold look flashed across Miles Law's steely blue eyes. He sat forward in his seat. Both officers saw the man's little body tense and Law suddenly seemed to them to be like a coiled snake, ready to strike.

'You were seen,' Carmen Pharoah explained calmly. 'You were being watched by someone, you see, and the person was able to fix your arrival at The Grange, and your entry into the house, very accurately. And we have a log of the time you made the emergency call to report Mr Garrett's body. There's almost an hour difference.'

'That's an hour for you to account for,' Webster added.

'The old woman who lives in the bungalow across the road from The Grange?' Miles Law sank back in his chair. 'Her? Was it her?'

'We can't tell you,' Webster explained. 'Sorry. That's for us to know and only us to know.'

'I dare say I should have known.' Law glanced up at the ceiling of his living room. 'My first cell mate, he said, "*Always assume you're being watched. Always, always assume you're being watched. Just because you can't see them, it doesn't mean they can't see you.*" So I should have known. I've seen her sitting in her front room looking out, but sometimes the window of that room looks like it's painted black due to the angle of the sun . . . you just can't see beyond the glass when that happens. I just forgot about her . . . out of sight, out of mind as they say because it was like that this morning. Do you know if she has any cars in that double garage by her bungalow . . .? I've often wondered,' Law asked. 'I've often wondered if there is anything in that garage because I've never seen the garage doors open.'

'We don't,' Carmen Pharoah replied, 'and we couldn't tell you even if we did. So, please stop avoiding the issue, Mr Law. Why did you delay calling the police for about an hour after you found Mr Garrett's body? Were you looking for something to steal? Were you looking for what you could fit into your pockets? Something you could drop out of an open window and hide it away somewhere to collect later?'

'Yes, I was,' Miles Law replied with what both officers thought was disarming honesty. 'That's exactly what I was doing. I was looking for anything that was worth stealing. I was having a good root around the house.'

'Be careful what you are admitting to doing.' Webster spoke coldly. 'Be very careful.'

'So, all right, I need to be careful about what I admit to doing.' Miles Law crossed one faded denim covered leg over the other. His thin but sinewy arms protruded from his blue T-shirt with a faded 'I love London' logo on the front. His shoes were a pair of worn and torn tennis shoes which had, it seemed to the officers, been relegated to being used as house slippers. 'You'll be doing your old criminal checks, if you have not yet already done them. I told the other guy this morning, tall, older guy with silver hair . . .'

'Mr Hennessey,' Carmen Pharoah prompted, 'that would be Mr Hennessey, he is our boss.'

'If that's his name.' Miles glanced at the floor then up at Carmen Pharoah. 'Anyway I told him, Mr Hennessey, I told him that I was known to the police. I told him I had form . . . like muchos previous track. Muchos. Mainly for theft so

132

there's no point in hiding it. That's what I thought. No point in hiding it because it's going to be discovered anyway. No point at all. So I told him.'

'Yes, we have in fact done all the checks on you,' Webster nodded. 'We are very thorough but you are not a serious criminal, Mr Law, only ever petty magistrates' court stuff and there has been nothing for a long time. In fact all your convictions are spent. Your record reads like you have turned a corner. It reads like you are a reformed character. We were impressed by what we read.'

'Well . . .' Miles Law leaned forward and rested his bony elbows on his knees, 'I reckon that I have calmed down a bit. I dare say that that is the old case . . . yes . . . I reckon I can say that I have calmed down with the years. But I've done a few things here and there since my last conviction, things that you don't know about.'

'We'll allow for that,' Carmen Pharoah replied icily. 'We know that that is always the case, but we can only proceed with what we know about.'

'But once a thief, always a thief.' Miles Law shrugged. 'That's the truth. All right, so I don't go on missions any more. I don't go out looking for windows to turn no more, none of that no more, never any of that again, but as I said, once a thief, always a thief. If the opportunity presents itself I'll grab it. If there's something of value left lying around, well, I'm the bogeyman that will pocket it. Once thieving is in your old system you can't get rid of it and I'll tell you plain, I don't want to get rid of it. It's been useful down

the years. Very useful. I've eaten because of it.'
Law paused. 'So . . . this morning I was inside
The Grange for the first time . . . I saw Garrett
had breathed his last, I saw that he'd been
dead for two or three days, so I thought what's
another hour? That's how I looked at it. What
was another hour in the great scheme of things?
So I went walkabout inside Garrett's house. It
was . . . it still is . . . a house full of goodies, a
real treasure trove. I mean, talk about Aladdin's
cave . . .' Law paused once more. 'I started early
in life, I did. Very early. I was a juvenile delin-
quent appearing before the juvenile bench. Mind
you, you'll know that, you'll have read that. I
did minor acts of theft, then I got into forcing
windows and doors of sheds and garages . . .
then I moved on to breaking into people's houses
and I got away with it most of the time. I was
making a good living at it. You know I once
broke into some geezer's house and his old coin
jar was overflowing, like he'd been putting off
counting all the coins and putting them into those
little plastic bags before taking them to the old
bank and paying them into his account. That is
one tedious job, so I reckon he was putting it off
. . . silly man . . . he won't be making that
mistake again. He didn't even hide it; he just left
it in an old margarine tub on top of a low wardrobe in his bedroom. It was a weight to carry
once I was out of the house with it, but once I
had counted it I worked out that I'd have to put
in a good month or six weeks' honest work to
earn what was inside his margarine tub and I
was in and out of that house in less than fifteen

134

minutes. You see, that's the attraction of thieving, getting in fifteen minutes what an honest man would take a month to earn. But I knew I'd get caught eventually because no one gets away with it for ever. I knew I'd do time if I carried on. So I joined the army.'

Webster nodded. The neatness of Law's living room suddenly made sense. Once a soldier anxious to pass inspection, then, like a thief always being a thief, one is always a soldier anxious to pass inspection.

'I had no convictions for twelve months,' Law continued, 'and so I was accepted to serve in HM Forces. I thought that once I was a soldier with a job to do, I'd stop thieving . . . and I did. That's exactly what happened. When I was in the army I stole nothing, not once, partly because there isn't much to steal in the army, everything is kept locked up, but mainly because the army is not a clever place to be a tealeaf. It's not a clever place at all. It's not the military discipline that keeps you in line, and that's strict enough, it's the unofficial barrack-room discipline. I once saw what happened to a thief. I'll never forget it. The boys broke both his arms and both his legs and smashed his fingers to pulp with rifle butts, kicked his teeth in and then dragged him across the depot and left him outside the guard house for the military police to find. He was in hospital for six months and then dishonourably discharged. He was also classed as being medically unfit for military service. I mean, you can't run at an enemy trench on two tin crutches, can you? So once I saw that then I kept myself on the straight

135

and narrow for the three years I was in the forces. I never got near to straying. Not once.

'So, anyway, once I was time expired,' Law explained, 'I couldn't get work, so I took to thieving again, turning windows, and stealing luggage from passenger trains. That was easy pickings, especially stealing suitcases from crowded trains. But I never got caught and so I was able to keep applying for jobs. Then finally, after years of trying, I got a start with a small haulage contractor, driving a heavy goods vehicle. I learned to drive HGVs in the army and got my HGV licence from them, so I settled down and then, after a few steady years on the road, I lost my driving confidence.'

'You mean you lost your licence?' Carmen Pharoah continued to glance discreetly around the room, looking for detail with her trained police officer's eye.

'No. I mean I lost my confidence,' Law repeated.

'An accident,' Webster asked, 'a fatal accident, you mean? Something you were involved in?'

'You could say that.' Law forced a smile. 'It was classed as a disaster, not an accident, and yes, I was involved in it.'

'You mean seven or more persons died in a single incident?' Carmen Pharoah clarified. 'Up to six fatalities then the incident is classed as an accident, so seven or more people lost their lives in a single incident?'

'Yes . . . eight persons, in fact . . . enough to make it a disaster.'

'What happened?' Webster asked, sensing that Miles Law needed to talk.

'Well . . . it was like this.' Law took a deep breath. 'I was driving my rig so I was, just me in the cab of a fully laden articulated vehicle. I was running pre-cast concrete beams to a building site up there in the north-east up around Newcastle way, so I was driving up the A1 near Northallerton . . . not far from here, in fact. Just two lanes in either direction, not three lanes like on a motorway.'

'Yes . . . yes.' Webster nodded. 'I know the A1 quite well. It's not my favourite road.'

'Mine neither.' Law looked to his left. 'It wasn't before the incident and it's definitely not now. Anyway, it was a Sunday afternoon, and so traffic was light, mainly cars and bikes and one or two other HGVs. I was driving along, feeling well content and happy. It was an easy drive, a bit dull, but easy, and I was getting double time for working on a Sunday. I mean there was no traffic to speak of, like I said, and then . . . it all happened so suddenly, but sometimes that's how it happens. It all happens right out of the blue . . . suddenly with no warning . . . no build-up.'

'It can be like that,' Webster replied calmly, 'as you say, suddenly, out of nowhere, from calm to confusion in an instant. So what did happen?'

'It all began with that damned woman, that wretched, stupid female. It all began with her.' Law once again leaned back in the chair and looked up at the ceiling. 'She just ran out of the bushes at the side of the road . . .'

'Suicide,' Carmen Pharoah offered, 'she was committing suicide?'

137

'Well . . .' Law paused, 'murder–suicide really because she was holding up this infant in her arms . . . he was just a few weeks old. His life hadn't really started.'

'Oh . . .' Carmen Pharoah put her hand up to her mouth. 'Do you know, I think I recall this incident? I was not living in York at the time but it made the national news.'

'I remember it also. I remember it very clearly. Folk talked about it for a long time afterwards,' Webster nodded. 'So you were the lorry driver?'

'Yes. Little me. The one and the same.' Law looked at Webster and turned his eyes upwards once more, looking at the ceiling. '"*The A1 Disaster*" and "*Disaster on the A1*" were the sort of headlines the newspapers ran with. But that woman . . . the way she looked at me with this stupid, brainless grin on her face and all the while holding up her child like she was holding up a trophy she'd won at a sports competition. She was like that. Just like that. I had no time to stop. No time at all. I stood on the brakes but I am sure I hit her before the brakes began to apply and then . . . then I did the most stupid thing imaginable. I still swerved to try to miss her, even when it was a hundred per cent certain that I was going to hit her, I still swerved . . . and I swerved to the right, not to the left. It was the infant I was thinking of and as soon as I turned the wheel I knew, I just knew, I shouldn't have done that, especially to the right. It was an instinctive thing but I still knew I should have kept the rig going in a straight line, or even swerved to the left and into the side of the road. I lost control

138

at that point. I crashed through the central reservation like it wasn't there; I went through it like a hot knife through butter . . . a forty-ton lorry, laden, going at sixty miles an hour. I mean, it would take more than a thin strip of metal to stop that monster, and I went through the barrier just as a car was coming the other way. A young family was in the car, parents and two children. The children were pre-school age in child safety seats in the back . . . all killed by my tractor unit and just as a motorcyclist and his girlfriend, both in their early twenties, were overtaking the car. Their bike went under my trailer, they didn't. Nothing was happening, a nice smooth run up the A1, light traffic, dry road surface, good visibility, and then suddenly, eight people were dead, all died within a few seconds of each other. The combined ages of all the fatalities was over one hundred years . . . just over. These days individuals can live longer than that.' Law took a deep breath. 'No blame was attached to me. The coroner "regretted" that I had not kept my vehicle going in a straight line while bringing it to a controlled halt but he said that my action was "understandable" and the police didn't prosecute me.'

'They wouldn't,' Webster commented. 'Not for that. As you say, in the heat of the moment your action was understandable, even if a little ill-advised.'

'But it still finished me with driving,' Miles continued. 'After that it was just the old dole for me and odd jobs until I started working for Garrett.'

'I . . . and my colleague are both sorry to hear about that accident, it was a bad experience for you.' Carmen Pharoah re-focused the interview. 'But it still doesn't answer our question. So I will ask you again. Why did you delay calling the police for so long after you found Anthony Garrett's body?'

'I am answering it,' Miles spoke firmly. 'I am telling you the reason. But if you insist, the delay was because I was having a good rummage round his house, that's what I was doing. I was enjoying having a good poke around, knowing that I had all the time in the world.' Law spoke calmly and matter-of-factly. 'No quick in-and-out before the householder returns. Not that morning. No one was going to disturb me . . . and Garrett was dead. Like I said, he'd been dead for a few days . . . so I was looking for stuff I could steal, like only a thief would look around a house searching for stuff which I could stash somewhere outside and come back later with a hired van. I can still drive enough to do that, especially if there's some good money to be had, and Garrett's house was full of good money.'

'Again . . .' Webster cautioned Law, 'be careful of what you are saying, Mr Law.'

'Oh, I am being careful,' Law smiled. 'I am being very careful. You see, I didn't steal anything in the event, even though there was a lot of stuff worth stealing, a lot of high-value, low-bulk items. Just the sort of swag a thief dreams about. And I bet Garrett didn't come by that lawful like . . . that old boy was a real tealeaf, so he'd be reluctant to notify the police of all that might have been stolen, even if he was still alive.'

'You know that, do you?' Carmen Pharoah spoke with a disapproving tone.

'Well . . . it takes one to know one.' Law continued to smile as he tapped the side of his nose with his left forefinger. 'It takes one to know one.'

'Yes . . . your criminal record,' Webster growled, 'mainly for theft in one form or another.'

'And that being not one-tenth of what I actually did do, like all folks with criminal records,' Law replied coldly, and impressed both officers as being a man who could change from being a warm personality to a cold personality, and back to a warm personality again, and do so in an instant. 'Being convicted is like a form of taxation; you keep most of what you half-inch, then you get a fine or a few months inside. And the majority of those with criminal records just have not been caught. Even from school days I was always on the nick, except when I was a soldier, like I said. I learned that in the army the military police don't take you into custody so much as rescue you from your mates. But you see, I was curious as to what Garrett had stashed away in his house so I couldn't resist the curiosity I felt, but I thought that there was no point in stealing anything because I have not got a future. I mean what point, what purpose, what reason is there? No point at all.'

'You don't have a future?' Carmen Pharoah repeated. 'What do you mean? Are you suffering

141

from a terminal illness? I must say that you look very fit, very fit and healthy.'

'Thank you. In fact, I do feel very fit, all that open air, all that physical work for Garrett.' Law smiled a smug smile. 'But no, I don't have a future and you know, I don't feel at all bad about the fact. To tell you the truth, I feel very good about it. It's like all my little concerns and issues are being lifted from my shoulders, all of them, and all of them all at once. You see, it's like this for me . . . it's like this.' Law paused. 'It's just that I have seen too much death. I have seen too many dead bodies, and when I saw Garrett's body with all those flies crawling on it and buzzing over it, I knew then that it was going to be the last dead body I would ever see. The very last one. No more dead bodies for me.'

'Too many dead bodies?' Webster queried. 'From the army, you mean?'

'Yes . . .' Miles Law nodded, '. . . and from before that . . . and afterwards. I've just seen too many . . . just too many . . . more than enough for me, anyway.'

A silence descended within the small room within the small cottage.

'You see,' Law explained, 'I reckon it all started with my dad, my old man, and what an evil, bullying swine he was. Totally evil. Anyway, I went out early one morning when I was about eleven or twelve and I saved my old life, so I did. I saved my old life by doing that. I got back home about midday 'cos I was getting hungry and I saw that there was a crowd round our house on the estate we lived on. There was a couple of policemen among the crowd. Anyway, it turns out that the postman called about an hour or so after I had left the house, and as he pushed the letters through our letter box he got a strong blast of gas. He banged on the door and got no answer. So he alerted the next-door neighbours who called the police and when I got back home the police were trying to force the front door, but I knew where the spare set of keys were kept hidden in the back garden. They were under the garden shed. So I grabbed them and unlocked the back door which the spare keys opened. A great cloud of gas came out of the house when I did that. The back door opened into the kitchen you see and there was my old man with his head in the gas oven. I let out a cry, but I still went further into the house rather than running back out into the garden. I saw my mother and sister stabbed to death . . . blood . . . blood every-where. So going out for a walk saved my life like I said, but they were the first dead bodies I saw, but not the last. So after that it was chil-dren's homes for me, one after the other, each one stricter than the last because I was difficult to control, and then I got into thieving . . . then I went for a soldier . . . idiot that I was and so I saw more dead bodies. I served in Northern Ireland during "the troubles" so dead bodies were not uncommon.'

'You shot people, you mean?' Webster probed.

'Shot at more than shot, I can say that. I did three tours of Northern Ireland with the Royal Logistical Corps . . . the "Loggies", and I saw what terrorists can do to each other.' Again Law

143

paused. 'Once we came across a car which had been set on fire, totally burned out, with four bodies inside, all chained together so they couldn't escape. The sergeant, Wilkinson, he had it in for me, he just took an instant dislike to me from day one and he told me to pull the bodies out of the car. I cut the chain with a bolt cutter and pulled the bodies out of the car, one by one, whilst the rest of the platoon looked on. A burned corpse falls apart if you don't handle it correctly. I found that out the hard way. Wilkinson, he wouldn't let anybody help me . . . that was just Wilkinson . . . evil swine, like my old man . . . totally evil. It was the work of the UDA, so our officer told us. The bodies in the car were identified as known members of the IRA.'

'I see,' Carmen Pharoah replied softly. 'That sort of experience can cause dreadful emotional scarring.'

'It gets worse. It gets much worse. Do you want to hear the rest? Well, I'll tell you anyway. It was tit-for-tat in Northern Ireland in those days, so about one week later don't we come across pretty much the same thing . . . a burned-out car with four charred bodies inside it, chained up like the first four men, with the chain looped through the steering wheel, so they couldn't escape the flames, so they were all burned alive. The second time it was the work of the IRA and the victims were identified as members of the UDA, but we were the platoon which found the second car and guess who Sergeant Wilkinson ordered to pull out the four corpses one by one and lay them on the grass?

It's not the sort of thing any twenty-year-old should have to do, no matter how much he's been toughened up by the army.'

'I'll say,' Webster replied sympathetically. 'As you say, that sort of thing is not the sort of thing a young boy should be made to do.'

'Anyway,' Miles Law smiled, 'rough and natural justice being what it is, that ever so nice Sergeant Wilkinson got his head blown off by a sniper a few weeks later, and a few weeks after that I became time expired. I left with an honourable discharge and my papers were stamped "*conduct exemplary*". After that I saw no more dead bodies until that female ran out in front of my lorry one Sunday afternoon, holding up her infant with a *didn't-I-do-well* look on her face. Anyway, that day I got out of my cab just as other cars were stopping and folk were arriving and calling the emergency services. I walked round the scene in a sort of daze. The family in the car were crushed by my tractor unit, and the motorcyclist . . . he'd lost his head . . . literally . . . his head was lying about twenty feet from the rest of him. She remained intact, his pillion rider. She was dead all right, just as dead as dead can be, but all in one piece . . . and the woman and her infant . . . they were both just part of the same bloody mess, the two of them just mangled up together. So when I found Garrett's body, I knew it would be the last dead body I would ever see. I wanted it that way and I still want it that way. I've seen enough dead human beings. I can't get the images out of my head. I don't want to see any more. So I saw no reason why I shouldn't take a quick gander round his house, see what bling he has worth nicking, but knowing I wouldn't be nicking anything. But once a thief . . . like I said. And he was long dead, anyway. He was long past caring.'

'The last . . . what do you mean?' Webster probed. 'The last body that you will ever see? How do you know, you're still relatively young? I hope that you're not going to do anything stupid.'

'No . . . no, I am not going to do anything stupid,' Miles Law replied calmly, 'just the opposite in fact. I will be doing something so very, very sensible. So very sensible. I've got a gun,' he added in a calm matter-of-fact manner.

'Where?' Carmen Pharoah suddenly sat forward. 'Where is it?'

'Yes . . . and like . . . so very, very like I'll be telling you.' Law continued to speak calmly. 'Like I am really going to do that. But I can tell you that it is not in this house or in the garden either. You're welcome to search, you don't need a warrant, you have my permission, so feel free.' Law waved his arms in a gesture of invitation. 'You won't find it and it's in pieces. It is reduced to what is that expression . . . an irreducible minimum. The parts are all well separated from each other and they're all wrapped up in oily rags, as are the bullets. I acquired it when I was in Northern Ireland, and I have kept it safe and well hidden. It's a Colt .45. It makes quite a mess of someone's head, but there is no danger at all, none at all, of it being found by anyone. It's safe where it is . . . I mean the bits are safe where they are.'

'That's still no guarantee,' Carmen Pharoah

advised. 'It's no guarantee, Miles. No guarantee at all.'

'No guarantee of what?' Miles Law asked curiously. 'What is not guaranteed?'

'Escape,' Carmen Pharoah replied quietly. 'If I am right in thinking that you intend to kill yourself so as to free yourself of the images you mention, it's no guarantee you'll succeed.'

'Escape?' Miles Law eyed Carmen Pharoah with caution.

'Well, let me put it like this,' Carmen Pharoah explained. 'I can't say that I am a practising Christian, I can't say that at all, but I do find myself firmly believing in the continuation of consciousness after mortal death, and we all have our guilt, all of us. None of us is free of it, and we all have our regrets, and yes, some of us have seen terrible things which we cannot drive from our mind's eye . . . really awful sights.'

'Yes,' Law nodded, 'those bodies . . . those sights . . . my parents and my sister . . . those men in the burned-out cars . . . that carnage on the A1 that Sunday afternoon . . . nineteen all told. I counted them. Nineteen all told.'

'Yes, and they're all part of your consciousness, Miles, and if you go ahead and top yourself you might very well take those images and all your guilt and your regrets into eternity with you because consciousness continues. So blowing your head off is no guarantee of escape from it all,' Carmen Pharoah explained slowly. 'That's what I mean, Miles. I have often wondered if people who do what you say you intend to do arrive in eternity to find everything they hope to escape from has arrived with them.'

Miles Law's mouth opened slightly. 'I confess I have never thought of it like that. That's a new angle.' He paused. 'But it didn't stop the jockey . . . it didn't stop him.'

'Which jockey?' Carmen Pharoah asked. 'What on earth has horse racing got to do with all this?'

'That jockey who was riding the King's horse in the 1913 Epsom Derby when that suffragette woman flung herself in front of it. She killed herself for the suffragette cause. You must have seen the film of it,' Law explained. 'It's a famous bit of newsreel footage.'

'Emily Davison,' Carmen Pharoah advised. 'That was her name, and yes, I have seen the footage, quite a few times, as you say. It's a famous bit of film.'

Law inclined his head, 'So that was her name, Emily Davison. I probably have heard it but it didn't register.'

'Emily Wilding Davison,' Carmen Pharoah added, 'to give her her full name.'

'I'll try to remember that,' Law replied. 'But you know I never knew how she could tell which was the King's horse. I mean, racehorses are like cows in that they all look the same to me. I can tell a Shetland pony from a Suffolk Punch but racing horses . . . they're all much of a muchness to me.'

'The jockey's colours,' Carmen Pharoah explained. 'He wore a shirt of many coloured patches while the other jockeys wore plain white shirts. She

148

recognized the jockey's colours, not the horse as such.'

'Well, how about that,' Law smiled. 'Isn't it true . . . every day is a school day. So I thank you for that. But the jockey, you know that he committed suicide? He said that he couldn't drive the image of that wretched woman from his mind, and he killed himself in an attempt to rid himself of the memory.'

'I didn't know that.' Carmen Pharoah sank back in her chair. 'That is really very interesting. So, two suicides in that case. A double tragedy.'

'Yes,' Law nodded, 'as you say, there were two suicides but with a fair bit of time between them, that has to be said. He didn't top himself until the 1950s. He was an old guy by then, he had not much time left anyway, but he had struggled with and fought with the memory for fifty years and when he couldn't cope with it anymore, he iced himself.' Miles Law paused. 'But the point is, I know exactly why he did it. Like him, I just can't drive the images from my mind . . . all those images . . . I just can't get them out of my mind. They haunt me, especially at night when I can't sleep. It's always worse at night. Always.' Law took a deep breath. 'So you see, all that stuff in Garrett's house, so much of it was so easy to lift, probably still is . . . it would have been so easy to help myself to a lot of it . . . stash it somewhere outside, just behind the house . . . before calling the police, but why? What for? I knew when I saw Garrett's body that I had seen my last corpse. So that's the answer to your question. That's why I waited before

149

dialling three nines . . . it's because there's no pockets in a shroud. You can't take anything material with you, but I wanted a good look round the house, to see what I could have stolen if I had wanted to steal. I mean, just because you've stopped eating doesn't mean you can't still look at the menu.'

'Dare say that's a neat way of putting it,' Webster commented. 'It really sounds like you need someone to talk to, but if nothing else, do remember what my colleague said about the continuation of consciousness and the taking of your guilt and regrets and things witnessed into eternity with you, that mortal death is not necessarily an escape from all that mental anguish.'

Miles Law pointed a low finger at Webster as if to say, 'I hear you', then he added, 'That is food for thought, like I said, that had not occurred to me, but it's real food for thought.'

Webster drove at a slow and steady speed from Miles Law's cottage westwards into Millington, which he and Carmen Pharoah noted seemed to occupy a natural hollow in the landscape. It appeared to the officers to be a neatly kept and a prosperous village with one or two new buildings which, by their design and colour of brick, seemed to blend sensitively with the older buildings. Carmen Pharoah was particularly taken by such touches as a stretch of elevated pavement separated from the road by a gently sloping grass bank, and she was also amused by a huge wooden spoon of about six feet in length hanging beside the front door of one of the houses.

'We'll have to report him for his claim about owning a firearm,' Webster commented. 'The boss will want to know about that.'

'Yes,' Carmen Pharoah nodded, 'in fact we can't not report it. We'll put it in writing.'

The remainder of the journey back to Micklegate Bar Police Station was passed in a comfortable silence with Carmen Pharoah and Reginald Webster being wholly content in each other's company and both enjoying the journey through the rich summer fields in warm weather and under a near cloudless blue sky.

After completing their reports of their visit to Miles Law, both Webster and Carmen Pharoah signed out for the day and both returned to their respective homes.

George Hennessey cradled the mug of tea in his hands as he read the file on Francis Badger which had been sent up to him from Records by the collator as he had requested. Francis Badger, he read, did indeed have a 'history of violence' and seemed to Hennessey to be a person of considerable interest in respect of the murder of Anthony Garrett. He had convictions for attempted murder, grievous bodily harm, threatening behaviour and other similar crimes, but he also seemed to have calmed down, not having been prosecuted for, by now, over ten years.

Hennessey noted Badger's address to be in the village at Great Givendale, and a glance at the map of the Vale of York showed that Great Givendale and Millington, where Garrett lived, were perhaps four miles apart by winding road, in other words a one-hour walk for a man or woman in their forties with no physical infirmity. Hennessey closed the file and sat back in his chair. 'A person of interest,' he murmured to himself. 'A person of great interest indeed.'

Reginald Webster, suddenly feeling very tired, drove thankfully to his home in Selby. He turned his car into the cul-de-sac on the new-build estate where he lived and sounded the car's horn as he approached his house. It was, he knew, especially as a serving police officer, strictly speaking an offence to sound a car's horn unless as a warning, but his good neighbours knew why he did it and none had ever objected or made any complaint. As he parked the car the door of his house opened and a long-haired Alsatian bounded out of the house and nuzzled his head against Webster's legs, having been trained not to jump up at people. Webster reached down and patted the dog's head, and fondled its ears, and man and beast walked up the driveway together and into the house. Inside the house Webster's wife, Joyce, approached with open arms. He reached out and touched her shoulder whereupon man and wife embraced.

Joyce Webster was not able, nor did Reginald Webster permit her, to prepare hot food, but it being summer a beautifully and carefully prepared salad awaited him.

After he and his wife had eaten, Terry was declared officially 'off-duty' and Reginald Webster took the Alsatian for an hour-long walk through the woodland which stood near their home. Terry explored the undergrowth and Webster, with the dog's lead slung over his shoulder, recovering some energy enjoyed the late summer afternoon, with the sun's rays filtered by the rich canopy of leaves and delighting in the strong woodland scents. He was, he found, permanently in awe of his wife's courage, she having lost her sight in a car accident whilst she was studying the history of art at Edinburgh University and yet considering herself fortunate in that of the four passengers in the car, only she survived. Her courage caused Webster to continually feel a confusion of reverence and humility, and of pride and devotion. He found that she provided him with a purpose and a fullness which marriage to a sighted person could not, he believed, have been possible.

Carmen Pharoah returned to her flat in a modest but, she always found, a 'cosy' development on Marygate between Bootham Bar and the River Ouse. She peeled off her working suit and gratefully took a hot shower, and then re-dressed in jeans, training shoes, a blue T-shirt and a wide-brimmed summer hat and with a small handbag slung over her shoulder left her flat and took a bus out to Strensall and from there she walked for an hour and a half along country lanes to Haxby and from Haxby took a bus back to York. She enjoyed the walk; she enjoyed the landscape of rich rural England, so different from the East London of earlier in her life when she often felt swamped by the endless buildings and

153

the seemingly incessant traffic, the fumes and the ill tempers.

Later she ate a homemade, previously prepared, lasagne and at ten p.m., after watching the news headlines on the television, she retired for an early night. She lay abed listening to the sounds of the night, the solid reassuring 'ee-aw' of the railway trains entering and leaving York Station, the good-humoured laughter of the homeward-bound pub goers and later, to the click, click, click of a woman's high-heeled shoes walking calmly along the road and which sound told her that, outside, in the ancient city, just as sleep enfolded her, all was well, all was very well indeed.

George Hennessey drove home to his house which stood detached from the neighbouring proper-ties on the Thirsk Road in Easingwold. Upon turning into the drive he heard a dog barking excitedly in response to his car's tyres crunching on the gravel. He exited the car, leaving one of the windows wound half down, and let himself into his house by the front door. Oscar, his black mongrel, jumped up excitedly at him and he bent down and patted the dog's head and flanks. Once inside the house he walked through to the rear of the house and let Oscar out on to the back lawn and then returned to the kitchen and made himself a pot of tea.

'Well, I don't mind confessing it's been quite a day, really quite a day,' he said as he stood on the patio of the house watching Oscar crisscross the lawn as the dog followed an interesting scent before then trotting to where Hennessey stood and sitting lovingly at Hennessey's feet. 'Really quite a day,' Hennessey repeated. 'In fact I find it difficult to believe that it was just this morning that we were called to a house in Millington, that's to the east of York . . . a man was in the house with a bullet in his head. It was a large house, set in its own grounds, mid- to late-Victorian era I thought. He seemed to be monied and he seemed to live alone. Turns out he is, or was, known to the police, to the Metropolitan Police especially, but the man they sent up to see us didn't seem to me to be up to much as an officer. He couldn't provide any insight.' Hennessey sipped his tea as Oscar barked at a blackbird which had landed on the lawn. The bird promptly flew away. 'The evening television news will feature it, and we hope that that might generate a few leads and the *Yorkshire Post* will carry it tomorrow. We especially need to know why the victim served only three years for murder . . . which he did,' Hennessey continued, '. . . and we definitely want to know about the three women who called on him on the day he was murdered which we have deduced was Saturday last, just before midday, probably in the late forenoon. The name of the house in which the deceased lived, by the way, it is not a particularly original name, but its name is The Grange.' To an observer George Hennessey would appear to be a middle-aged man who was talking to himself, while drinking a mug of tea, a man who was rambling on, quite contentedly, to himself. It was not though the case, dear reader. It was not the case at all.

George and Jennifer Hennessey had been married for only two years, and when Jennifer was heavily pregnant she had sat down one afternoon and had designed the rear garden of their home. The flat, dull expanse of lawn which was the extent of the garden at the back of the house when they had moved in, she decided would be divided in half, width-ways. The first half, near the house, would remain as lawn, a hedge of privet would, she had decreed, be planted across the garden to divide the near half from the further half, with access between the two parts by means of a gateway set into the privet. Beyond the privet would be a shed for the housing of gardening tools and the remainder of the garden be given over to an orchard of mixed types of apple trees. The final ten feet would be left to return to nature but a small pond would be dug, pond water introduced and then amphibians in turn introduced to the pond.

Then Jennifer died. Just three months after their son was born she collapsed, suddenly, whilst walking in the centre of Easingwold. Good people rushed to her aid assuming that she had fainted, it being a hot summer's day, but no pulse could be found. An ambulance was called and Jennifer Hennessey was rushed to hospital where she was pronounced to be deceased upon arrival, or 'condition purple' in ambulance-crew speak. A post-mortem was carried out but no obvious cause of death could be determined and so the pathologist had written 'sudden death syndrome', which is as close as current medical knowledge can come to explaining why a perfectly healthy young woman with all the world to live for should collapse in the street with whatever life force was within her having been suddenly extinguished. So suddenly that she was probably deceased before she lay on the pavement.

After the funeral Hennessey had scattered his wife's ashes on the rear lawn of the house and had then set about landscaping the garden according to her design. It had also become his custom to stand on the patio upon his return from work and tell her of his day. The previous summer he had told her of a new love in his life and assured her that no one could ever replace her, but he hoped that she was pleased for him. Upon saying that he felt himself enveloped by a warmth which he could not explain as coming from the sun's rays alone.

'I think that I'll send Carmen Pharoah down to London,' he continued. 'I am sure that she can obtain more information about Mr Garrett, the deceased. Yes . . . yes, I'll do that. If there's anything to be dug up, Carmen will find it.'

Later, having dined on a home-made chicken salad, and having read more of the book about the Boer War, being the latest acquisition to his by then impressive collection of books about military history, he decided that the evening had cooled sufficiently to take Oscar for a walk, knowing very well how black and brown dogs suffer in the heat. Later still, having exercised his dog, and, dear reader, himself in the process, by a walk of half an hour out, and half an hour back, which would have pleased his doctor, George Hennessey strolled contentedly into Easingwold for a pint of brown and mild at the Dove Inn, just one, before last orders were called.

It was Wednesday, 22.15 hours.

Four

Thursday 22 June, 09.20 hours – midnight

In which information about the three women who called on Anthony Garrett is obtained, and George Hennessey is once more at home to the courteous reader who comes to learn about his host's delights.

Thompson Ventnor stood fully square on to the man who he found to be short, overweight and who was both casually and untidily dressed. In fact, Ventnor found him to be the archetypal taxi driver, as the man professed himself to be. He said, 'This is a little cloak and dagger, isn't it?'

'What do you mean?' The man spoke in a strongly sibilistic manner, pronouncing 'what' as 'her-what'.

'Well . . .' Ventnor glanced around him. The side of the pub the Horse and Trumpet was to his right hand, to his left was a privet hedge which Ventnor noted was composed of an interesting mixture of yellow and green bushes which he estimated to be about four feet high. Beyond the hedge, clearly seen, were the decaying remains of a petrol filling station. On the fourth side of the car park in which he and

159

the man stood facing each other was the B1246 Pocklington to Driffield road, and a road so light of traffic that it was clear to Ventnor why the petrol station had been forced to close down. At that time in the morning the road was in fact utterly free of traffic and only birdsong filled the air. The only vehicle in the pub car park was a motorcycle sidecar combination which Ventnor saw belonged to an earlier era. The man he stood talking to was in his forties, yet the motorcycle and the black-painted sidecar could, Ventnor thought, have belonged to the man's father. It had an oily piece of sacking draped over the seat and the rear wheel, and as a machine it just looked to Ventnor to be 'tired'. Very tired indeed. 'Well,' Ventnor repeated, and then he explained what he meant, 'people who have information to give usually come into the police station and they usually ask about any reward. They do not, usually, want to meet in a pub car park, miles from anywhere, and they don't usually insist on just one officer meeting them. So that is why I feel that this is all a bit "cloak and dagger".'

'You cannot be too careful.' The man pronounced 'cannot' as 'ha-not' and 'careful' as 'hare-full'. 'You are alone? I hope you're alone. I want you to be alone.'

'Yes . . . all alone,' Ventnor remained calm, 'as you requested, there's just me, all by myself. Just me alone.'

'And,' the man continued, pronouncing 'and' as 'h-and', 'you have not got a mate hiding out of sight with a camera or with one of those long-range microphone things? I've seen them on television.'

'No,' Ventnor replied, 'and I have not got a tape recorder hidden inside my jacket. So, enough games. Let's cut to the chase, shall we? You said that you have information about the murder of Anthony Garrett of The Grange, Millington. So what have you got to tell us?'

'Yes. Where's your car?' The man was insistent, and he looked anxiously from left to right as he spoke. 'Where did you leave it? I can't see it.'

'In the layby about one hundred yards back that way.' Ventnor pointed to his left as he felt his patience thinning. 'And you're in danger of being run in for wasting police time. So come on, what have you got to tell me? I have other things to do and I have not got all day.'

'I can't be too careful,' the man wheezed. 'I'm a gypsy. I can't be too careful.'

'A gypsy?' Ventnor brushed a fly from his face. 'What do you mean? Are you a traveller? A member of the travelling community?'

'Reckon I do travel,' the man shrugged, 'but not very far. I mean that I am a gypsy cab driver. Anyway I saw on the TV last night that you are looking for information about the murder which took place in Millington. So I contacted you, but I am an illegal taxi operator.'

'Ah . . . I see.' Ventnor nodded. 'I understand you now. Quite illegal.'

'Yes,' the man nodded, 'quite illegal. Very illegal. So I don't, I don't want to give no name and it's why I covered up my bike's number plate with that bit of sackcloth, so you won't know who I

161

am, and it's also why I can't get no reward because I can't give you my identity,' he panted, pronouncing 'identity' as 'hi-dentity'.

'Fair enough,' Ventnor brushed a fly from his face, 'but I assure you, we have bigger fish to fry right now than to want to bother about your little fly-by-night money-making scam. So you tell me what you can. You do that and I won't tell the taxi cab licensing people all about you.'

'Or the Social Security,' the man panted. 'I'm drawing the dole, you see . . . I have emphysema . . . I have it bad,' he patted his chest, 'can't work. They can't know about me moonlighting as a gypsy cab operator either.'

'But you can drive a car?' Ventnor smiled. 'You can do that.'

'Yes, it's about all I can do. So I make a little beer money, but it's not much really.' The man looked about him nervously. 'I've got to keep the car on the road, you see, so like after petrol and insurance and all the rest of it there's not a lot left over out of the fares . . . and there's not a lot of fares to be had. Not a lot at all.'

'OK . . . so what have you got to tell us?' Ventnor pressed.

'You sure you're alone?' the man asked in a fretful manner.

'Quite sure,' Ventnor breathed deeply, 'and you're on thin ice now. You're really testing my patience. I've had quite enough of your games, so spill, now, or I'm taking you into custody for wasting police time, and the illegal taxi operation, and there'll be more for us to find out about you

162

because there always is more to find out about felons. Always.'

The man wiped the sweat off his face and then wiped his sweat-covered palms on his grimy white T-shirt. He wore baggy and much faded denim jeans and torn with age tennis shoes. His crash helmet, not being in plain view, Ventnor reasoned, must be hidden from sight in the sidecar of his motorcycle combination.

The man shrugged. 'I'm saying nothing but I know you have spies everywhere. I know that about the police. You have spies everywhere. Everywhere.'

'And a very long arm,' Ventnor growled. 'In fact, you have no idea just how far the long arm of the law can reach. So, one last time before I book you for wasting police time, tell me what you know.'

'All right . . . all right,' the wheezing man held up his fleshy, sweat-soaked palm. 'Last Saturday morning, it was, I was touting for fares outside the Holderness Arms Hotel . . .'

'By the racecourse,' Ventnor confirmed, 'that hotel?'

'Yes . . . yes,' the man panted, 'that one. Not many people seem to know of that hotel. It's quite small as hotels go is the Holderness Arms Hotel, not many people know it.'

'I'm a cop,' Ventnor replied icily. 'We know where everything is. It's our business to know where everything is. So . . . you were touting for illegal fares at the Holderness Arms Hotel on Saturday last in the morning . . . then . . . then what happened?'

'Well, then I was leaning on the bonnet of my car, that's the gypsy cabby's signal that he is for hire . . . when it's wet we just sit at the wheel.'

'I know,' Ventnor sighed. 'I know that. Just carry on.'

'So these three women approach me.' The man took another clearly painful breath. 'They were weird. I could tell. Like they were really weird.'

'How?' Ventnor pressed. 'In what way were they weird?'

'Well, first off they were dressed identical to each other, and they were, all the three of them, the same height, all the exact same height. I'd say about my height and I am five feet seven inches tall.'

'All right.' Ventnor reached for his notebook and the ballpoint pen. 'Five feet seven inches . . .'

'Yes, boss,' the man wheezed. 'But they had heels, so allow for that.'

'And all dressed the same?' Ventnor clarified. 'You mean like a uniform?'

'Yes, boss, like a uniform but not a uniform . . . civilian clothing . . . they wore civilian clothing: red blouse, grey skirt, each had a black shoulder handbag, and each one was carrying a small yellow holdall. The handbags were on their right shoulder and the holdalls were in their left hand.' The man continued to speak in his distinctive manner and pronouncing 'shoulder' as 'h-shoulder'. 'Small holdalls they had, boss, not huge kitbags, nothing like that, and the holdalls didn't seem very heavy, I could tell that there was not much weight in the holdalls.'

'All right,' Ventnor commented. 'This is very good. Carry on.'

164

'So then it gets a bit weird,' the man glanced about him nervously, 'really weird.'

'What do you mean?' Ventnor asked keenly. 'Really weird? How? In what way was it really weird?'

'Well, boss, it was like this.' The man took a breath and seemed to Ventnor to be experiencing difficulty in doing so. His eyes darted from left to right. 'Are you sure that you are alone?'

'Quite sure,' Ventnor calmed himself. 'Very, very sure. Just tell me what you brought me out here for.'

'All right . . . so they asked me was I free,' the man continued.

'Free?' Ventnor repeated.

'So I said, "*Well, I charge, I charge money, but I'm for hire. I'm free in that sense, free to be hired,*"' the man explained as he continued to look from left to right. 'So they smiled and said, "*Point to you.*"'

'So what was weird about that?' Ventnor put his pen in his mouth and sucked the end. 'Explain what you thought was weird about those women.'

'Well, what was weird, boss, what was weird, is that they all spoke at once . . . all three spoke but they didn't seem to have rehearsed what they were going to say,' the man explained. 'I mean they didn't know what I was going to say, "*Well, I charge, but I'm for hire,*" but they, all three, responded at the same time with the same words, "*Point to you.*" It was totally very strange. Those three women were very strange.'

'Yes,' Ventnor wrote on his notepad, 'that does

sound strange indeed, very strange. So then what happened?'

'Well, then they said . . . again all three at the same time,' the man continued, "*Can you take us to Millington? It is a village to the east of York, more than ten miles from York.*" So I said, yes, I know where that village is but I'm a gypsy. I work only for cash and I can't give receipts either,' the man explained. 'It is strictly cash only, I told them, and no receipts.'

'OK,' Ventnor replied, 'were they happy with that?'

'Yes, they were, in fact they said "*ideal*", in that way they had of all speaking all at once . . . all three said "*ideal*" at the same time. Weird.' The man took another painful breath. 'So they gets in, so they do, one in the front beside me and the other two side by side on the rear seat. So I drove them out to Millington and not a word was spoken during the journey. Not a word. Silence all the time. Then we get to the village and I slow down and say, "Where in the village? Where do you want to go?"' The man once again looked nervously about him. 'So they all said, all three at once, "*A house called The Grange,*" so I said, "I don't know where that is, I'll have to ask." I have learned since I've been driving my gypsy cab that there are two good places to ask for local directions, one is an estate agent and the other is a postman. They both know all the little streets, they both do . . . all the little out of the way nooks and crannies.'

'I'll remember that.' Ventnor smiled so as to encourage the man to continue talking. 'That's a useful tip to remember.'

The man beamed with pride, boyishly so, thought Ventnor. 'So there was no estate agent that I could see, don't get them in villages anyway, but there was a postie doing his walk. Postmen have walks, milkmen have rounds. So I left the cab and got directions from the postie. A really friendly bloke he was. Very eager to help. So I returned to the car with good, clear directions and drive on through the village. On the other side of the village I see the house, just as the postie described: blue painted, pale blue, and well set back from the road . . . old building, maybe Victorian era, up on a bit of a hill, but more a sort of slope up to the house from the road, with lawn and shrubs . . . quite a well-kept garden, I thought.'

'Yes . . . yes.' Ventnor nodded. 'I know what you mean. I've been there. Carry on . . .'

'So I halt at the side of the road and the three women all say at once, "*No, turn into the drive please and then stop just beyond the gateposts. We want you to stop just beyond the gateposts.*" Again, it was the same, all three spoke at once, all three saying the same words at the same time, with no indication that they had rehearsed them. So I do as they say. I mean, they're paying customers, aren't they? So I turn into the drive,' the man pronounced 'into' as 'h-into', 'and then I stop, like they asked me to do. The drive was gravel and the cab's tyres crunched on it but there was no reaction from the house. It was the sort of sound that would make a dog bark if there was a dog in the house.'

'All right,' Ventnor nodded again, 'so they get out of the car, then what?'

'Yes, boss, at the same time and without saying anything, but they all leave their little yellow holdall bags in the cab. Then it gets even more strange – they all begin to walk up to the big house, but they start weaving in and out of each other's paths, not staying in a line like I had expected them to do, a shoulder to shoulder line, I mean. I saw that the one who had sat next to me was the one on the left of the line when they started walking, but after they'd taken about fifteen paces I couldn't say which of the three she was, with nothing to tell them apart. I tell you, I just couldn't,' the man explained. 'So they walk up to the house, very calmly, always moving in and out of each other's path. Then, when they reach the house, two stand by the front door, one either side of the steps leading up to the door, but not at the door itself.'

'Yes . . . yes,' Ventnor replied, 'I know what you mean.'

'They stood like a pair of sentries, so they did, facing out, you know, with their backs to the house, not moving, not talking that I could see from where I was sitting at the bottom of the drive. Anyway, the third one goes up the steps and she knocks on the knocker, or she rings a doorbell . . . but whatever she does the door opens almost immediately and she walks in and the door closes behind her. The two other women just stay where they are, just looking straight ahead and not moving at all.'

'Like sentries,' Ventnor repeated.

'Yes, like they were guarding Buckingham Palace.' The man anxiously looked to his left and right.

'I'm alone.' Ventnor raised his voice. 'Just me. I told you I am alone. Stop worrying.'

'Can't ever be too careful,' the man wheezed, 'those long-range microphones, those cameras with telephoto lenses. Can't ever be too careful.'

'Just carry on,' Ventnor pressed. 'Just try to calm down and tell me what happened. You're doing well.'

'Well then . . . seems like the one that went into the house came back out again more or less straight away. I mean that. Straight away. She wasn't in for more than a minute,' the man wheezed, 'and like I mean sixty seconds. Less, possibly less than sixty seconds. She emerges, shuts the door behind her and walks down the steps.'

'So . . .' Ventnor wrote on his notepad. 'So, she pulls the door shut behind her? It wasn't closed from the inside?'

'No, sir, it looked to me like she pulled it shut behind her. In fact, I am pretty sure that the woman pulled the door shut behind her. Pretty well certain.'

'All right.'

'So then all three of them start walking at the same time and once again they mix them-selves up as they walk, in and out of each other, weaving like.'

On a whim Ventnor turned around and his eye was caught by a hawk circling over a wheat field which then folded its wings and dived into the crop, then re-emerged and flew away towards a line of woodland. He saw a vastness of golden corn, a line of green foliage, all under a blue, almost

169

cloudless sky. He returned his attention to the wheezing man. 'So then what did those three women do?'

'Well, then they walked back to me and my cab, and continued walking in and out of each other's path, weaving, so that when they got back to the car I couldn't say for certain which of the three had entered the house. They then got back into my car and I tell you plain, I wouldn't have known if the one that sat in the front passenger seat was the one who had sat in the seat on the drive out to Millington. Even that close, I still couldn't tell one from the other two. So I said, *"Back to York, ladies?"*, and they said, *"No,"* talking at the same time, they said, *"Take us out into the country. Find somewhere remote for us. Really remote. Well out of the way."* So I drove east, further away from York, and then turned on to a "B" road, then I found an even narrower road with woods on either side. Then they said, *"This will do. This will do very nicely. It is just right, in fact. Just what we need."* So I stopped the cab and as they got out, this time they took their small yellow holdalls with them and they walked into the greenery and were lost from sight.' The man pronounced 'sight' as 'h-sight'.

'Interesting,' Ventnor murmured. 'I think I can guess what you are going to tell me, but do go on . . .'

'Well, they came back after a while during which time I see smoke rising from the trees . . . but when they come back into view they're all dressed in casual clothing – jeans, T-shirt, sports shoes . . . and all different. One had a red T-shirt,

170

the others blue or green. Their hair was different, shorter and darker, so they had been wearing wigs . . . and they were not carrying their hold-alls, just their handbags. They got into the cab and they speak at the same time and say, "*Take us to our hotel, please.*" So we go back to the hotel and the journey again passes in silence . . . they pay the fare . . . no tip or anything, just what I ask for. I thought that was tight-fisted because the Holderness Arms Hotel might be small but it's not cheap, not by a long chalk, it's not cheap. That's why I go there looking for customers. So I hang around, sitting on my car. I needed the money.'

'Sitting,' Ventnor echoed, 'sitting on it?'

'Leaning, then . . . just a manner of speaking. I was hoping for another fare and then half an hour later those three women come back out of the hotel, still dressed casually, but this time each of them is carrying a small suitcase, same style but different colours.' The man looked around him.

'I'm alone!' Ventnor raised his voice. 'Stop worrying. I am quite alone.'

'All right.' The man took another difficult breath. 'So they see me still there and recognize me and they say . . . all three at once, "*You're still for hire, we see?*" So I said, "*Yes, I'm still for hire.*" So they say, "*Well, in that case, can you please take us to the railway station?*" So I say "*yes*" and so that's what I do. I run them to the railway station. I drop them as near as I can because I don't want to be noticed by the licensed operators who'd report me at the drop of a hat. They pay me and they walk from my cab into the

171

station foyer. They didn't tip me again then either. Not one tip despite two trips.'

'So where did you take them after you left The Grange?' Ventnor continued. 'Can you find that exact location again, do you think? It's vital, absolutely vital, that we investigate where they burned their clothing. I mean vital.'

'Yes, I can. It's not too far from here. Just you and me. I can do that. We can go now, but only if we use your car. I won't take my bike, well it's Dad's old bike really, because I don't want you to read the number plate. You can trace me that way. Just can't be too careful. Just can't be too careful.'

'Fair enough.' Ventnor pocketed his pen and notepad. 'Come on, we'll go there now, then I'll drop you back here. My car's this way . . . not far . . . in a layby and a hundred yards that way, like I told you.'

George Hennessey sat at his desk and smiled warmly at Detective Constable Tobias Sherwood. He saw a youthful officer, very youthful to hold the rank of detective constable. He also saw Sherwood to be tall, narrow-faced, with a striking head of neatly cut ginger hair, a man who seemed a trifle nervous as if possessed with a healthy respect for authority.

'Well,' Hennessey began, having invited Sherwood to sit on one of the chairs which stood in a semicircle in front of his desk. 'Allow me to congratulate you on your promotion, and to welcome you to our team.'

'Thank you, sir.' Sherwood, Hennessey felt,

172

had a soft speaking voice and, Hennessey thought, warm brown eyes. 'I am very happy to be out of uniform – I'd rather be detecting crime than directing traffic.'

'Oh, indeed, indeed,' Hennessey replied as he glanced over Sherwood's service record. 'A watch leader after just two years. Not bad. Into CID after just a few years in uniform. Accepted into the police on your first application. That's virtually unknown these days. Acceptance upon third application is considered creditworthy, but on first application, that is virtually unheard of.'

'Well, I did have some experience before, sir. I was a kibbutz volunteer for a while. I also worked in a refugee camp in Rwanda. And I was employed by the probation service. So I was hardly a fresh-faced teenager just out of school. That might explain my good fortune in respect of joining the police on my first application. The police like newly appointed officers to have a bit of experience on their CVs.'

'Indeed,' Hennessey replied. 'No bad news on your service record either, none at all. No reprimands, no disciplinaries, nothing.'

'No, sir.' Tobias Sherwood snorted briefly. 'Not yet anyway.'

'Not yet?' Hennessey held eye contact with Sherwood. 'Do you plan to be a management problem?'

'I hope not, sir,' Sherwood replied. 'I just meant that no one is perfect.'

'Well, anyway, welcome. I will introduce you to the others as soon as I can, but right now, you and I have a visit to make. Grab your jacket.'

Driving out to Great Givendale, with Hennessey at the wheel, Hennessey told Sherwood about the murder of Anthony Garrett and of the sudden emergence of Francis Badger as a 'person of interest'.

'And practically the same village.' Sherwood glared out of the window to his left at the rolling green landscape of the Yorkshire Wolds, under a blue and near cloudless sky. 'Both from London, both have a connection with each other, no matter how tenuous, are both within an hour's walking distance of each other's house.'

'Quite a coincidence,' Hennessey conceded, 'but a coincidence nonetheless.'

'I've known similar,' Sherwood replied. 'The probation officers' course I did was two years at a university and was a graduate-only course. In the course year I was in, there were two female students who looked similar and who gravitated to each other as similar-looking people tend to do.'

'Yes, I have also known that to happen.' Hennessey slowed to negotiate a tight bend.

'Anyway, long story short, it turns out that not only did they come from the same town, but grew up in houses on the same, very long road, went to the same primary school, the same high school and the same university, though at different faculties, and the first time they met was when they met at their second university to do the probation officers' course, there being just one year age difference to explain why they hadn't met previously. After that they were inseparable.'

'I can imagine.' Hennessey accelerated out of the bend.

'So like I said, I have encountered coincidence and can accept the coincidence of Badger and Garrett settling down close to each other, but also being unknown to each other.'

'As you say . . .' Hennessey slowed for another tight bend. 'But Badger must have seen Garrett when he was walking or cycling or driving past Garrett's house. Garrett didn't leave his property much we believe, but he was no hermit either. He would go outside to talk to his gardeners and the cleaning ladies and neighbours when he had to. It explains how Badger found him.'

'If he found him, sir,' Sherwood commented. 'He's still only a person of interest.'

'Well, we'll see what he says,' Hennessey growled, and then fell silent.

The woman was late middle-aged, probably, thought Yellich, about to qualify or having just qualified for receipt of the state pension. She was visibly frightened and spoke in a shaking voice whilst wringing her hands. 'You know I could get into an awful stew for this. Really I could, a really awful stew.'

Somerled Yellich and Carmen Pharoah had driven out to Millington and had parked by the entrance to The Grange. They had ducked under the blue and white police tape which was still strung across the gateposts and had walked slowly up the long gravel-covered drive to the house. At the house they had exchanged pleasantries with the youthful-looking white-shirted constable who stood at the foot of the steps which led up to the front door, the house still deemed a crime scene. Somerled Yellich and Carmen Pharoah had then walked leisurely around the house to the rear and, upon examining the hedge at the back of the house, were able to detect the narrow gap in the privet through which a person could pass through sideways-on to said privet, as had been described by Mrs Staples of 'The Maids' cleaning services and also reported by Harry Millom, the principal gardener.

Once on the further side of the privet hedge, Yellich and Carmen Pharoah had cast their eyes across the landscape towards the village at which point Carmen Pharoah had said, 'You know, I think I can detect it, I can see a path ahead of us . . . it's not a clear path but more like a track of worn-down grass.'

'So can I, I think,' Yellich had replied, noticing not a clear pathway but a route identified by means of trampled grass stalks which wound between shrubs and bushes. It seemed to him to be a distinct route across the landscape. Without a further word being said, Yellich and Carmen Pharoah had begun to walk, now side by side, now one behind the other, as they followed the pathway which had, in the event, brought them to the edge of a small council-house estate at the edge of the village. Specifically it had brought them to a development of ten small garages, each large enough to contain a family-sized car and which were arranged in a semicircle around a concreted-over area and which stood at the end of a cul-de-sac. The two officers had emerged into the semicircle of garages between two of the units. The door of one of the garages was seen

176

to be open. The two officers had calmly approached the open garage and had encountered a middle-aged man working on the engine of a car within the garage. They had introduced themselves.

'How can I help you?' The man had stood. He had been seen by Yellich and Carmen Pharoah to have a thin, clean-shaven face and was of a relaxed and a warm manner.

'We're just following up on some information,' Yellich had replied. 'It's nothing for you to be alarmed about. Doubtless you will have heard about the unfortunate incident at The Grange?'

'Ah, yes.' The man had reached for an oily cloth and wiped his hands upon it. 'It's quite a turn up for the books for that sort of thing to happen in Millington. I have lived here all my life and that is the first murder that has taken place here in living memory . . . death by natural causes, of course . . . accidental death, yes . . . but murder in our quiet little village, never . . . as I said . . . not within living memory. So a strange business all right, a very strange old business.'

'Did you know the deceased at all?' Yellich had asked.

'Only by sight . . . I never did speak to him. I never had any reason to speak to him. He always seemed to me to be a very private person,' the man had explained. 'A very private person, all right . . . yes, a very private sort of man.'

'We are led to believe that Mr Garrett, the deceased, the man who was murdered at The Grange, was in the habit of walking from his house, specifically from the back of his house,' Yellich had explained, 'towards the village. We have just followed the path we believed he took and it has brought us here. Did Mr Garrett have some connection with these garages, do you know?'

'Yes, I do know.' The man had smiled and once again wiped his hands on the oily rag he held. 'He rented a lock-up here; number eight . . . that one over there.' The man had pointed to a garage with green-painted doors which stood opposite to his garage. 'I work here, you see, I make a living repairing cars. I like working for myself. I do repairs, I do servicing, I do engine rebuilds, I do de-coking . . . I do all that sort of thing. I have a good customer base and a long enough list of cars waiting to be sorted out. I've got work for at least six weeks at the moment. I make a decent enough living but I declare my income.' He had held his hand up in a defensive gesture. 'I'm not frightened of the revenue people giving my books a good going over. Not frightened at all.'

'I'm sure,' Yellich had replied warmly, 'but good for you anyway.'

'But, Mr Garrett . . . yes, he rented unit number eight,' the man continued. 'I have got to know the other garage renters because I work here each day. I've seen 'em come and I've seen 'em go.'

'So who does he rent the garage from? The local authority . . . the housing department of the same?' Carmen Pharoah had asked. 'They are clearly council garages. So I assume that he rents from the council's housing department.'

'Nope.' The man had then put the oily cloth down on the bodywork of the car on which he was working. 'Nope, you assumed incorrectly,

178

miss. What he does is a bit illegal, actually what Garrett does, or did, is not illegal, what the people who rent the garage to him do, is illegal. They're breaking the rules of the game, not Garrett.'

'What do you mean?' Carmen Pharoah had asked.

'Well, it's hardly Serious Crime Squad stuff,' the man had explained. 'It's not like you could make a TV drama out of it, but the tenant who rents the garage fell ill some time ago. He had a massive stroke, poor bloke, so that was his driving days behind him. He sold his car but his wife didn't tell the council, so they're renting it out for a little more than they pay the council, well a lot more really, probably about twice as much I think, going by something she once said to me. The rent we pay as council tenants is a low rent, nominal really, but the tenant of number eight is renting it out at commercial rates. A bit naughty but, like I said, it's not really the sort of thing the Serious Crime Squad would be interested in.'

'I see,' Yellich had murmured. 'I presume he keeps a car in there, in the garage?'

'Yes, he does, a little blue five hundredweight van.' The man had glanced up at the roof of his garage and had rolled his eyes. 'All that money he must have, would you believe it? I mean the house he lives in, the money he must have and yet he sneaks along a path in open country to a little council-owned garage and he scuttles away in a little blue van. He goes away for all the day. He leaves in the mornings and returns after I have packed up for the day, but I know that he has returned that night.'

'How,' Yellich had asked, 'how do you know that?'

'The garage is double-locked, as you see.' The man had extended a forefinger towards garage number eight. 'Two hasps, both padlocked, as you see. When he leaves for the day in his van he locks up using one padlock and hasp. The other padlock he leaves locked to the garage door but does not double-lock it as such. When he returns he double-locks it. He is very methodical. So I have seen him drive away for the day. We say "Good morning" to each other, so he's not worried about being seen, then later I have packed up for the day and his garage is still single-locked. But when I return to my garage the following morning, I see that his garage is by then double-locked. So he has returned after I had finished work and double-locked his garage and then walked back to The Grange. It was not like he was hiding, like I said, he wasn't frightened of being seen, but at the same time he didn't advertise his movements. That was the impression I got anyway, but I don't know folk as well as I know cars and so I might be wrong there. Cars are much easier to understand than people.'

'That is quite interesting,' Yellich had replied. 'So who is the official tenant of the garage which was used by Anthony Garrett?'

'Mrs Docker, sweet old soul really, hardly a criminal but she clearly found a way of getting a little money in to supplement her pension,' the man had advised. 'Her house is just down there, house on the corner, number five, Elm Tree

Drive . . . yellow door, with large plant pots either side of it. You can't miss it.'

Somerled Yellich and Carmen Pharoah had thanked the man for his information and had indeed found the address in question with consummate ease. They had identified themselves to the frail-looking lady who answered their knocking on the door. She had begun to shiver with fear and said that she could get into an 'awful stew'.

'Don't worry,' Somerled Yellich replied calmly, 'we won't report you.'

'We promise,' Carmen Pharoah added equally calmly. 'We just need a little information.'

'We understand you rent a garage to Mr Garrett of The Grange?' Yellich asked.

'Yes, I do.' The woman seemed calmer follow-ing the officers' promise not to report her. 'Do come in.' She led Yellich and Carmen Pharoah into her house and when all three were seated in her small living room Mrs Docker asked if it was true what was being said in the village about Mr Garrett.

'Yes, it's true,' Yellich confirmed. 'So look, we'll tell you what to do . . . just give us the keys for the garage. I assume you have a spare set?'

'Yes, I have spare keys for both padlocks. My husband put the second lock on. In fact, I have two spare sets of keys for the garage.'

'Right . . . well, let us have one spare set, and then wait for a week and then tell the council that you want to give up the rental on the garage.'

'A week?' Mrs Docker whimpered. 'That long?'

'Yes,' Yellich explained. 'It's a crime scene. We'll have to examine it carefully, inch by inch, the garage and Mr Garrett's motor vehicle, then we'll take away anything we need to take away.'

'Oh, I see.' Mrs Docker's voice still shook slightly with fear. 'I'll get a set of keys for you. Then I'll wait a week and tell the council we don't need the garage any more. Only the pension doesn't go far and Mr Garrett's cash for the rent of the garage has been very useful . . . it made all the difference, just those extra pounds coming in. It's been a lifeline for me and Mr Docker. He's in bed right now.'

'How long have you rented the garage to Mr Garrett?' Yellich asked.

'About two years . . . yes . . . about two years since Mr Docker had his stroke and we sold his car. Yes,' she repeated, 'I'll go and get the keys . . .'

In the garage Yellich and Carmen Pharoah found the small blue van, as the self-employed car mechanic had described. They also found a male wig, a false beard and a pair of spectacles with clear, non-corrective lenses.

'A simple yet effective disguise,' Carmen Pharoah commented. 'I mean it's quite sufficient to do the trick, especially if you are not going to hang around too long, and if you're not being looked for or you are not expected. Or both.'

'As you say . . .' Yellich surveyed the garage. 'There seems to be nothing of interest to us apart from the van and that disguise. We'll secure the premises and notify SOCO.' Yellich and Carmen Pharoah vacated the garage and Yellich locked it behind them. They nodded their thanks to the self-employed car mechanic who gave a cheery 'thumbs up' sign by means of reply and then he returned his attention to the engine of the car he was working on. Life in 'quiet little' Millington went on.

'So you have not been such a good lad, have you, Francis?'

Badger shrugged. 'I have done some things.' He sat in an old chair, wearing a white T-shirt and a pair of faded denim jeans which had been severed at the knees. He was barefoot. His home was decorated with what appeared to the officers to be a collection of junk items, as if scavenged from a waste tip, and it smelled strongly of damp. 'Some you know about, some you don't know about.'

'Attempted murder,' Hennessey quoted Badger's criminal record from memory. 'Five years, out in four. That was a lenient sentence.'

'There were considerations.' Badger sniffed. 'He attacked me.'

'Grievous bodily harm, two convictions of,' Hennessey continued, 'and various other felonies, too numerous to recite.'

Hennessey and Sherwood had found Badger's home address without difficulty. It had revealed itself to be a pre-fabricated house with white asbestos walls and a flat roof which had been liberally smeared with tar. It stood at the top of a stony, deeply potholed driveway and was surrounded, Hennessey thought, being 'swallowed' by out-of-control vegetation.

'So,' Hennessey continued. 'Do you know a man called Garrett? Anthony Garrett?'

'I'll say so,' Badger snarled. 'Of course I know him. He arranged for my father to be killed . . . to be murdered.' Badger eyed Hennessey and Sherwood coldly, both of whom had chosen to remain standing despite Badger's invitation to sit down.

'Did he?' Hennessey replied softly. 'Or can it just be the case of your father being in the wrong place at the wrong time?'

'Same difference, if you ask me.' Badger snorted.

'It isn't actually, there's a big difference, but we won't go there. So why,' Hennessey asked, 'did you leave London and come to Yorkshire?'

'The police advised me to leave London until I had cooled down over the death of my dad. I was still one of theirs in those days. They heard I was looking to buy a shooter, you see. They said it was bad enough for my mum to lose her husband, she didn't need to lose her son as well. They said they would take care of Garrett. I suppose they were right. If I had killed Garrett it would not have brought Dad back. Mum was from this part of the world – we always had family holidays on the Yorkshire coast and odd weekend visits to York so I felt a sense of belonging to this area. It seemed a second home from London. So I came here and here I stayed. Simple as that.'

'So you have calmed?' Hennessey probed.

'Possibly, but I didn't do well did I . . . I mean, look at what I've got to show for my years.' Badger had a drawn, gaunt look; he seemed to Hennessey to be malnourished, his long strands of black hair were greying at the roots. 'To think my dad wanted me to follow him into the police. Thank God he isn't here to see this.'

'Who owns this house?' Hennessey asked.

'A local farmer. I rent it. It's nothing so the rent is nothing,' Badger explained. 'I keep the rats out. Suits both of us.'

'Do you live alone?' Sherwood queried.

'Yes. I mean, who'd live here?' Badger sighed.

'So where were you late last Wednesday morning?' Hennessey probed.

'Wednesday? Why are you asking?' Badger became defensive. 'Cops always ask that when some turn has gone down, and I done nothing. What happened last Wednesday?'

'Anthony Garrett was murdered,' Hennessey explained.

'Good.' Badger's jaw sagged and gasped. 'Good,' he repeated.

'He was living in Millington,' Sherwood advised.

'That's the next village!' Badger gasped. 'Only an hour's walk, possibly less if you put a wriggle on.'

'We know,' Hennessey growled.

'All the time I was up here, so was he . . .' Badger sat back in his chair and glanced up at the low, mould-covered ceiling of his home. 'Well, I have heard that the world is a small place but I never knew it was that small.'

'Yes . . . as you say.' Hennessey continued to press Badger. 'So Wednesday last in the late forenoon, where are you?'

'Am I a suspect?' Badger smiled.

'Yes,' Sherwood replied. 'You could say that.'

'Well, it was my signing-on day at the dole office. I signed on at ten thirty a.m., that's my signing time. Then I went for a quiet drink with my girlfriend.'

'OK.' Hennessey nodded. 'That's easy to check. Which pub did you go to?'

'The Royal Oak.'

'And the name and address of your girlfriend?' Sherwood asked. 'We'll need to talk to her to confirm your alibi.'

'So you met "Mr Paranoia" . . .' George Hennessey raised his eyebrows. 'It certainly sounds like you did, anyway.'

'It seems so, sir,' Ventnor replied. 'I mean, long-range microphones, cameras with telephoto lenses, me hiding my fellow officers behind trees and in the bushes, but nonetheless, tortured soul that he might well be, the wretched man did give some good information. The hotel, I would hope, will be able to help us identify those three women.'

'Yes . . . yes, I was thinking much the same thing.' Hennessey glanced to his left and he saw a lone elderly female solemnly walking the walls of the ancient city. 'And a pile of charred clothing . . . I like the sound of that. It does seem very interesting. What did you make of it?'

'Well, I didn't get to within six feet of the remains of the fire, I didn't want to contaminate it prior to SOCO examining it, but I couldn't see anything promising,' Ventnor replied. 'It might not have anything to do with the women, of course. The fire might be totally unconnected.'

186

'All right . . . you'll be able to take SOCO to the location, I assume?' Hennessey asked.

'Yes, sir, I broke the branch of a sapling by the roadside close to where the fire was as a sort of marker. I'll find the location again easily,' Ventnor advised with a confident tone.

'Good, good. So if you can take a SOCO team back there asap, do that before anything gets too disturbed. Then return and find Reginald, he's in the CID corridor, at his desk, writing up his visit to Miles Law. I'll have to visit him, Mr Law, I mean, because DC Webster notified me of something significant but not relevant to the murder of Anthony Garrett. But if you and Reginald can visit the hotel in which the three women stayed, see what the staff there can tell you about them . . . but the priority is to get SOCO back to the pile of burnt clothing so do that before anything else.'

'Yes, sir.' Ventnor stood, as did George Hennessey.

'You know it is so strange how police officers make my modest little cottage seem even smaller than it already is.' Miles Law shrugged as he and George Hennessey sat in Miles Law's elongated living room. 'But then I dare say that it is a small cottage to start with and police officers tend to be on the large size but you do suddenly make me feel as though I am living in a doll's house.'

George Hennessey had driven out of York and, following Carmen Pharoah's directions, had found Miles Law's cottage without difficulty. He parked his car outside, at the kerb, and walked up the short path and knocked politely but authoritatively on the door, using the classic police officer's knock of: 'tap, tap . . . tap'. Miles Law answered the door promptly. Hennessey introduced himself whereupon he was invited inside the cottage, warmly so, having to stoop to enter the doorway. Law invited Hennessey to sit and he then said, '. . . it is so strange how police officers make my modest little cottage seem even smaller . . .'

'I think I can guess why you're here.' Miles Law now looked across at the wall opposite to where he sat. 'In fact, there's no guessing. I reckon I know why you're here.'

'Oh . . .?' Hennessey raised his eyebrows. 'Why might that be?'

Miles Law held eye contact with Hennessey. 'The gun I have in my possession. The gun which I unlawfully possess. The gun I told the other two officers about.'

'Yes,' Hennessey nodded very slightly, 'that is indeed why I am here, Mr Law.'

'So the officers did report me,' Law spoke calmly. 'They said that they would have to do that.'

'They had to, as they said,' Hennessey explained. 'They had no option but to report you. But thus far the issue is still unofficial, which is why I am visiting you myself. The other officers verbally reported you being in possession of a firearm. It has not yet been written up as an official document. If you don't hand it over, then we'll visit in force. If you don't surrender it you'll be issued with a court order compelling you to do so.'

'And if I fail to surrender it despite the court

order?' Law asked. 'What happens then? I dare say that's contempt of court, isn't it?'

'Yes,' Hennessey replied, 'and it guarantees prison time . . . and I don't think prison is for a man like you. I mean, what have you been in life . . . a soldier, a gardener, a long-distance lorry driver . . . used to open spaces and travelling? Could you adjust to a cell for two or three years?'

'Not easily,' Law sighed. 'I was stupid in my youth, but now . . . my age . . . no, you're right, I would find it difficult.'

'I imagine there's no point in obtaining a search warrant, is there?' Hennessey probed. 'Not if what you told the officers is true.'

'It was . . . it is true,' Law replied firmly. 'The gun isn't here, not in the house, the outbuildings or the garden, nor is it in Garrett's garden.'

'So just what level of risk does it pose?' Hennessey queried.

'None. It's in pieces. I dismantled it and wrapped each piece in an oily rag, then placed each piece in a plastic container and then buried each container in separate locations. The bullets have a box all to themselves,' Law explained, 'and I buried them deeply, no one will stumble across one.'

'That's reassuring,' Hennessey replied, 'but it is still an issue. We will have to assume custody of it at some point.'

'I should also tell you,' Law continued, 'that if . . . when I do reassemble it, I won't point the gun at anyone.'

'Again, the officers told me that.' Hennessey paused. 'Have you sought help with your demons,

189

Mr Law? Have you talked to anyone . . . a psychologist . . . someone from the Samaritans?'

'No . . .' Law breathed deeply. 'The only thing that might stop me topping myself is something the lady police officer said. That there is no guarantee that death is an escape from your demons. If your consciousness continues so will your demons.'

A silence then developed between the two men, broken, eventually, by Hennessey who said, 'Well, I have done what I came to do. Advice has been given.' He stood slowly. 'I have made a request. Please think very carefully about things, Mr Law, please think very carefully.'

George Hennessey knew what Miles Law meant when, as he drove back towards York, a motorcyclist came up behind him then, when it was safe to do so, overtook him with a roar. The sudden appearance of the motorcycle caused him to be transported back in his mind to his boyhood . . . to Greenwich, south-east London and the practice of helping his beloved elder brother to clean and polish his equally beloved motorbike and how he would be rewarded for his effort by being taken a ride on the pillion, usually up Trafalgar Road and across the river by Tower Bridge and round the sights, St Paul's Cathedral, the Houses of Parliament, and back across the river via Westminster Bridge. Then . . . then there had been that terrible, dreadful, fateful night, which had changed his life for ever, and not for the better. He recalled with awful clarity how he lay abed one evening listening to Graham kick-start the Triumph into life and drive away, climbing through the gears, as he drove towards the *Cutty Sark*. Then in the silence he listened to sounds outside, the horn of a ship on the river, a drunken Irishman walking up Colomb Street reciting his Hail Mary's. Then later still the loud and unexpected knock . . . the classic policeman's knock he would later come to use . . . tap, tap . . . tap . . . then those awful voices. His mother's dreadful wailing and his father coming to his room to tell him, whilst fighting back tears, that Graham had 'ridden to heaven to save a place for us'. A few days later there was the incongruity of a summer funeral to attend . . . of grief among the rich foliage and the flitting butterflies, of the sound of 'Greensleeves' being played by an ice-cream van in some close by but unseen street. He was later to meet again the incongruity of a summer funeral when he was obliged to be the chief mourner at the funeral of his beloved wife, carrying their first born in his arms as he did so.

'The Black Swan.' Sheila Perry presented as a much younger woman than Francis Badger. 'We went to The Black Swan.'

'Sure,' Hennessey confirmed.

'Of course I'm sure. Why wouldn't I be?' She was in her mid-to-late twenties, Hennessey guessed, she wore her hair in a combed-up style with a plume rising from the top of her head. Like Francis Badger she wore faded denim and a T-shirt. Her home was a cluttered back-to-back in Holgate, so that one stepped through the front

191

door and then directly into the living room, thus from street to living room in one stride.

Hennessey's eyes were caught by the bulging and inexpensive shopping bags, one in blue and white check pattern, the other in green and white. He also noticed that Sheila Perry eyed the bags nervously. Hennessey advanced on the bags and opened them.

'Do you have a warrant to look in those bags?' Sheila Perry spoke with a resigned tone of voice, as if realizing the question was futile.

'We don't need one,' Sherwood replied. 'You invited us in, remember.'

Hennessey peered into the bags. He saw bottles of expensive malt whiskey. He saw items of clothing still with the price labels attached. He saw large joints of frozen beef and lamb. 'Been out shopping, Sheila?' He smiled. 'Do you have receipts for all this?'

'I don't keep receipts.' Sheila Perry folded her arms and looked down at the dirty carpet.

'Really? It matters not,' Hennessey replied. 'We can take them all back to the supermarket and they can tell us if they have been scanned through the till or not.'

'All right, you've got me. Again. I'll be going down for this. Last time the magistrate told me that just one more conviction for shoplifting and I'll be going to gaol. If I go to gaol I will lose this tenancy then I'll have to go to a hostel. There's some really heavy girls in those places . . . all that bullying and thieving . . . no wonder so many homeless people prefer to sleep rough. But I've done nothing bad. I never stick needles in myself. I never sold my body. But you can't survive on the dole, not without a bit of stealing.'

'So which pub were you and Francis Badger in last Wednesday at midday?' Hennessey pressed.

'I told you,' Sheila Perry replied indignantly.

'Tell us again,' Sherwood pressed.

'The Black Swan,' Perry replied. 'We was in The Black Swan.'

'Really, because Badger said that you were in The Royal Oak.'

'I meant The Royal Oak,' Sheila Perry replied in a desperate tone. 'I get those two pubs mixed up.'

'You can't mix them up,' Hennessey replied patiently. 'One is as old as olde York itself. The other is post-Second World War, and they are on the opposite sides of the city. All right, put some shoes on. We're arresting you for shoplifting and when you're at the station you can tell us all about a murder.'

'Murder!' Perry reacted with distinct alarm. 'Murder? I have not done no murder. What murder?'

'We'll explain at the police station.' Sherwood picked up the shopping bags. 'Right, now you can decide whether you'll be working for yourself or against yourself.'

Reginald Webster and Thompson Ventnor stepped, one behind the other, into the foyer of the Holderness Arms Hotel. It was, they found, a small hotel but one which had the confident air of a large, well-established institution. The walls were of dark panelled oak adorned with horse brasses, all highly polished. A solid table, also of darkly stained oak, stood against the wall

193

opposite the staircase and seemed to the officers to be the resting place of delivered mail, whether for the hotel or for guests. The carpet was of a dark purple shade and was of a deep pile. The air within smelled strongly of furniture polish mingled with the soft scent emanating from the flower arrangement in a cut-glass vase which stood on a doily on the table, surrounded by unopened envelopes. The receptionist welcomed Webster and Thompson with a radiant though, the officers felt, a superficial smile. She was smartly dressed in a white blouse and a red skirt. 'Can I help you, gentlemen?' she enquired with a softly pleasant speaking voice.

'Police,' Webster replied as he and Ventnor showed their ID cards. 'Is the manager available, please?'

'The manageress,' the receptionist politely corrected Webster. 'Mrs Bloodworth prefers things to be kept as traditional as possible. I'll see if she is available.' She picked up the phone which stood on the right-hand side of the reception desk and pressed a two-digit number. When her call was answered she announced the arrival of the two police officers, listened for a few seconds and then said, '*Yes, ma'am,*' and then gently replaced the handset. 'Mrs Bloodworth,' she advised the officers, 'will be here directly, gentlemen.'

Mrs Bloodworth, when she descended the staircase within sixty seconds, revealed herself to be a tall, slender lady, possibly in her sixties, Ventnor thought. She had a sharp, angular face, wore her greying hair pinned back and had a

194

serious cold-eyed, stone-faced expression. If she wasn't the manageress of a small independent hotel, then Ventnor could easily picture the woman as the headmistress of a traditional all-girls' school. Webster, similarly, had the immediate impression that Mrs Bloodworth would not stand any nonsense from anybody. Guests included. 'The police, I understand?' She held her hands together in front of her, as she eyed both Webster and Ventnor with curiosity, but she betrayed no trace of alarm. 'How can I help you, gentlemen?'

'We are making inquiries in respect of recent guests at your hotel, madam,' Webster replied. 'There is an issue of confidentiality. Is there somewhere a little more private where we can talk?'

'Well . . . my office upstairs is so very cramped,' Mrs Bloodworth replied. 'It will not be able to accommodate us three . . . but . . . but . . . the dining room is not being used at the moment and it has been cleaned and the tables set for dinner so I think we might use that.' She extended her right arm, indicating the door to the right of the reception desk. 'We can talk there, I think.'

'Ah yes . . . those three ladies,' Mrs Bloodworth sniffed when standing in the dining room with the door closed behind them, and the officers having explained the reason for their visit. 'We will remember those three guests for a long time to come methinks . . . they were very strange ladies . . . a strange trio indeed.'

'Strange?' Webster asked. He glanced round the dining room, noting twelve tables with four chairs at each table, a thick dark blue carpet, matching velvet curtains which hung from the ceiling to the floor and a long, narrow garden, neatly kept, on the further side of two tall windows at the far end of the room. As with the foyer, the dining room smelled heavily of furniture polish. 'What do you mean, madam? Strange in what way?'

'Strange in the manner in which it was as if all three shared one mind. It is the only way to describe them, one mind between the three of them. They spoke in unison but without any indication that they had rehearsed from a pre-planned script,' Mrs Bloodworth explained. 'And they also seemed to move as one when it was possible to do so. In fact I think that one of my waitresses put it very well when she said that watching them eating was like watching one woman sitting in front of two mirrors . . . and you know that it really was like that. It was not unlike it at all. If one cut a piece of meat and then forked it to her mouth, the other two did the same thing at the exact same time, so it was not the case that two were following the lead of the third. It was more, as I said, as if one mind, one brain was shared between the three bodies. It was most strange. Most, most strange indeed.'

'What name did they give?' Ventnor asked as he took his notepad and ballpoint from his jacket pocket.

'Middlemiss,' Mrs Bloodworth replied without hesitation. 'We won't forget that name in a hurry either . . . quite appropriate we thought – an odd number of women has to have a "middle" miss.' She permitted herself a brief smile at her own joke.

196

'Indeed,' Webster replied dryly. 'When did they arrive?'

'On Friday last. That is to say the Friday just gone, a week ago tomorrow,' Mrs Bloodworth advised. 'They booked three separate single rooms, so I dare say they could act independently if they so wished. They took their evening meal with us, eating as one, and then they retired for the night. On the Saturday, the following morning, they came downstairs all dressed identically, and each carrying a black shoulder bag. They took a late breakfast, then they went back up to their rooms and returned soon after, this time each was carrying a small yellow holdall type of bag and they left the hotel. They returned a few hours later but by then they were dressed differently from each other, in casual clothing and without their yellow holdalls. They went straight to their rooms and collected their belongings, just a small suitcase each, and then came downstairs and settled their bill and left the hotel in the early afternoon.'

'Did they provide an address?' Webster noted the ornate patterned ceiling of the dining room.

'As good as.' Mrs Bloodworth followed Webster's gaze. 'The ceiling is authentic, you might be interested in knowing. The building dates from the eighteenth century,' she explained. 'But the ladies in question, their address . . . they paid by a company credit card . . . Middlemiss, Middlemiss and Middlemiss, Solicitors.'

'Solicitors!' Webster echoed. 'They were lawyers!'

'Yes . . . so it would seem,' Mrs Bloodworth replied. 'I'll retrieve a copy of the invoice we gave them, and from that you can obtain their company address. They were, probably still are, Londoners by their distinct accents, very East End I thought, not your usual solicitor's speaking voice . . . but the invoice . . . if you'll please wait here, gentlemen, I'll collect it for you.'

Hennessey and Sherwood sat side by side in front of a highly polished wooden table. Opposite them sat a pale-faced and worried-looking Francis Badger. Set in the wall beside the table was a tape recorder. The twin spools spun slowly and silently. The red recording light glowed.

'I am Detective Chief Inspector Hennessey of the Vale of York police. The place is interview room one at Michelgate Bar Police Station. The time is eleven fifteen a.m. I am now going to ask the other persons present to identify themselves.'

'Detective Constable Sherwood of the Vale of York police.'

'Keith Thrower of Thrower, Wortley and Wilkinson Solicitors of St Leonard's Place, York.'

'Francis Badger of . . . of wherever . . . My home is temporary anyway.' He spoke with a nervous, shaky voice. 'And I done nothing wrong.'

'Francis Badger,' Hennessey began. 'We have arrested you in connection with the murder of Anthony Garrett.'

'I know.' Badger's reply was sullen. He gazed round the interview room, which had an orange-coloured hessian wall covering and only artificial lighting. 'You told me.'

'Francis,' Hennessey continued. 'Your alibi doesn't hold together. It is full of holes. Yes . . .

it is true that your signing-on time at the dole office is ten a.m. each Wednesday, but the Social Security people have confirmed that you did not sign on last Wednesday. You claim to have had a drink with Sheila Perry in The Royal Oak, yet Shelia Perry says that you were in The Black Swan. And just to give you the benefit of the doubt, we checked the CCTV of both pubs and neither of you were in either pub that day at that time. Both pubs keep their CCTV tapes for fourteen days, you see,' Hennessey added by means of explanation. He paused. 'You've got form, Francis, and you and Sheila Perry can't agree on an alibi. But, look at it from our point of view. You have a motive, you have the opportunity, we just need the means . . . but we will get there. What did you do with the gun? Throw it in the river?'

'I did not murder Garrett.' Badger's voice grew stronger. 'I did not murder him. I didn't know he lived in the next village until you told me.'

'You still lack evidence of the means, Chief Inspector.' Keith Thrower spoke with calm, self-assured authority.

'So what did you do with the gun?' Hennessey pressed Badger. 'Sell it in the York underworld, if you didn't throw it in the river?'

'No comment.'

'Really, Mr Hennessey.' Thrower held eye contact with Hennessey. 'I must insist that you either charge my client or release him.'

'We'll do neither. We can hold him for forty-eight hours, and then we'll decide what we'll do. Meanwhile, we'll see what else Sheila Perry has to say.'

'You arrested her?' Badger became alarmed.

'Yes. She's in the cells. You sound worried, Francis. What does she know that you do not want us to find out?'

Hennessey and Sherwood sat side by side in front of the table in interview room one. Sheila Perry and a young and smartly dressed man who had introduced himself as Barry Elderkin of Elderkin and Hargreaves Solicitors sat beside her.

'The possible charge is murder if you were there with Badger,' Hennessey explained. 'Even if you did not pull the trigger, you're still guilty of murder. If you helped to plan the murder, helped obtain the weapon or got rid of the weapon for him, you're guilty of accessory. Murder will get you life; accessory will get you at least five years, so forget about the three months for shoplifting. Forget that . . . you're in the top league now, Sheila.'

Sheila Perry paled.

'Your alibi has been disproven and that alone makes you a person of interest.' Hennessey paused. 'You know we could offer you something here . . . how about if we make the shoplifting charge disappear?'

'You can?' Sheila Perry looked hopeful. 'You can do that?'

'Yes. If you turn Queen's evidence against Francis Badger, help us find the means – by which I mean the gun – he used to murder Garrett . . . and then we are able to identify and eliminate . . . then you can walk.'

be more on the ball than the officer he sent up to photograph Anthony Garrett's arm,' Hennessey explained.

'That tattoo you mean, sir?' Ventnor clarified. 'To photograph the tattoo on Anthony Garrett's arm?'

'Yes . . . "Pilot". So he got his photograph which scratched an itch and we got an explanation for the tattoo, but it transpires that Mr Allardyce knows a little about Anthony Garrett.' Hennessey outstretched his arms at either side of his shoulders. 'I hope, and in fact I am certain, that Mr Allardyce will be more forthcoming to Carmen. He indicated that he'd be more than happy to talk to her, preferring face-to-face contact rather than telephone contact, so I am sending Carmen. As you say, she won't object at all.'

George Hennessey signed out and drove sedately home. As he approached he smiled and felt his heart leap as he saw a silver BMW parked half on and half off the grass kerb outside his house.

'I didn't expect to see you for a few days yet.' Hennessey had entered his house to be warmly greeted by Charles and Oscar. Later, whilst father and son sat on the patio at the rear of the house and Oscar followed a clearly interesting scent across the recently mown lawn, Hennessey sipped his tea from his favourite pint-sized mug, and repeated, 'Not for a few days.'

'Yes, we concluded early.' Charles Hennessey also sipped from a mug of tea. 'The defence put up a "cut throat" argument.'

'What is that?' George Hennessey watched his dog crisscross the lawn, his nose to the grass.

203

'Well, as you know, I was acting for the Crown in this case; a young infant only a few weeks old had been murdered. His parents were both heroin addicts. So he hadn't got a good start in life. Anyway, medical evidence was conclusive that the injuries had been perpetrated by one person and one person only,' Charles Hennessey explained, 'but they couldn't say which one. So one parent was guilty and one was not guilty. They both pleaded "not guilty" and each blamed the other. So they were both acquitted. They both walked free. No one was happy with it, even the defence counsels, but they had a job to do and they did their job by exploiting the law's fear, nay the law's terror, of wrongful convictions. Both could not be convicted without knowingly convicting an innocent person. So there was no justice for the little snapper, and, like I said, no one was happy. The judge's reluctance in dismissing the case was plain to see and hear, and the defence counsels, both friends of mine, apologized for having to do that when we met in the robing room after the trial but, as I said, they had a job to do and they did it. It was a classic example of a "cut throat" defence. So we concluded early. They pleaded NG, the medical evidence was heard and they were acquitted, all over in less than thirty minutes.'

'I can understand your anger.' George Hennessey continued to sip his tea. 'So, tell me, when do I get to see my grandchildren again?'

'When we meet your lady friend,' Charles Hennessey replied warmly, and smiling widely. 'You keep promising me that we will.'

'That's emotional blackmail,' Hennessey complained, also in good humour, 'quite below the belt and unfair. Totally unfair.'

'You keep promising, father,' Charles Hennessey pressed. 'It's time to deliver.'

'Soon,' George Hennessey replied. 'Soon.'

Thompson Ventnor returned home by bus to his semi-detached house in Bishopsthorpe. As he opened the front door he stooped to pick up the post which had been delivered to his house in his absence and he found himself, as he did so, pondering how different is the life of the modern postman to the life of a postman when he was one such in the early part of his working life. In his day, a postman had to rise at four a.m., he recalled, and had to walk or cycle to the sorting office and be out on his 'walk' before six a.m., so that the essential mail, needed by businesses, could be delivered by nine a.m. or as soon as possible thereafter. But, these days, all essential mail is delivered electronically thus freeing the modern postman to work normal office hours. Thompson Ventnor, though no longer a postman, found he had mixed feelings about the change. Certainly, he had to concede, the hours of the modern postman are more civilized, but not for them is the tranquillity of the still and empty pre-dawn streets, when there was just him, the occasional fox and the cheery milkman who was always ready with a wave of his hand or a hushed 'good morning, squire' if they were close enough to talk, without waking the slumbering householders. On that afternoon the mail which had awaited Ventnor's return home was all unsolicited 'junk mail'. He opened each envelope and took the pre-paid reply envelope from each one, as was his usual practice, and put it on one side. These he would drop into the post the following day, knowing that the company concerned would have to pay for the return postage of the envelope and which practice would serve to help to keep down the cost of the postage stamp he would have to buy for any personal mail he would have to send.

He went upstairs to his bedroom and changed out of his work suit into a lighter Italian-design summer-wear suit. He returned downstairs and went into his kitchen where he put a pre-cooked chicken tikka with rice, labelled 'serves two', into the microwave. He reflected that 'serves two small children' might be a more accurate label, for the entire contents were just sufficient for a single meal for him. Having eaten, he left his house and walked away with a casual glance at his untidy front garden and, making a silent promise to 'do something about it', took a bus back into York whereupon he caught another bus which took him beyond the edge of the southern suburbs, where he alighted. He walked perhaps a hundred yards along the country lane until he came to the entrance of a driveway which was flanked by two huge white-painted gateposts. He walked up the drive, dwarfed, he felt, by the thick vegetation growing on either side of the roadway until he came to a large Victorian-era house which stood at the top of the drive. The house, he thought, could best be described as 'Gothic' and it was, he thought, typical of Victorian houses, being a ramshackle architectural mess with a complicated roofline and turret windows. Ventnor entered the house by the front door. He signed in the visitors' book to state his presence in the building in the event of a fire and walked across the deeply carpeted foyer and began to climb the wide staircase, nimbly taking the stairs two at a time. As he ascended a young woman in a blue smock was descending and he and she smiled at each other as they passed.

On the first floor of the house he walked to a certain door and opened it. The room was, as usual, too warm in his view to be healthy but he knew that regulations dictated the temperature therein. In the room elderly men and women sat in armchairs which stood against the walls and faced outwards. The room was thickly carpeted and had a flat-screen television attached to the wall which, at that moment, was tuned into a commercial channel which was broadcasting a panel quiz game. As he entered the room an elderly man sitting in a corner recognized him and his face seemed to light up with delight, but by the time Ventnor had crossed the floor and knelt beside the man, the man seemed to be lost again in his own world. 'Hello, Dad.' Ventnor spoke softly, knowing the elderly man could not understand him but he said it anyway. Ventnor later spoke to the duty staff who advised him that 'Mr Ventnor' was stable and was 'not presenting any issues'. Ventnor thanked the staff for their care and walked back down the stairs to the foyer where he signed 'out' in the visitors' book.

He returned to York and went to The Green Dragon for a pint of beer, then to The George for another beer and finally to The Three Cranes for a third pint. It was his habit to walk from pub to pub having a beer in each, rather than standing alone at the one bar drinking beer after beer after beer. He did not like the image of himself that that practice would present, accurate as it may be. Eventually he fetched up at Caesar's Nightclub, which, being midweek, had few guests. He bought one woman a drink who told him, proudly, that she was older than she looked, produced a photograph of her grandchildren and spoke obsessively about her 'new' grandson. Another woman, who had been drinking all evening and was clearly on the verge of being escorted from the premises, kept forcing her eyes to focus on his face and kept repeating, 'You look familiar, darlin'.' The third woman he spoke to was sober and softly spoken and demure. She, early in their conversation, used a slender finger with a loud red nail varnish to pull down her silk scarf to reveal an Adam's apple. 'I'm not a woman yet,' 'she' told him, 'but I am having the surgery. I'm definitely going to have it done . . .'

Finally Thompson Ventnor gave up and walked home.

Alone.

It was Friday, 00.00 hours.

Five

*In which more is learned of the Middlemiss
sisters and the urbane and always too
kind reader learns of Carmen Pharoah's
demon, and the locating of Anthony
Garrett's home is explained.*

Carmen Pharoah enjoyed the thrill of home-
coming as she stepped from the train at King's
Cross railway station, always finding London to
be a mothering city, as well as being her home
town. She took the Victoria Line underground
train from King's Cross to Victoria where she
left the subway system. She then walked the short
distance to the junction of Victoria Street and
Broadway and thence to the headquarters of the
Metropolitan Police at New Scotland Yard. She
stepped lightly up the wide and gently inclined
flight of steps and walked beside and beneath
the iconic revolving triangle at the entrance of the
building. The white-shirted constable on duty
at the reception desk remained stony-faced as
Carmen Pharoah approached him. At the desk
she introduced herself and showed her warrant
card as she did so. 'To see Detective Chief
Inspector Allardyce,' she explained. 'I believe
that I am expected.'

'Yes, ma'am.' The constable picked up the phone which sat on the enquiry desk and jabbed a four-figure internal number. When his call was duly answered he advised of the arrival of Carmen Pharoah at the reception desk, listened for a few moments and then said crisply, 'Yes, sir.' He replaced the handset, softly so, and looked up at Carmen Pharoah, and said, 'Can you take the lift to the fourth floor please, ma'am? Mr Allardyce will meet you at the lift shaft.' The constable then indicated to his left.

Carmen Pharoah thanked the constable and proceeded to do as she had been asked. On the fourth floor she stepped out of the lift and was indeed met by a particularly well-built, muscular man in plain clothes. He held out a meaty right hand and smiled. 'I'm Detective Chief Inspector Allardyce, Nigel Allardyce. You are Ms Pharoah from the Vale of York Police?'

'Yes, sir.' Carmen Pharoah accepted his outstretched hand and found his grip firm but not crushing.

'This way please, Carmen. First names suit you?' He indicated for her to accompany him as he walked down a quiet corridor carpeted with brown hardwearing fabric.

'Oh, yes, Nigel,' Pharoah fell into step with Nigel Allardyce, 'first names are much preferred in fact, much preferred, and it is what I am used to except with our boss who likes to keep things formal.'

'Good . . .' Nigel Allardyce spoke with a soft London accent. 'My office is just down here, a little further along the corridor and as you'll see,

210

it offers a splendid view of the backyards of all the surrounding buildings. I must confess that that is quite an interesting sounding name you have there, Carmen, if you don't mind me saying. Carmen Pharoah . . . it does have a distinct ring to it.'

'Not at all,' Carmen Pharoah replied. 'In fact, I get many such comments. I started out in life as Carmen St John, and I became Carmen Pharoah upon marriage.'

'Just here, here's my little bolthole.' Nigel Allardyce indicated an open door and invited Carmen Pharoah to precede him into his office. 'And a London accent to boot. I confess I didn't expect that.' Allardyce sat in the chair behind his desk and invited Carmen Pharoah by hand gesture to sit in one of the two chairs which stood in front of his desk.

'Oh, yes.' Carmen Pharoah sat down and placed her bag on the floor beside her feet. 'Yes, London born and bred. I'm a good East End girl from Leytonstone, third-generation British, our family emigrating from St Kitts in the West Indies. In fact, I once served in the Metropolitan Police. I wasn't here, at "the Yard", but I was in the Met.'

'Really?' Nigel Allardyce beamed his approval. 'Really?' he repeated.

'Yes, really.' Carmen Pharoah glanced around Nigel Allardyce's office and she found it to be like all police officers' offices, neatly kept and functional, the only softening which appeared to be allowed in the room being a small cactus plant in a terracotta pot which stood atop the grey Home Office issue filing cabinet. 'I had a few jobs upon leaving school, this and that, nothing spectacular, then I applied to join the police. I got in on my third application.'

'That was quick,' Nigel Allardyce commented, 'that really is quite impressive. I beat you by one application but I have known some very good officers who got in only upon their seventh or eighth application, so third application is not bad, not bad at all. You can be well pleased with yourself on that score, well pleased.'

'Thank you, Nigel.' Carmen Pharoah began to relax in the company of Nigel Allardyce.

'So what drove you from London, or what attracted you to the north of England?' Allardyce leaned back in his chair. 'Or is that something personal you'd rather keep to yourself?'

'My husband was killed,' Carmen Pharoah replied, in a flat, unemotional matter-of-fact manner. 'And no, I don't mind talking about it.'

'Oh . . . I am so very sorry,' Allardyce groaned. 'That was more than a little insensitive of me. It is quite an injustice . . . I mean, you seem to be far too young to be widowed, again, if you don't mind me saying.'

'I have known younger . . . but no need to upset yourself, Nigel. He, my husband, also worked for the Metropolitan Police. It's how we met. We met when both of us were working,' Carmen Pharoah advised.

'He was a police officer? Not killed while on duty, I hope?' Allardyce asked. 'It being a constant fear for all police families, it is a constant nagging fear.'

'No . . . and no,' Carmen Pharoah replied. 'He

212

was an accountant with the Met. He was killed by a drunken driver when he, Thomas, my husband, was crossing the road, when he was coming home from work one evening after working late. He actually worked here, in this building, and we met when he visited the station I worked at, being Whitechapel, Jack the Ripper territory, as it was in 1888. He visited to check the station accounts. It has to be said, in fairness, that there was an element of culpability on both sides that has to be acknowledged. The driver was travelling at an excess speed and he was under the influence of alcohol, but my husband was wearing dark clothing and he was also Afro-Caribbean, like me. You see our skin absorbs light, it does not reflect it like the skin of Europeans does, and he was in the car's path. He had stepped off the pavement and into the road. The driver stopped rather than tried to drive on and escape justice . . . but if my husband had waited at the kerb to let the car pass . . . I am sure my husband must have seen that the car was travelling at speed and it would have been sensible to keep out of its way as it approached. I go over it again and again in my mind . . . if he had only waited a couple of seconds, then crossed the road after the car had passed, but he must have thought that he had time to cross the road in front of the car.'

'You would,' Allardyce spoke softly. 'It's a tragic story, and you will keep going over it in your mind. It will stay with you for the rest of your life.'

'Yes . . . I have come to realize that.' Carmen

Pharoah paused. 'He was so proud, he was proud of being the first black accountant in the Metropolitan Police. He was the only black student on his accountancy degree course at Cardiff University where he took a very good degree . . . an upper second.'

'Not bad,' Allardyce nodded. 'My son is at Derby University, he's studying computer science, dare say that that is the way forward, computers I mean. He's hoping for a 2:1.'

'Good for him,' Carmen Pharoah replied, 'but, as my husband's father told us . . . he gave us a lot of good advice, he said, "*You're both black, and that means you have got to be ten times better just to be as good, that's just the way of it,*" and my husband was particularly keen to prove himself to be just as good. And he was succeeding . . . and then he steps in front of a speeding car. I can be just as angry with him as I can be angry with the driver of the car. As I said, there was culpability on both sides.'

'So that tragedy drove you out of London?' Nigel Allardyce calmly stood and walked to a small table by the window of his office and picked up an electric kettle and shook it so as to test its contents. 'Tea or coffee?' He switched the kettle on and selected two mugs from a metal tray on which stood a number of brightly coloured mugs.

'Tea for me, please.' Carmen Pharoah reasoned that office-produced tea in Nigel Allardyce's office, like all office-produced tea anywhere in the world, would be marginally less awful than would office-produced instant coffee. 'No . . . it

214

was the guilt I felt,' she explained. 'And still do feel. It was guilt that caused me to flee north, and I accept that guilt is a very poor reason for doing anything, but it was the guilt of it.'

'Guilt?' Allardyce poured boiling water into a mug containing a single teabag. 'Why should you feel guilty? You were not there.' He added a drop of milk to the mixture.

'I don't know myself; well I didn't at the time, anyway.' Carmen Pharoah leaned back in her chair as Nigel Allardyce handed her a mug of hot tea. 'But I have subsequently found out that what I felt is called "survivor guilt". It's the feeling of guilt which sets in when you live and someone else doesn't. Widows feel it, as do widowers, after a long and successful marriage, so do soldiers who have survived combat when their comrades in arms didn't. I felt I had to pay a penalty for my husband's death, and most especially for his early death. That will always seem so dreadfully unfair. So I applied for a transfer to the north of England because it's cold up there and because I saw television adaptions of *Nicholas Nickleby* and of *Wuthering Heights*, and in those programmes I saw all that rugged moorland landscape in that driving rain and high wind and I thought that that is where I deserve to be, not in the soft south . . . and only when the guilt for Tom's death leaves me will I be permitted to return to London, which I consider to be my home. That is what I feel.'

'So is it that cold . . . as cold as they say?' Nigel Allardyce carried a mug of tea back to his chair. 'And is it as rugged as it appears? I confess it's always seemed to be like a very hostile landscape.'

'Well . . . it can get a bit cold, but then London also has its cold spells. I mean Old Father Thames has frozen solid in the past, the last time being in 1947 I believe, in the post-war 1940s anyway. So it's not really much colder,' Carmen Pharoah sipped her tea, 'and the landscape . . . well, the Vale of York is a landscape of flat fields and low rolling hills, very similar to parts of the south of England. The landscape of the Brontë sisters does exist and I find it quite a brutal landscape, always I find it to be unforgiving. I think you have to be born to that landscape.' She enjoyed the warmth of the tea.

'Well, I'll take your word for it.' Nigel Allardyce also sipped his tea. 'I went to Derby when I drove my son up there to start his university course and I have never been further north than that and I don't want to go any further than that either. I am a southerner and am only happy in the Saxon south. I make no secret of it. So,' he said after a pause, 'the reason you are here is one Mr Garrett, Mr Anthony Garrett. Also known as . . . well, he has quite a string of aliases, so we'll just refer to him as Anthony Garrett. The important thing is that we both know who we are talking about.'

'The one and the same.' Carmen Pharoah nodded her agreement. 'As you say, Nigel, so long as we both know who we are talking about. My governor, Mr Hennessey, he's another Londoner by the way . . . originally from Greenwich but I don't know what made him swap

216

London for York, but I think it was because he married a Yorkshire lass.'

'Really? We do get about, we Londoners, despite having a reputation for being poor travellers. What is that saying? "*Londoners don't travel well because they have already arrived*"? Or something like that. I need this . . .' he sipped his tea, '. . . even if it doesn't taste like tea, but it's hot and the colour is right, and it's been a hectic morning.'

'Yes . . . but my boss, Mr Hennessey,' Carmen Pharoah continued, 'he said the officer you sent up to York to photograph Anthony Garrett's tattoo wasn't really able to help much in respect of what information he could provide. We still feel a little in the dark about Garrett. We need to know more about a man who was so obviously murdered with pre-meditation.'

'Yes . . . Harry Kelto.' Allardyce shrugged. 'What can I say about Harry? He's an officer who makes up the numbers rather than being someone to give a responsible job to. Harry wasn't able to help much because he didn't know much but I needed a photograph of Anthony Garrett's unique "Pilot" tattoo. I needed it for personal reasons. It's only the photograph of that tattoo when he was on a slab which would calm the demons in me and the demons in the people on the floor above this one, and the demons in the people on the floor above them. For some personal reason I can't explain, his DNA or his dental records or fingerprint ID just wouldn't cut it. It had to be the photograph of that tattoo.'

217

'I think I can understand that,' Carmen Pharoah replied softly. 'It's become personal.'

'Yes . . . personal.' Allardyce clenched his fist. 'He's been a thorn in the side of the Metropolitan Police, and particularly the Serious Crime Squad, for years now . . . and I mean years. From even before I joined, and I have been in the SC Squad for longer than I'd care to admit.'

'Can you tell me why Garrett served only three years for murder?' Carmen Pharoah asked. 'It is something that puzzles my boss, Mr Hennessey and, quite frankly, it puzzles the rest of our team also and equally. Mr Hennessey specifically asked me to ask you about it.'

'Oh . . . well, the answer is that it is all about Garrett. It's all about him. I'll tell you about him, so you may as well get comfortable,' Allardyce sighed. 'So where do I begin . . .?' Allardyce turned and glanced out of his office window. 'Where do I start?'

Carmen Pharoah followed his gaze. She saw the blue sky with scattered clouds at three-tenths, in Royal Air Force speak, and her eye was particularly caught by a Qantas 747 jumbo jet airliner, distinctive by the white kangaroo logo on the red tail plane, which was making its final cautious, slow approach to Heathrow Airport with a slightly nose-up attitude and undercarriage safely lowered. No one, she pondered, drawing on her own experience of flying, no one was talking on that aeroplane at that moment. The passenger cabin would be in complete silence. The passengers in the window seats would be staring out and down at the roof tops and the streets and the famous buildings of London town, some seeing the city for the first time, some enjoying their home-coming . . . but no one, not one single soul, would be talking.

'Well, Anthony Garrett . . .' Allardyce turned back from the window and held eye contact with Carmen Pharoah, then broke it. 'He was a crim-inals' criminal. He knew the rules and he had a hand in every major crime which took place in this city . . . well, practically every major crime. He was to London what Al Capone was to Chicago in the 1930s. He was never part of any job as such. He never actually took part is what I mean, but he was the Mr Big behind the scenes, pulling the strings. If a major turn went down you could be pretty well almost one hundred per cent certain that Garrett was the fixer who had put the team together, worked out the job and took a generous cut of whatever was half-inched. He held the London underworld in the grip of fear. He was one of about three crime lords in London before his arrest but he was definitely the biggest, the most powerful, and his tentacles were everywhere and they didn't seem to have any boundaries. No limits at all. He didn't keep to one part of London as it was in the 1960s when the Kray twins ruled London north of the river and the Richardson gang ruled the south of the river. It wasn't like that. Anthony Garrett *was* London crime, and I mean Greater London crime.'

'I see.' Carmen Pharoah drank her tea and was finding it not the unpleasant experience she had been anticipating. 'The Krays were before my

219

time but I have heard of them . . . and I have read about them. Charlie Richardson's gang was also before my time but I have heard about his gang as well as the Kray twins.'

'Who hasn't?' Nigel Allardyce smiled. 'Well, what copper anyway? We heard about Garrett's firm from felons who were willing to talk but they were obviously in great fear of the man . . . getting information, hard facts, getting evidence which would have stood up in court . . . well, the words "blood" and "stone" come readily to mind.'

'I know what you mean,' Carmen Pharoah replied. 'As you say . . . like drawing teeth. You paint a clear picture of the man, totally out of reach, and clearly knowing how to stay out of reach.'

'Yes, this is why the good people on the floors above my humble floor were all particularly anxious to see the photograph of the tattoo. It is the one thing we wanted to see. So we sent Harry Kelto north with his box Brownie and, now, finally, it is as though a ghost has been laid.'

'So the murder for which he was convicted?' Carmen Pharoah pressed. 'What was the story there? It does seem somewhat out of character for him to get himself convicted.'

'Well, yes . . . yes, it was out of character, as you say.' Nigel Allardyce clasped his hands together. 'It was quite a turn up for the books, and, as you say, quite out of character for him to get himself caught like that, totally bang to rights. I can't say he let his heart rule his head because he hasn't got a heart, or he didn't have

220

one. So I'll just say that in respect of the murder he committed, he seemed to let his emotions get the better of him, they totally ran away with him. He was always so calm, so calculating, from what we could learn, so always in control and then for just one incident, he loses all self-control. The incident was outside the criminal world and was a so-called "domestic". In short, he murdered his wife. He was by all accounts a so-called "control freak" at home. It was alleged, for example, that his wife couldn't breathe without his permission . . . that would have been an exaggeration, of course, but it does shed light on the sort of man he was. Anyway, the upshot was that his wife eventually had had enough, she grabbed the kids and escaped to the safety, she thought, of a women's refuge. Garrett was given the phone number of the refuge so that he could phone her and arrange access meetings with the children. You know the number, arrange to meet in a neutral public place, collect the children and then return them at a pre-arranged time or date.'

'Yes.' Carmen Pharoah nodded her head. 'Quite the usual arrangement in such circumstances. Quite normal.'

'Yes, but Garrett,' Allardyce continued, 'was not the sort of man to take his wife walking out on him lying down. He took it as a personal slight. He could treat her like a dog but she could not leave him, especially she could not leave him *and* take the children . . . it seemed he had that sort of attitude. You will doubtless have come across it?'

'Many times,' Carmen Pharoah replied, 'many,

many times. Too many times really, especially when I worked in the Female and Child Unit. In fact, I often failed to see what some women ever saw in the man they married.'

'Yes, I am sure you saw much of that sort of thing.' Allardyce unclasped his hands. 'Well . . . to cut a long story short, it seems that Anthony Garrett had a mate and said mate had a mate who worked for the telephone company and in his position with the phone company he could access the addresses of the ex-directory numbers.'

'Oh . . . no . . .' Carmen Pharoah put her hand to her mouth. 'I think that I can guess where this is going . . . but please, don't let me interrupt. Please continue.'

'Yes,' Allardyce folded his arms in front of him, 'you'll be guessing correctly, I'm sure. But just to confirm, Garrett asked his mate to obtain the address of the refuge from the ex-directory phone number. So said mate asked his mate who worked for the company if he could provide the address of the refuge so he could let his mate have it so he could go round to the refuge and talk to his wife and rescue his marriage. Anyway, the prize idiot that he clearly was acceded to the request and gave out the address of the hostel, or refuge, to his friend, who duly passed it on to Garrett.'

'Yes,' Carmen Pharoah groaned, 'I did indeed guess correctly.'

'Anyway, it was the case that Garrett's idea of rescuing his marriage was to go round to the hostel taking a twelve-inch carving knife with him. He burst into the hostel, smashing his way in like the lock wasn't there, demanding to know where his wife was. Someone pressed the alarm which connects directly to the police station but it didn't help Mrs Garrett. He found her in the television lounge and plunged the knife into her chest a multitude of times, claret spilled everywhere, so I was advised . . . women and children screaming. You can well imagine the scene . . . total panic . . . mayhem, pure mayhem. Then, job done, he sits down and watches television waiting for the police to come and fondle his collar.'

'An awful, terrible story, very annoying really.' Carmen Pharoah drained her mug of tea and placed it on Allardyce's desk. 'That was a tragedy which could have been so easily avoided. A bit more common sense on the part of the phonecompany employee and it wouldn't have happened. Did the Crown Prosecution Service prosecute the idiot employee of the phone company?'

'No, no they didn't,' Allardyce shook his head. 'There was believed to be no criminal intent on his part. He didn't accept a bribe, for example, and they decided that no purpose was to be served by prosecuting him. As you know the CPS will only prosecute if there is a purpose to be served. The man lost his job, of course, and was not likely to get another one, not one that was worth having anyway . . . and the press and the television news were all over it like a London fog and one camera crew caught a few seconds of footage of him running along the front of his house and then down the side of the building to the safety of his back garden. So, for him, that was like guilt in a goldfish bowl. Every way he turned he'd come face to face with someone who knew what he had done . . . all his relatives, close and distant, his friends, his neighbours, all his colleagues . . . no matter how junior . . . there was just no escape for him . . . and how his enemies would gloat.'

'As you say,' Carmen Pharoah replied, 'all the damage that could be done was done. There was no purpose to be served in prosecuting him. I can see that now, but it still makes me angry.'

'As you say . . .' Allardyce opened and closed his palms. 'Everyone was a loser in that situation. The wretched Mrs Garrett lost her life when she was probably less than halfway through her life expectancy. Garrett lost his liberty by collecting his nominal life sentence for murder, and the telephone company employee lost his job and probably any prospect of future employment. Just losers all round, and arguably and most irritatingly, the least damaged of the three was Garrett himself. The judge didn't set a minimum tariff and so he was out in just three years, and he came out to the fortune which he had squirreled away, with his multiple bank accounts and a large property portfolio. He came out to a lot of money waiting for him.'

'So how did he manage to obtain such an early release?' Carmen Pharoah's eye was caught again by another airliner slowly and steadily descending towards Heathrow Airport. 'Even for a so-called "domestic" that is a very early release; I mean there was clear pre-meditation on Garrett's part.'

'Well,' Allardyce reclined in his chair, 'you ask

the question . . . It seems that Garrett, who played by the rules when he was on the outside and had displayed loyalty to anyone on his side of the fence, rapidly grew to dislike being a guest of Her Majesty, and he let it be known to the police that he would be willing to scratch our backs if we would scratch his. He would give us some very good information in return for early parole, and Wormwood Scrubs isn't the most comfortable of Her Majesty's guesthouses.'

'Ah . . . I see,' Carmen Pharoah nodded slightly, 'now the early parole makes sense.'

'Yes, and being the Mr Fix-it that he was, he knew a great deal but he made it plain that he would only talk to the police if he was moved out of London. If he was seen making too many trips to the agents' room for an hour at a time and arrests happened shortly afterwards then, he argued, the lags would get suspicious and his life would be in danger. So he was moved north.'

'To Full Sutton,' Carmen Pharoah advised, 'just outside York.'

'Ah, I did wonder where he went.' Allardyce folded his hands together once again. 'I could have found out very easily, but I never got around to it. I was only interested in the information that was streaming down from the north.' Allardyce paused. 'So, once in the north and because of that then in some degree of safety, he began to come up with the goods, and he began to name names, and to tell us where we'd find things. He wouldn't give a statement, and he wouldn't enter the witness box but, as I said, he told us who did what and where we'd find evidence which would put people away, and he told us who'd be a good bet to lean on to persuade to turn Queen's evidence, which we did, and which we got. In fact, Garrett gave shedloads of information and because of that information we managed to shut down a few firms, and we solved many cold cases and one or two gangland murders. We managed to put a lot of people away and so it was a most welcome result. So, as I said, it was all very scratchy back time. Garrett had come up with the goods and he promised more once he was on the outside and so strings were pulled, words were put in ears, and, hey presto, he was released on licence. He continued to give good information after he was released. We'd drive up north and meet him in supermarket car parks or other public places. We would meet once a month, or once every six weeks, that sort of frequency, he would dictate the point of rendezvous and it was never the same place twice. We continued to make some good arrests and obtain prosecutions, and then he stopped contacting us. We knew that he had quite a lot of money put by, mostly in property, and he could raise a lot of cash when he wanted to by selling one of his houses. Sadly he was not liable for an asset-seizure order because the crime for which he was committed did not involve theft or extortion.'

'I see,' Carmen Pharoah replied. 'So he went to prison a rich man and he came out a very short time later still a rich man. No assets could be seized, as you say.'

'Yes, in a nutshell. But he was no longer safe.' Allardyce leaned forward and rested his elbows on his desk. 'You see the jungle drums had started to sound, and they sounded loud and clear. The underworld started putting two and two together, they considered who had been arrested and convicted, which cold cases were being closed, if the bodies which had been dug up from shallow graves in Epping Forest, where evidence was found by the police, which evidence was found plastered into the walls of which person's house, or dug up from the concrete of some person's back-garden pathway, as if the police knew where to find it. I mean, exactly where to look. One common denominator was Anthony Garrett, who had been removed to another prison in the north. It was rapidly realized that Garrett had turned supergrass. So the knives were out for him. Contracts on his life were issued but no one knew where he was. Then just a few months ago, perhaps going back about eighteen months, that sort of time, he started being seen in London. He was disguised, but it was Garrett, so we were told. So now it seems that he was traced to his hidey-hole and someone fulfilled a contract. Someone has drilled him, job done and money collected. The mighty has fallen. Do you have any leads at all, can I ask?'

'Just one, just the one line of enquiry.' Carmen Pharoah adjusted her position in the chair. 'At about the time he was murdered he was known to have been visited by three women who we have discovered to be the solicitors of a firm of solicitors in the East End of London called Middlemiss, Middlemiss and Middlemiss.'

'You are joking!' Allardyce shot backwards in

his chair and did so with a sagging jaw and dilating eyes. 'Tell me you are not serious!'

'Very serious.' Carmen Pharoah thought Allardyce's surprise to be genuine. 'Very serious indeed,' she continued softly, 'my governor wants me to call on them, to put the cat amongst the pigeons, if you like, make them flap a little, just to see how they react when they realize that we have tracked them down. You sound as though you know about them?'

'Know them!' Allardyce, having collected himself, once again leaned forward. 'I'll say we know them. I'll say we know them. They are real criminals' lawyers. I mean lawyers for real criminals. If you ask me they are very low-minded lawyers, all three of them. You see they come from the East End, and so they grew up among criminals and their peers became criminals. Each took a law degree from one of the new universities, not from an old, much respected, ivy covered institution which produces High Court judges and the like, but they qualified just the same and they set up their firm in the East End and they rapidly developed a reputation for getting their clients off the hook on technicalities, so much so that they became known as the "Loophole Ladies". They became part and parcel of the underworld as much as any criminal and were fully accepted by them because they'd gone to the same tough council schools as their clients. They didn't defend their clients via barristers, if it got to court, as the more conservative high-minded members of the legal profession would do, but they would find loopholes for their clients to slip through.

228

Theirs is a more cynical, low-minded approach to law. They won't do civil cases, only criminal work. Civil cases, like house conveyancing, would be too much like hard work for them, so only criminal work, much easier for the "Loophole Ladies". They're not fat cats; they only work for Legal Aid.' Nigel Allardyce paused. 'The ladies . . . now what I am about to tell you, and this is just between you and me and the gatepost. Fair enough?'

'Understood.' Carmen Pharoah drew her finger across her mouth. 'Totally within these four walls.'

'Thank you,' Allardyce nodded. 'Well, within these four walls, as you say, we believe that they actually do more than help their clients after they, the clients, have committed a crime. Information has come our way from more than one source that the ladies actually advise their clients on how to plan their crimes – they are reportedly helping them avoid prosecution in the first place.'

'Now it is you who are joking,' Carmen Pharoah gasped. 'Lawyers can't do that!'

'Not joking at all,' Allardyce held eye contact with Carmen Pharoah, 'I kid you not. There is no evidence of that, of course, there is only one client and one of those "ladies" in the room at any one time so there are no witnesses and of course, nothing is written down. It's all verbal advice, all word of mouth.'

'They could get struck off for that!' Carmen Pharoah felt a growing sense of anger.

'They could be charged with a criminal offence such as aiding and abetting, or such as accessory before the fact,' Allardyce continued. 'It is a very

229

serious game that they are playing, very serious. It has huge risks involved. We have been told that they will also put criminals in touch with each other, so that if a gang planning a job suddenly needs a replacement wheelman, they'll contact the "Loophole Ladies" who'll tell them who to phone or they'll put them in touch with credible people who are prepared to sell alibis, or they will help young bloods contact a gunsmith, for which services the "ladies" will have an envelope of hard cash, in used notes of course, pushed through their letter box at night.'

'My . . .' Carmen Pharoah gasped. 'That is a dangerous game they play.'

'Their latest suggestion was to a team of ram-raiders who they told to alter the number plates of the cars they were to use to ram the windows of the shops they intended to raid.'

'Cloned plates?' Carmen Pharoah suggested. 'Every criminal knows the value of cloned plates.'

'Nothing so high-tech,' Allardyce grinned. 'No . . . what the ladies suggested was low-tech, ultra-low-tech at that. They allegedly suggested to the criminals in question, their clients, to alter the registration number of the vehicle or vehicles they intended to use with a few strips of carefully placed black adhesive tape, just prior to the crime. You see an "L" can be very easily doctored to look like an "E" as can an "F". A "3" can be made to look like an "8".'

'A "C" turned into an "O",' Carmen Pharoah offered, 'and a "P" into a "B".'

'Yes, exactly.' Allardyce nodded. 'So at night an ANPR camera might record a suspect vehicle with the number plate ENB 280, and the number goes straight into the Automatic Number Plate Recognition computer, but in fact the real number is LN6 230. The ruse won't fool the mark-one eyeball when close up so the felons still have to worry about traffic cops and the bobby on the beat, but it is sufficient to fool the camera, and if the tape is removed soon after the job, then the suspect car can be driven past the cameras without being recognized. Cheaper and easier than cloned plates. Anyway, we found that out about the Middlemiss sisters because a team of ram-raiders did what all criminals do eventually . . .'

'They slipped up, you mean?' Carmen Pharoah suggested. 'As they all do, if they commit crime often enough, they'll make a mistake.'

'Yes . . . as you say,' Allardyce smiled briefly. 'So at night the doctored plate was caught on CCTV, and the CCTV operator reported the false number which was only altered by one letter, an "L" to an "E" I believe, but once the tape had been removed that was sufficient to permit the vehicle to drive past the ANPR cameras without triggering the alarm. We knew the type of vehicle we were looking for, a Range Rover with a distinct non-standard two-tone colour scheme which they had used to ram-raid a jeweller's shop. Shortly after the raid two traffic cops saw a vehicle of that description tucked away in the driveway of a house in a cul-de-sac, so they investigated. They noted the similarity of the number plate of the car to the number plate sought. So they knocked on the door most gently and politely and the felons were surrounded by Rolex watches and diamonds and other assorted "bling" from the jewellery shop. So they were nicked and then, being sensible young men, decided to work for themselves. They were not going to turn Queen's evidence, but it was that team who told us about the Middlemiss sisters, the so-called "Loophole Ladies", and they told us that it was the sisters Middlemiss who had suggested altering the car's number plates with the short strips of black adhesive tape in the manner described. Very KISS.'

'KISS?' Carmen Pharoah queried.

'Keep-it-simple-Simon,' Nigel Allardyce explained. 'Using tape is easier than obtaining cloned plates which take time to fit and to remove, and if you can avoid being seen by constables in the immediate vicinity of the car, then all you have to do is to fool the CCTV operator. But, of course, all we had was hearsay, but useful hearsay all the same. We'd rather have it than not have it.'

'Of course,' Carmen Pharoah sat back in her chair, 'but so frustrating that it's only hearsay.'

'That's the word, frustrating,' Allardyce took a deep breath, 'and it was the same sort of hearsay which reached our ears about Garrett being seen in the East End, from Aldgate to all points east. It's the so-called "Ramsgate Factor", you see.'

'You mean the pull of your roots?' Carmen Pharoah clarified. 'That I can fully understand.'

'Yes, that's it,' Allardyce replied. 'You seem to feel it?'

'Well I dare say I do, I won't deny it,' Carmen

Pharoah admitted. 'I had many happy times in Ramsgate as a child. Our summer holidays were always spent in Kent . . . Ramsgate, Margate, Herne Bay. We went on educational and cultural trips as well as spending the days by the sea, trips to Canterbury Cathedral, for example, and other places of interest. So yes, I know of the so-called "Ramsgate Factor". I know it well, all too well.'

'So that's the pull which evidently made Anthony Garrett return for a day here and there, wearing a disguise, but he was seen and recognized as being Garrett, definitely Garrett, and if the "Loophole Ladies" were involved with Garrett's death, probably finding him for somebody to fulfil a contract out on him, they would have used their contacts to have him traced on their client's behalf. They wouldn't do the leg work themselves, not those three, they would most likely have used the "Ferret",' Allardyce explained. 'Him they would have used, most likely.'

'The Ferret,' Carmen Pharoah raised an eyebrow. 'He sounds . . . how shall I put it? He sounds to be a person of interest.'

'Oh, he is, in his own way. In fact, I'll take you to meet him, if you wish. But . . . but . . .' Allardyce held up an admonishing finger, 'do not go and visit the Middlemiss sisters, not alone, go mob-handed and then only if you have enough grounds for an arrest and have a warrant with you. I don't care what your boss wants you to do. You're dealing with lawyers who are as slippery as . . . as a boat-load of jellied eels.'

'I'll take your advice on that, it sounds like sound local knowledge.' Carmen Pharoah nodded. 'Thank you for that. I appreciate it. I'm sure my governor will understand.'

'So . . . let me ask you,' Allardyce pressed, 'do you have anything else to tie them to the murder of Anthony Garrett, other than the fact that they were in the vicinity of York at about the time he was murdered?'

'Yes . . . yes we do,' Carmen Pharoah advised, 'but I have been told to be discreet, to keep that to myself. I am sorry, but I am under strict orders in that respect.'

Allardyce held up his hand. 'I fully understand. Fully understand. Walls have ears and all that. But I'll buy you lunch in our canteen.' Allardyce stood. 'If we go now we'll beat the crush. It's hardly fine dining . . . it's hardly the Savoy Grill, but it will fill the gap. After lunch we'll pay a call on the Ferret.'

After a lunch which Carmen Pharoah found to be filling, but uninteresting, though better than the fare she was used to in the Micklegate Bar Police Station canteen, Allardyce drove Carmen Pharoah on a slow, halting journey from New Scotland Yard to Radland Road, Canning Town. Radland Road, Carmen Pharoah observed, was a short, straight road bounded by a well-kept recreation ground on the one side, and a row of new-build four-storey local-authority houses on the other. A bus shelter with multiple route numbers indicated that the area was well served by the public transport system.

'This whole area was bombed flat in the Second

234

World War.' Allardyce halted the car by the side of the road opposite to the bus shelter. 'They were dockworkers' houses, apparently. You must know the type, or have seen photographs of two up two down in terraces with backyards and shared privies. This part of London bore the brunt of the Blitz and after the war the new grew out of the old. It's a fairly good area to live now. The "Ferret" lives back there.' He jerked his left thumb over his shoulder. 'We'll have to walk I'm afraid. I couldn't park any closer, this was the nearest gap, but we're young and fit . . . we can cope with a short walk,' Allardyce added with a smile.

The 'Ferret' lived in a flat on the second floor of a housing block. Carmen Pharoah noticed it to be kept tidy but it was also spartan with inexpensive furnishings. She saw immediately why the man was called the 'Ferret'. He was short, he was very slender but muscular; he had a sharply pointed nose between a sloping fore-head and a very weak chin. His eyes were cold, piercing, predatory. Carmen Pharoah noticed how the man welcomed Nigel Allardyce as one might have welcomed a disliked relative: coldly, and it was, thought Pharoah, as if he talked to Allardyce because he had to talk to him. The 'Ferret' sat in an inexpensive-looking armchair by the side of an empty fire grate and did so in what Carmen Pharoah thought to be a feminine pose with both legs folded up beneath him. Carmen Pharoah noticed that the fire grate had, by the time she and Allardyce visited that summer, become a receptacle for anything small and combustible, cigarette packets in the main.

'You found Anthony Garrett.' Allardyce, having introduced Carmen Pharoah, drove straight to the point but he did so with a smile.

'You asking or telling, Mr Allardyce?' The 'Ferret' spoke with a strong East London accent. Carmen Pharoah noticed that he pointedly ignored her, probably she felt because she was a woman, or because she was black. Or both. Probably both, she decided, probably both. 'Are you asking or telling?' he repeated.

'It doesn't matter which,' Allardyce replied, 'we know you did. We have heard that he'd been seen in the Smoke and if there's one person who could run him to ground, it's you. You have that reputation. It's a skill you have. Something to be proud of.'

The 'Ferret' shrugged, though Carmen Pharoah thought that Nigel Allardyce's compliment clearly mollified the man. She also liked the way Allardyce worked, by appealing to people's vanity.

'So come on . . . it was you who found him, wasn't it?' Allardyce pressed. 'It would take someone of your skill to find a quarry like Anthony Garrett.'

'Yes, I found him, this I did,' the 'Ferret' smiled with self-satisfaction. 'It wasn't a hard old job, I've had harder jobs, a lot harder old jobs, but I found Garrett when half of London was looking for him, it was me that found him. Me. He offed his old lady, he did, he gutted her like a herring. He treated her like a dog so eventually she'd had enough and she grabbed her kids and walked out on him but no one does that to Anthony Garrett, like no one. So he finds out where she's living

236

and he goes round there and he separates her from her life . . . this he does, and he does so very messily and very publicly. So he is sent down the line to the "Scrubs". He collected life. Well, it was murder, wasn't it? He does a year in the old "Scrubs" then he gets transferred to another prison somewhere outside London. Then the Old Bill starts arresting a lot of good boys. The Bill start finding evidence where they would not normally look and that makes rumours fly most freely and most widely . . . this they do . . . most freely and most widely and many people suddenly want a chat with Mr Anthony Garrett because they think that only he will know where all the evidence is to be found. It is believed that he has turned into a grass, because he can't do his bird and wants back on the streets. But he has gone to ground like a hunted fox, and this is all about twenty years ago and the people stop looking for him because they don't know where to look. Things begin to die down for Garrett, they do.'

The Ferret continued to address Allardyce, persistently ignoring Carmen Pharoah. 'Then he is seen about a year ago now, rumours begin to circulate that Garrett is being seen from time to time. He just can't ever hope to stay away from dear old London town; he can't ever hope to do that. So he's been naughty, grassing villains up right and left, breaking the criminals' old code, so he is staying away. For many years he is staying away but then he must have thought it was safe for him to return. He is seen in disguise, so he thinks it is not fully safe for him in the

"Smoke", but safe if he has a disguise, but it is Anthony Garrett all right. It's like you see a geezer walking down the street and you clock him once and then forget about him, then two or three days later you suddenly realize it was Anthony Garrett you saw, twenty years older, and in disguise, but it was Garrett. It's the little things, the way he walks, the way he moves his body, little things like that which you can't hide with a wig. This you do . . . or someone clocks a geezer with long hair and a beard and spectacles standing at the bar in a battle cruiser minding his own business and then the next day he realizes it was Garrett at the bar, the geezer with a beard is Garrett. People begin to see him more and more often so he's feeling more and more safe. So I gets a job offer. This I do. A nice old job offer.'

'Who offered you the job?' Allardyce asked.

The 'Ferret' smirked and tapped the side of his nose with his right index finger. 'Them that asks no questions get told no lies.' He paused. 'But it's what I do, that's why they call me the "Ferret". It's not because I look like one, I've been told that often enough, it's also because I can get down any hole and whatever is down there I can ferret it out. Ferret, stoat, weasel . . . they're all the same. You want something out of a hole; you send one of those beasts down it. It is what I have become in life but I make some good money, and I made some very good money from those people who hired me to find Garrett. I don't splash it about. I live like this to look like I got nothing but I got a bank account with

238

some useful dosh in it. If I flashed my dosh there's folk who'd take it off me, so I look like I got nothing but I'll never go hungry. This is how I have lived for many years and no one has burgled my house, not once.'

'People?' Carmen Pharoah echoed. 'You said "people". So more than one person hired you to find Anthony Garrett? Two was it . . . or perhaps three . . .?'

The Ferret shot a cold and a piercing glare at Carmen Pharoah, and he pointed a long finger at her. 'I could order you out of my house. This I could do,' he snarled. 'You don't have no warrant. This I see. This I could do.'

'That's true,' Allardyce spoke calmly, 'but it's also true that I could bounce you into custody on any one of half a dozen charges. We have a good idea who those people are but we won't tell them it was you who told us who hired you. So if you want to stay safe when you go to the battle cruiser for a beer, tell us how you found him.'

The Ferret sat back in his PVC-covered chair as if he had been stung. He fell silent as if in protest, and then replied but did so clearly on his terms. 'I was told where he'd been seen,' he began. 'I know Garrett from the old days when I was a gofer for a small gang of villains . . . so he wouldn't recognize me. I was small fry when he was a very big fish, so I could recognize him. So I used to go to the pubs he'd been seen in, up West Ham, round here in Canning Town, over Stepney way . . . all over the East End really, Whitechapel, Shoreditch, Spitalfields . . . all over

I went. This I did. But I was given spending money to do that, so I wasn't buying my own beer. So who was complaining? Not I. Then I saw him in a battle cruiser in Whitechapel . . . this I do. Beard, spectacles, but it was him all right. No mistake, it was him in that boozer that day, standing at the bar enjoying his pint of good London beer. So I go outside and I wait for him to come out and I have not a long time to wait because soon he does so. When he comes out I tag along behind him. This I do. Down into the Tube he goes, down I go after him, and he goes to King's Cross and I follow him up to the main-line railway station. He stands in a queue for the mainline train and I stand behind him, just a little way behind him. When the queue starts to move I see it is for a train to Aberdeen and so then I peel off, smoothly, I do, and come back home to Canning Town where I feel comfortable and I go down to the boozer to have a pint because I know that I am by then on my way to earning my wedge, and a very nice old wedge it was, four figures, halfway to five figures, more than halfway to the big five, plus expenses. My clients, they wanted Anthony Garrett found all right. They wanted him bad.

'So then I wait. This I do. It is all I can do. I wait. I wait for three weeks, perhaps four, but I am always looking for him, and then I see him walking down Commercial Road, so I go to King's Cross and I buy a return ticket to Aberdeen and I wait for him to come to the railway station. It's a long wait, but I must wait if I want my wedge, and I wanted my money. This I do. He comes many hours later and he joins a queue for the train but I see he has joined the queue for a Newcastle train. So he is not living in Scotland. I join the same queue and I travel in the same coach as he does, sitting where I can see him, and he gets off at York.'

'I knew you were going to say that.' Carmen Pharoah crossed her legs and earned herself another angry glare from the 'Ferret', who clearly didn't like being interrupted. 'Otherwise it would be a member of the Northumbrian Police sitting here, wouldn't it? But please do carry on.'

After another pause, the 'Ferret' continued. 'So I follow him off the train and out of the station. This I do.' The 'Ferret' continued to address Nigel Allardyce, still ignoring Carmen Pharoah. 'He turns left and then enters a car park close to the railway station.'

'Leeman Road car park,' Carmen Pharoah offered. 'I know where you are.'

'So I wait at the entrance of the car park and he drives out in a little blue van, still with his beard and spectacles, and I am able to note a partial number plate XMS . . . easy to remember. Like XMAS but without the "a". So now I am too late to return to London in time for a beer at my local boozer and so I take a room at a small hotel which suits the likes of little me, and in the morning I go looking for a gypsy cab.'

'Oh, interesting,' Carmen Pharoah commented.

'Oh,' Nigel Allardyce turned to her, 'why is that?'

'It's not really important, more of a coincidence really.' Carmen Pharoah inclined her head towards

Allardyce. 'It is just that gypsy cabs have featured once in this investigation already.'

'Ah . . . I see,' Allardyce nodded. 'Sorry . . . please carry on.' He addressed the 'Ferret'.

'So,' the 'Ferret' carried on, 'the next morning I find a gypsy cab outside a hotel and I say to the driver that I want to book a ride and he says, *"To where?"* and I say I don't know and I don't know when and he says, *"You're having a laugh, aren't you, mate?"* so I say that I am not having a laugh and I offer him much money and then he becomes most very interested. Very interested indeed. So I say, *"Let me have your mobile phone number and I will phone you in a week or two and we'll meet by the car park near the railway station."* So this we agree to do.

'So about two weeks later, about, I see Garrett having a beer in the battle cruiser he likes a lot and as soon as I see him I travel to York. At York I phone the gypsy cab driver, who is called Roy, by the way, and we meet and wait by the car park. I told him it is going to be a long wait and he says he doesn't mind because he is being paid by the hour, not the mile. So we use the time to look at the cars in the car park and I see Garrett's little blue van is there and I point it out to Roy so he can recognize it then we go and wait by Roy's cab. This we do. Night falls and we continue to wait and then Garrett comes. We follow his little blue van, but it is night so we can get up close behind the van in the town because Garrett doesn't know he's being followed because all he sees is two headlights in his rear-view mirror. Roy is good anyway, like he's done this sort of thing before, and he lets two cars get between us and Garrett once we have left the built-up area, which is soon because York is like a big village compared to London. So we follow Garrett into a real village and he turns into a council-house estate and Roy says that he knows the estate. He says there is only one road in and the same road out. So at this news I am gleeful. My wedge is almost earned.

'Roy turns into the estate and we look for Garrett's little blue van which we think has to be parked somewhere because council houses do not have garages like the posh private house estates. But we cannot see a little blue van, no we can't, which muchly puzzles us both, so it does, until Roy has a think and he says that those estates sometimes have a few garages on them which residents can rent, so we drive around until we find the garages. So then we return to York and I pay Roy and he is pleased with what I pay him and I stay in a small hotel for the night, a different hotel to the last one, because I do not want to get known. Most certainly this I do.

'So the next day I take a bus to the village. I wrote the name of it down so I would not forget it. In the village I walked from the bus stop to the council estate and in the estate I walk to the garages. At the garages I stop and there is a man in mechanic's overalls who is working on the engine of a car and he eyes me most fiend-ishly but I smile and say hello to him most friendly. This I do. I then espy a path leading between two garages. It is not a proper pathway of concrete or bare earth, but a pathway caused by grass being much trampled. So I follow it. This I do. I come then to an area of wasteland, turned to neither building nor to farming, a natural area, and I see the path goes across this land and so I follow it. It comes out to a field of corn, at the side of the field is a hawthorn hedge so I follow the path which runs between the hedge and the cornfield and I see a large blue-painted house on the other side of the hedge with no other buildings beyond the house, but the path continues. So I think it is a good bet that this house is Garrett's house. This I think. So I wait. I hide and I wait. I look at the house and I find the kitchen, because I think that we all go into our kitchen more often than any other room during the old day. So I hide where I can see the kitchen. I can tell the kitchen because of the kitchen furniture, and racks of plates and rows of mugs from which to drink. I do not wait for very long, less than two hours, which in my line of work is a blink of an eye, and I see Garrett come into the kitchen but he doesn't see me. So I wait until he leaves the kitchen and then I stand up and return to the garages where the mechanic is still working on the car and he eyes me once again in a most fiendish manner, but this time I do not smile at him. I have no reason to smile at him. I have got what I have come to get and I do not need friends. Then I leave the estate and walk along the main road until I come to Garrett's house so as to obtain its name or street number. I see not a number but a name, 'The Grange', which I wrote down in my notebook, which I carry. This I do. Then by bus do I return to York. Then by train do I return to London. The next day I report my findings and those who have employed me to find Anthony Garrett are most pleased. Most pleased indeed. One job leads to another and my reputation is good. I am in a good way of business. This I am.'

'Dare say it's lucky we found you in, in that case.' Nigel Allardyce stood, as did Carmen Pharoah. 'Very lucky. Thank you for telling us what you have told us.'

Outside the 'Ferret's' flat, in Radland Road, Canning Town, Nigel Allardyce unlocked his car. 'Can I drop you near King's Cross?' he asked.

'No, but thank you,' Carmen Pharoah replied soberly, shielding her eyes against the sun's glare. 'I must go to where my husband lost his life, I must pay homage. If I see a florist I'll buy a bouquet of flowers, but if I don't see a flower shop it's of no consequence. But I must go and stand where it was he died. I'll find my own way to King's Cross later. I won't go and see the Middlemiss sisters, on your advice. I doubt my governor will be too upset that I did not "take the measure of them", not after what you have told me.'

'Keep 'em guessing.' Tobias Sherwood reclined in a deep armchair and raised his voice slightly so as to enable it to carry across the ocean of blue carpet which separated him from the four-seat settee upon which the young blonde woman sat. 'They are suspicious, of course, I expected that. I mean, no detective constable could afford a house like this and a Mercedes sports car. I don't take the car to work . . . that would be too much. But I have been visited by A10.'

'A10.' The blonde wore nothing but one of Sherwood's shirts, fastened at the middle by just two of the buttons.

'The anti-corruption squad,' Sherwood explained. 'Like a police force within a police force.'

'Ah, yes, also in my country we have the same.' The young blonde sipped her martini.

'But I stick to my story. I'll claim that I inherited the money before I joined the police, and I let them look at my bank account.' Sherwood sipped his malt whisky. 'But I kept details of the other account to myself and that black book is where they can't find it. They are suspicious, but cannot prove anything.'

'Like the Cayman Islands,' the woman suggested. 'Is it there?'

'A little closer but that's the idea. But . . .' Sherwood tapped the side of his nose. 'The less you know, the better.'

It was Friday, 15.43 hours.

Six

Monday 26 June, 14.34 hours – dusk

In which the three Middlemiss sisters return to York, a middle-aged couple enjoy each other's company in front of a log fire and a man has cause to wonder if a police officer's words of caution should be heeded.

The three Middlemiss sisters, who had given, and had been able to confirm, their names as Fiona, Felicity and Florence, were arrested by officers of the Metropolitan Police at their place of work shortly after nine a.m. on Monday 26 June in connection with the murder of Anthony Garrett. The sisters were taken to New Scotland Yard whereupon they were given into the custody of police officers from the Vale of York Police. Each was placed in a separate police vehicle and they were then conveyed in convoy to Micklegate Bar Police Station where they were placed in separate cells. After being given rest and refreshment under the terms of the Police and Criminal Evidence Act 1984 so as to prevent accusations of coercion and duress, the sisters were then escorted to separate interview rooms.

George Hennessey and Somerled Yellich entered interview room one and sat opposite Fiona

247

Middlemiss. She remained, Hennessey noted, calm and silent as he placed two blank audio-cassette tapes into the tape recorder, which was set in the wall behind the table at which he and Yellich and Fiona Middlemiss sat. Hennessey pressed the 'record' button and the red 'recording' light glowed softly and the twin tapes began to spool silently around.

'The date is Monday, the twenty-sixth of June, the time is 14.35 hours, the place is interview room one at Micklegate Bar Police Station in the city of York. I am Detective Chief Inspector Hennessey. I am now going to ask the other persons present to identify themselves.'

'Detective Sergeant Somerled Yellich of the Vale of York Police.'

'Fiona Middlemiss.' She spoke in a calm voice, thought Hennessey, but the East End of London accent was, he also thought, as clear as the bells of St Clement Danes.

'You have waived your right to legal representation. Is that correct, Miss Middlemiss?' Hennessey confirmed for the benefit of the tape.

'Yes.' Fiona Middlemiss remained calm. She was dressed in a black pinstripe suit with a three-quarter-length skirt and a red blouse. She wore dark-shaded nylons, and patent-leather shoes with small 'sensible' heels encased her feet. She wore a pearl necklace with matching earrings, and a gold lady's watch hung loosely on her left wrist. Her hair was short and dark. Her lipstick was of a pale shade. 'I am one, as you know, and I specialize in criminal law. I don't need legal representation.'

'Understood and noted,' Hennessey continued. 'You have been arrested in connection with the death . . . the murder of Anthony Garrett, of The Grange, Millington, in the Vale of York.'

'Yes,' Fiona Middlemiss's reply was clear. 'Yes,' she repeated, 'I know. The Metropolitan Police notified us of that this morning when we were arrested.'

'You were arrested having been identified as probably being one of the three ladies seen at the home of the deceased on the day it was believed that he was murdered. Were you and your sisters at Mr Garrett's house on Saturday the seventeenth of this month?'

'Yes,' Fiona Middlemiss remained stone-faced, 'yes, all three of us were there, me and my two sisters. Often we are taken as triplets but we are sisters, just one year apart. I am the eldest. Florence is the youngest. But yes, we were there on that day.'

'What is . . . or was your connection with the deceased, Mr Anthony Garrett?' Hennessey probed.

'He was our father,' Fiona Middlemiss advised, still betraying no emotion. 'And my sister Felicity murdered him.'

Hennessey and Yellich glanced at each other. Both officers thought that it could not be as easy as this. Especially not with three sisters who were well versed in criminal law.

'Would you . . .' Hennessey asked, 'like to tell us . . . and for the benefit of the tape, what happened?'

'Oh, yes . . . willingly, most willingly. You see, me and my sisters are always very willing to cooperate with the police.' Fiona Middlemiss paused. 'You see the background to all this was that our father was a tyrant, a bully, a so-called control freak. He was emotionally, verbally and physically violent in our home. I won't go into details; I'll let your imaginations, as clearly very experienced police officers, do that for me. Well, it went on for years and got worse, until Mummy could no longer cope and she picked up me and my sisters and ran to the Housing Department offices. She told them the whole sad story and so they found us temporary accommodation in a refuge for battered wives and their children. We found ourselves crammed in a box room but at least it was a room of our own, and for once we had no one to be in constant fear of. The hostel, or refuge, was an old Victorian house with some huge rooms where three or four families shared one room, with a dormitory for boys over the age of eleven in the attic. It was more like a hospital with beds in wards than a hostel. There was a self-catering kitchen and a TV lounge. Anyway, Father found out where we were. He did that by . . .'

'Yes,' Hennessey held up his hand, 'we know the story there. Do go on, please.'

'Yes . . . but talk about naivety . . . I mean naivety is just not the word, giving the address of the hostel to help Father rescue his marriage . . .' Fiona Middlemiss glanced downwards at the floor and shook her head. 'You know Mummy was still in her thirties when she was murdered, and her mother, Granny Middlemiss . . .'

'So you took your mother's maiden name?'

Hennessey clarified. 'I was going to ask you about your surname.'

'Yes, we changed our surname by deed poll as soon as we came of age. We didn't want his name. We didn't want to be Garretts, none of us did, not after what he did to Mummy.' Fiona Middlemiss returned her gaze to Hennessey, while also glancing at Yellich from time to time. 'Well . . . Mummy . . . she was just a lovely woman, a lovely parent, and Father . . . well, as I said, he was just the opposite. But to continue, Granny Middlemiss was alive when Mummy was murdered, and she, Granny Middlemiss, went on to live into her nineties . . . so there was no reason why Mummy should not have had a long life. You see the greater part of Mummy's life was probably still ahead of her. She could have had another fifty-plus years of life, she would have seen her daughters married, she would have had her grandchildren, all that was robbed off her by a man who thought that she was his possession. Anyway, Father collected his nominal life sentence but was paroled after just three years. How he managed that we don't know but there were rumours flying about that he was helping the Old Bill, too many felons who had worked for him were getting arrested, and there was talk of contracts out on him, but no one knew where he was. He'd gone well to ground all right. Well to ground.'

'Yes,' Hennessey nodded, 'he vanished off the radar one year after he was released from Full Sutton Prison. We understand he had the means to do that?'

'Yes . . . he had plenty of money put by,' Fiona Middlemiss confirmed. 'Or rather plenty of assets rather than money in the bank, assets usually in the form of property, houses which he could sell using an agent whenever he wanted a cash injection. Then, about a year ago, rumours began to circulate that he'd been seen in London, visiting his old haunts. He was older of course, and he was disguising himself, but people were sure it was him; even our clients mentioned it to us, like . . . "I'm certain I saw your old man walking down Commercial Road, long hair, beard, spectacles but I am sure it was him. He has that walk as if he expects people to get out of his way . . . sure it was him", that sort of thing was said to us. So we hired someone we use now and again if we want someone found. He's good at it.'

'The "Ferret".' Hennessey nodded. 'Yes, we have – well, one of my team has met him, but he was very discreet. He didn't say who he was working for, but we did assume that it was you and your sisters who had hired him.'

'And I won't admit or confirm that it was the "Ferret".' She pointed to the tape recorder. 'I won't have him drawn in as an accessory, even if it was him, and he certainly didn't know Felicity was going to murder him. I must make that very plain for the benefit of the tape. He was hired to find someone. He didn't ask why we wanted Anthony Garrett found, and he was not told why.'

'All right,' Hennessey held up his hand, palm outwards, 'we're not interested in him, anyway. He's not in the frame for anything if he was

252

genuinely in ignorance of why he was finding Anthony Garrett.'

'Which he was, if it was him,' Fiona Middlemiss added, 'if it was him.'

'So why did you three visit him?' Hennessey leaned forward, resting his elbows on the tabletop.

'Because he had murdered Mummy . . . because we wanted to tell him what we thought of him . . . because we wanted him to know that we knew where he lived and that we'd be making no secret of his address when we returned to London. Now that, let me tell you, Mr Hennessey and Mr Yellich, that would have put the fear of God into him. As I said, there are many knives seeking him and now they'd know where to look. People knew he'd been talking to the police,' Fiona Middlemiss added, 'and he would know that he was a dead man if found. He was a bully, and like all bullies, he was a coward. He'd have to run away and start all over again, and he wouldn't like that because he would know that for him it was a case of "he can run but he can't hide", not with the man we use to find people. We know a few criminals, we know what the East End villains think of him . . . we are people's lawyers.'

'Yes,' Hennessey growled, 'we have heard about your law firm, and the advice it gives.'

Fiona Middlemiss grinned broadly. 'We help our own. We are three good East End girls. We have not turned our backs on our roots.'

'So . . . the next question,' Hennessey continued, 'is why did only your sister Felicity go into the house? Why did you and Florence stay outside?

We have interviewed the taxi driver you hired to drive you out to Millington. He gave us that information.'

'I see.' Fiona Middlemiss remained calm, and seemed utterly content.

'And a neighbour was also observing you from her house on the opposite side of the road. She also states that only one of you went into the house.'

'Really!' Fiona Middlemiss beamed enthusiastically with evident satisfaction. 'That really is most useful.'

'Useful?' Hennessey queried. 'Why should that be useful?'

'It just is, as you will shortly find out,' Fiona Middlemiss replied calmly. 'But to answer your question, when we got to the house, we felt only one of us needed to go in and to tell him what we came a long way to tell him. It just needed one of us to let him know that he had been found, and then walk away, leaving him to absorb the implications of that information. None of us wanted to see him. None of us wanted to go into his wretched house, so Felicity volunteered. Florence and I waited outside. Very soon after she had entered the house Felicity re-emerged and the three of us walked back to the taxi.

'Both myself and my sister Florence were in total ignorance of what Felicity had planned, of the fact that she carried a gun in her handbag, that she had shot Father and murdered him, because we did not hear any gunshot from within the house. Both Florence and I were totally ignorant of all those details.

254

'I daresay that we visited Father, each of us being in a state of . . . what can you call it? Cold wrath, that would describe our attitude, our emotions. Our plan being to make his life as hard and as miserable as possible, but not to murder him. My sister did that of her own volition, but it was not part of the agreed plan, because all three of us subscribed to the notion that even if you hate someone, let them live. It just would not be in our interests to kill him, but it would be very pleasant to know that we had placed him in a state of constant fear, knowing that he could never hide and never be safe.'

'So why did you drive out into the countryside and burn your clothing?' Yellich asked as he sat back in his chair.

'Because we knew we'd feel contaminated just going into his house, and we found that even waiting outside made us feel contaminated, so we took a change of clothing,' Fiona Middlemiss explained. 'And fire is a great cleaning agent. We are going to have the monster that was our father cremated, not buried, like Mummy is buried. We will visit Mother's grave and lay flowers on it, but the old man, his evil is going to be consumed with fire and his ashes will be scattered on a rubbish tip.'

'So when did you know that Felicity had murdered your father?' Hennessey, like Yellich, reclined in his chair.

'Not until it was announced on the national news, and picked up by the London media.' Fiona Middlemiss also leaned back in her chair. 'It was not until then that we found out what our sister had done. And I can tell you that it came as quite a surprise. Neither I nor Florence realized that Felicity was capable of doing that. It was really quite a shock, I can tell you. Quite a shock.'

'She said what!' Felicity Middlemiss gasped. She looked at Hennessey and then at Yellich and then back to Hennessey. 'That little minx! Well I never . . . I don't know what to say, I really don't.'

'So you deny that it was you who murdered Mr Anthony Garrett,' Hennessey sighed as he and Yellich exchanged glances.

'Of course I deny it,' Felicity Middlemiss insisted. She was dressed in identical clothing to Fiona Middlemiss although, unlike her sister, she exuded a delicate aroma of perfume. 'I waited outside with Fiona. It was Florence who went into the house, so as to give Father a piece of our mind and to tell him he'd better start packing his bags because knives would be travelling up from London within hours of the three of us getting back there.'

Hennessey turned to look at Yellich and he said, 'I see.'

Yellich held eye contact with Hennessey. 'I see as well,' he said. 'I see as well.'

'The little minx!' Florence Middlemiss, who was dressed identically to her two sisters, gasped when told by Hennessey that her sister Felicity had informed the police that she, Florence, had murdered their father. 'It was Fiona who murdered our father. Felicity and I waited outside while she went in to tell him what we thought of him and that we'd be telling the world where he lived so he'd better start house-hunting.'

'And you didn't know she carried a gun in her handbag?' Yellich spoke in a resigned manner.

'Of course I didn't know,' Florence Middlemiss replied indignantly. 'Of course I didn't know. I wouldn't have accompanied her if I did. Neither would my sister Felicity. That would have made us accomplices.'

'Like father like son,' Yellich commented as he sat in one of the chairs in front of Hennessey's desk, sipping tea from a mug decorated with the Virgo sign of the zodiac.

'What do you mean?' Hennessey glanced at the clock on the wall of his office, noting it read 18:47.

'Well, I was just thinking aloud really,' Yellich explained. 'You see, if it was the case that Anthony "Pilot" Garrett earned his nickname by being able to "navigate" him and his mates out of trouble with the naval authorities, if his daughters didn't have his influence in their lives when they were growing up, then they certainly inherited his cynical low-minded attitude to the law and they used it to get away with murdering him. So, like father like son, or in this case, like father like daughters.'

Hennessey snorted a brief laugh. 'Yes, I dare say that there is a certain irony there, but I am still annoyed that they got away with it.'

'Once my father told me,' Yellich sipped his tea, 'he said life is about winning and losing. Some you win, some you lose, and even if you

257

win fifty-one and lose forty-nine per cent that's still a won game, but you should try for a sixty per cent plus win rate, but I fear we have to chalk up the case of the murder of Anthony Garrett to a loss. We'll win the next few but, "the Crown versus Fiona, Felicity and Florence Middlemiss" is a trial which I doubt will ever happen.'

'I doubt it.' Hennessey glanced to his left, out of the window of his office at the walls of York. 'I doubt it also.'

Later that evening, a middle-aged man and a middle-aged woman sat quietly sipping wine in front of a small log fire in the hearth of the woman's lounge. They had both agreed that even in the height of summer a log fire had a certain comfort.

'You had to let them go?' The woman took a sip of wine from her glass.

'Had to is the expression,' the man repeated. 'Had, being the operative word. We didn't like it; the Crown Prosecution lawyer from whom we took advice didn't like it either. But we had to let them go. My son visited me last week; he was upset about a case up in Teesside where an infant was murdered by one of his drug-addict parents. Medical evidence could only say that one person had murdered the infant, there was nothing which could tie one specific parent to the murder, forensically speaking. Each parent blamed the other, so one was innocent, and given the fear that the law has of unsafe convictions, then the CPS could not proceed against either of them. It is, I was told, what in

258

law is called a "cut throat" defence.' The man paused and took a small log and tossed it on the fire. 'So we were in the same situation with the Middlemiss sisters. They executed a pre-planned "cut throat" defence with great skill as only three cynically minded lawyers could. Only one entered the house, two independent witnesses confirmed that, all three claim to have been outside the house with one of her sisters as the third entered the house, all three claim no prior knowledge that the third was in possession of a firearm, nor of the third's intention to murder their father. So two were innocent of murder and two were innocent of conspiracy to murder before and after the fact, in the eyes of the law that is.'

'It's a safe bet that the gun, the murder weapon, is as irrecoverable as the clothing they were wearing when they murdered their father.' Hennessey placed his right hand on the back of his neck and rubbed it gently from side to side. 'My guess it that it will be at the bottom of a river somewhere up here in Yorkshire. It would have been too risky for them to keep it with them any longer than they had to. If they did take it back to London it will be at the bottom of the Thames, but one way or the other its gone. And whatever Badger and Perry were up to that same day, we'll either convict them or we won't.'

'But in your eyes?' the woman asked. 'What do your eyes tell you?'

'My old eyes tell me very clearly that they knew how to get away with murder.' The man glanced up at the high-beamed ceiling of the room. 'Little wonder that they are known as the "Loophole Ladies". They also know of the law's terror of unsafe convictions. Only one is guilty, but which one only they know. And it was no wonder that Fiona Middlemiss was delighted to learn that they had a second witness to all three arriving but also to only one entering the house, and which one, the witness could not tell. Just as the driver of the gypsy cab could not say which one of the three had entered the house.' The man paused and sipped his wine. 'I dare say that the only compensation is that there is an element of rough justice in the whole affair in that Anthony Garrett was no saint. It is likely that many bodies lie in shallow graves in Epping Forest, on his orders, and that many weighted bodies were heaved over the side of small boats in the Thames Estuary in the hours of darkness, also on his orders, but the fact is that the Middlemiss sisters got away with murder.'

'Will they really get away with it, do you think?' The woman drained her glass of wine.

'Yes . . . yes, I think they will. The only possibility is that at some point in the future one might turn on the others and give information, but the likelihood of that happening is slim to zero, given those three. It's like they have one mind. They won't implode. Not those three. They burned all the clothing they wore when visiting the house thus making sure that there was no trace evidence left for us to find, and doubtless as soon as they got home they each showered and would have scrubbed themselves raw. They wouldn't have left anything to chance. So yes . . .

they most likely will get away with it. I don't like it, but that's it.'

'Well . . .' Louise D'Acre inclined her head to one side, '. . . little feet have stopped scurrying . . . it's gone pleasantly quiet. Shall we go up?'

'Yes.' George Hennessey put his wine glass gently down upon the coffee table and glanced out of the window and saw that it was filled from side to side and top to bottom with a bright orange sunset. 'Yes,' he repeated, 'let's go up.'

Miles Law sat in the lounge of his small cottage and also glanced out of his window, and also saw the sunset filling the window frame. He cradled the gun he had lovingly reassembled and ensured it was well oiled. He had checked the weapon was loaded . . . not a full clip, just two bullets but he'd only need one. With a gun as powerful as the one he held, which, it was reported, 'could blow a hole in a brick wall', he'd definitely only need one. He curled his finger around the trigger. 'I wonder if she was right?' he said to himself as he lifted the gun to the side of his head. 'That lady cop . . . I wonder if she was right . . . that you take all your guilt and your regrets and all the awful sights you have seen, you'll take them all into eternity because consciousness continues . . . and that those things are part of your consciousness . . . and because of that mortal death is no escape from them?' He looked around his small living room and glanced once more at the sunset.

'I wonder if she was right?' he said again.

'I wonder if she was right?'
'I wonder if she was right?'
'I wonder if she was right?'
'I won—'